Vengeance

The phone beside Flynn rang. A thin, cruel smile formed on his lips as he reached out his hand to answer it. He hardly missed the little finger absent from his hand. On occasion it ached, phantom pain, but he paid that no mind.

Pain, after all, was his stock in trade. He'd made a good living inflicting it on others. Death, despair and pure sweet pain. He pressed the phone receiver to his ear. "Well?"

"Rourke's in Ireland."

"Is he now?" The four-fingered hand squeezed the receiver even tighter. A grim smile played at the corners of his mouth as the nebulous fog of his thoughts coalesced into an idea.

It was more a dark dream than a plan, but it pleased him. He would need patience. But at the end of the bloody road of vengeance he saw so clearly in his mind's eye, Flynn could also see the destiny he had always known would be his someday. Total victory.

ABOUT THE AUTHOR

For Linda Stevens, story ideas ideally start with questions like "What if?" or "Then what?" and can be inspired by anything and everything. In the case of *One Step Ahead,* the inspiration was *Shadowplay,* Linda Stevens's first book for Intrigue. Ever since Flynn, one of the villains from *Shadowplay,* evaded justice, readers have been asking what nastiness he'd turn his talents to next, and who would dare match wits with him. *One Step Ahead* certainly answers both questions and more. Linda Stevens lives in Colorado Springs, Colorado.

Books by Linda Stevens

HARLEQUIN INTRIGUE
130—SHADOWPLAY

One Step Ahead

Linda Stevens

Harlequin Books

TORONTO • NEW YORK • LONDON
AMSTERDAM • PARIS • SYDNEY • HAMBURG
STOCKHOLM • ATHENS • TOKYO • MILAN

Harlequin Intrigue edition published February 1991

ISBN 0-373-22156-8

ONE STEP AHEAD

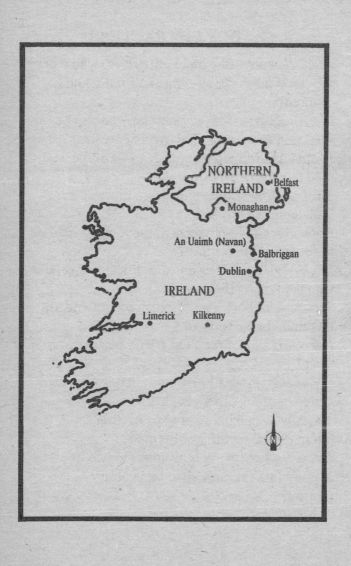

CAST OF CHARACTERS

Annie Sawyer—She owed Patrick Rourke a debt she could never repay—but she finally had a chance to try.

Patrick Rourke—Would his many talents be sufficient to withstand his many enemies?

Flynn—He wanted Rourke dead—and he was used to getting his own way.

Brady Adair—Loose ends from his past were threatening his future.

Colin Farrell—Were there limits to what he'd do to protect his investment?

Michael Adair—He wanted political power, but who would pay the cost?

Casey—His work came highly recommended, but could he be trusted?

Derry—Had Rourke's old friend betrayed his trust?

Orren Hagen—He knew too much for his own good—and for other people's.

Gerald—Was Annie's boss protecting international security or his own?

Bruce Holloway—Was his interference in Annie's mission prompted by jealousy or treason?

Chapter One

Iowa

Gun in hand, Patrick Rourke slipped into the motel room, closing the door softly behind himself. Everything appeared to be as he'd left it, but still he moved cautiously, checking under the beds, in the small closet, even behind the faded floral curtains. Satisfied his uninvited guest hadn't brought a friend, he turned toward the bathroom and the sound of the shower roaring full blast.

He didn't know anyone in this small town, so who the hell was in his bathroom? Carefully, Rourke eased the door open. Thick hot steam poured from the room. With his heavy automatic at the ready, he stepped over the navy-blue flight bag on the floor in front of him and silently approached the tub. He curled his fingers firmly around the heavy, opaque shower curtain, ready to yank it aside.

"That you, Rourke?" a distinctive voice from his past inquired.

It couldn't be! Resisting the urge to rip the curtain down, Rourke pulled it back slowly, revealing his visitor. Heedless of his presence, she stood beneath the steady flow of the shower, water cascading down her sleek back. It was hard to look away from that alluring scene.

"What are you doing here, Annie?"

"I'm flattered you remember me, Rourke," she replied, her eyes still closed as she continued to rinse shampoo out of her curly brown hair. She wasn't embarrassed by his presence. But, as she'd once told him, growing up in a household with nine brothers and sisters and only one bathroom had given her an acceptance of little or no privacy early in life.

Annie smiled. It was all part of her plan. The best way to handle Patrick Rourke was to keep him off balance, and that was not an easy task by any means. Annie Sawyer was prepared to use every means at her disposal.

"Forget you, Ms. Sawyer? Never!" With some difficulty, Rourke was managing to look the other way while pulling the shower curtain shut over the distracting view. "I never forget anyone who's almost gotten me killed. Now answer the question."

"You make it sound as if I'm a member of a club." She turned the water off and wrapped one towel around her hair, then began gently blotting the water from her body with another. "A large club. Are there that many of us?"

"Why are you here, Annie?"

She smiled. "I'm here to keep you in line, Rourke."

"In line for what?" he asked suspiciously.

She pulled the curtain open and stepped out of the bathtub, a white towel wrapped snugly under her arms. The room was so small they were almost touching. Her eyes met his, intently serious.

"You can't just kill those men, Rourke."

He glared at her. Patrick Rourke had always had an intimidating hardness about him, especially when he was angry, as he clearly was right now. But along with that anger she could see other emotions etched on his handsome face. Surprise, for one. That pleased her, as did the slight trace of wariness in his eyes. She stared up at him for a moment longer, then grabbed a bottle off the counter and walked into the bedroom.

Rourke didn't bother asking Annie how she knew about the men he would soon be pursuing. They both had their sources. Some of them were even the same ones. "What makes you think homicide is what I have in mind?" he asked, following her. That towel wrapped around her shapely torso was too short, on both ends.

"Who said I did? I'm just telling you, that's all."

"And how do you propose to stop me?"

She sat down on a bed and squeezed a dollop of lotion into the palm of her hand. "Any way I have to."

He raised his dark eyebrows slightly. "You'd kill me?"

Annie studied him; he was still lean, muscular and handsome. His hair, slightly longer than the last time they'd met, was still dark and thick. But there were deeper lines around his gray eyes. He didn't look as if he had found any inner peace in the past six years.

"No," she replied at last.

Rourke watched her rub the creamy lotion between her hands before smoothing it over her calves in long strokes. He wasn't sure if she was making a show of it for him or not, but either way, he was enjoying it too much for his own good.

"You don't have great legs."

She flashed him a quick grin, not offended by his comment. Attacking was a good defense and it meant she was getting to him. Her legs were like those of a professional athlete or dancer, well honed and tight.

"I agree. Too many muscles from running around in the hills as a child. But they have their uses."

He leaned nonchalantly against the back wall, his arms crossed over his chest. "Is that what you intend to do? Run after me?"

"Actually, I'm going to be right beside you this time," Annie returned candidly. "Maybe even one step ahead."

"Good luck."

"I won't need it," she told him, standing up and walking back into the bathroom. "I'll have you with me."

Shaking his head, Rourke crossed the room and took a seat in one of the two wooden straight-back chairs on either side of the small table near the window. The curtains were drawn tight. In the bright bathroom lights, and without makeup, she looked quite young and vulnerable.

Too vulnerable. "Annie, you're not cut out for this kind of thing."

"I know."

She hadn't changed, as honest as ever. "Do you even know why I'm after these men?" He didn't give her time to answer. "They're trying to murder an innocent child who was a witness to their previous killings. You're way out of your league. Even more than the last time."

Annie came back into the room wearing only a fuchsia T-shirt that hung halfway to her knees. She began briskly toweling her hair. His announcement didn't surprise her. The child was one of the reasons she wanted to help him.

"I never did get a chance to thank you for not telling the complete story about that little incident." She smiled. "Or rather *any* story." It had infuriated her superiors no end that Rourke hadn't filed a report. And they'd been even more annoyed to realize they couldn't force him to, either, mainly because they couldn't find him. Rourke had never been a government employee like her.

"My mistake," he said curtly. "Forget it."

"No way." Annie looked at him, serious now. "I'm not here just to pester you, Patrick. I'm here to help. According to my boss, the hunt for Bridget Houlihan has intensified."

Rourke sat up straight. He glared at her, his body tense. "How did you come by that name?" he demanded.

"I told you," she replied, taken aback by harshness of his tone. "My boss. Gerald."

"And how did *he* get it?"

She shrugged. "He didn't say. What's the big deal?"

"My friends and I take great pains to keep her name out of files, especially government files. And it's a big deal because Bridget is the most important thing in the world to me. Dammit! What else do you know about her?"

"Nothing! I didn't even know how much she meant to you!" But Annie was glad to hear it; perhaps there was hope for him after all. "If it makes you feel any better, I did check the files after Gerald briefed me on this. Zilch. I assumed this was another of your causes."

"It is. The only one I care about." Annie's reassurance had made him feel better, though. He leaned back in the chair with a sigh. "I suppose your boss must have people in Ireland who heard the same rumors we did. But how did he connect them to me and my search for these four men?"

"He didn't say."

"It seems there's a lot he doesn't say," Rourke observed.

Annie went back to toweling her hair, carefully avoiding his gaze. She was aware Gerald was being closemouthed. It annoyed her a lot. He hadn't even told her what Rourke had just let slip—that this search was for *four* men. This didn't seem like the time to admit it, though. Rourke was leery enough as it was.

"I'm capable of finding things out for myself," Annie told him. "And of helping you and your friends on this."

"We don't need your help," Rourke informed her tersely. "She's being well taken care of."

"Knowing what I do about Russ Ian and Jack Merlin, I'm sure she is. But they can't do that forever. You need my help and connections if you're going to find these men before they find Bridget."

What was the use? Annie certainly seemed to have all the facts she needed to give him a hard time. She was too stubborn to quit, and she still believed she owed him something for saving her career. He'd just have to find a way to lose her.

Thinking of Annie's career brought to mind a very intriguing notion, as well as a way to misdirect her attention. "About that report I never filed. Are you going to thank me tonight?"

She looked at him through a riot of tousled brown curls. "I don't repay favors that way."

"Too bad," he murmured.

Annie threw the damp towel at him and was pleased when it smacked him in the chest. "Why? You don't even like my legs," she retorted, combing her hair with her fingers.

"I never said I didn't like them, I just said they weren't great." He dropped the soggy towel on the floor, remembering how she'd looked in the shower with a cascade of water trickling down her breasts. "There are other parts of you I like much better."

She didn't look at him as she pulled down the covers of the bed farthest from the door. "Too bad. You already blew it."

"Your government too cheap to buy you your own room?" Rourke asked, watching as she slid between the white sheets.

"I can't keep an eye on you from another room."

"Or your hands."

"Wishful dreams," she responded, closing her eyes.

Rourke decided to switch his line of attack. "Since I doubt your interest in the men I'm looking for is purely humanitarian, you must be after something else. You want them, too, don't you? Why? Who are they? What else have they done?"

"I don't know," Annie replied, rolling onto her back with a heavy sigh. "My boss believes you're going to eliminate these men when you catch up with them. He doesn't want that to happen, so my orders were to find you. I did. Now I'm supposed to stay with you. And I will."

"That remains to be seen. One thing for sure, Annie. You'd better get some answers before something you don't know rears up and bites you. Or you could find yourself dead.''

Annie agreed with him. Quite often in the past she had worked blind, but not this time. In the morning she was going to do just as he suggested and ferret out some answers.

Right now she desperately needed sleep. Her overseas flights had been repeatedly delayed by bad weather and she hadn't slept much in the last seventy-two hours. Though there were a lot of unanswered questions about Patrick Rourke as well, she did know she was safe with him.

Or reasonably so. She could practically feel him watching her as she drifted off to sleep. It wasn't an unpleasant feeling at all. In fact, she rather liked it.

Rourke stayed in his chair, his eyes on the slender form covered by an ugly, faded, floral-print bedspread. This was a disturbing development, one he could have easily lived without. He hadn't thought about Annie Sawyer in a very long time, didn't particularly want to think about her now, or rather about the trouble she evidently planned on causing him.

But he would never forget those legs. For three nights he'd stared at those legs, encased in sheer black hose and red spiked heels. She'd been the only thing worth looking at in the ratty, depressing, partially burned out neighborhood they'd stationed themselves in on that fateful night long ago.

Though buried six years in the past, Rourke's memory of the occasion was still very strong. He could see Annie, her legs barely covered by a black leather miniskirt, standing patiently on the street corner waiting for their contact. Two other men had been positioned close by, revealing themselves only when someone tried to pick her up. Such was her allure that they had to replay this little scene quite a few times, but their size easily discouraged all comers.

Annie was there because she was the only woman agent available who fit the description of a much-needed go-between. As usual, Patrick was there for his own reasons. Those reasons had seemed all-important at the time, but not one of them had been worth what had almost happened when she had frozen on him at a crucial point. It was the closest he'd ever come to having his head blown off. And the closest he ever intended to come.

Only the luck of the Irish had saved him, and he wasn't going to tempt fate twice. Tomorrow he had a very important date to keep, one he would keep alone. So, tonight he intended to run like the devil was after him. Indeed, the devil would be after him in a way and, memorable legs or not, Rourke wanted to be as faraway from her as he could get.

ANNIE AWOKE TO A QUIET motel room the next morning. Too quiet. A quick check assured her that Patrick had, indeed, flown the coop.

"Damn," she muttered, but without much rancor.

In fact, she'd expected as much, had resigned herself to chasing after and finding him again just as she had last night. Like arranging to be caught in the shower, it was part of a thoughtful but flexible plan she had formulated to gradually wear down his resistance.

Patrick Rourke was wild, untamed and unpredictable in his movements. Tracking him down and gaining his trust wasn't going to be easy, but then, she'd never taken the easy way out in her life.

And she did owe him her career. A career she'd come to thoroughly enjoy. If the supposed facts of their fiasco six years ago had come out at the time, that precious career would have been over before it had even begun. Rourke had known this and he'd covered for her by disappearing. Her own account of the proceedings had been somewhat inaccurate, but believable, and there had been no one to refute her claims.

Now she had an opportunity to repay the favor. Patrick needed her help. He just hadn't admitted it to himself yet, that's all. And she already had a very good idea of where she might find him.

Annie washed her face and got dressed, preparing to meet what would undoubtedly be another exhausting day. Still, she was excited and looking forward to the hunt.

"You're a smart one, Mr. Patrick Rourke," she said, looking at her reflection in the bathroom mirror. Then she grinned broadly. "But so am I."

Chapter Two

Kentucky

In some circles, he was considered a genius. While he wouldn't go that far, Patrick freely acknowledged he had pulled off some brilliant ploys in his day. For a little while, he had even allowed himself to forget that in other circles, both he and the slip of a girl beside him had some equally brilliant enemies.

He didn't much like the idea, but he had Annie to thank for waking him up to that harsh reality. She was hot on his trail, and that meant others might be, too. This was not the time to be taking foolish risks. He stood a chance of losing the most important person in the world to him.

Granted, Bridget Houlihan could melt ice with her sweet, coaxing smile, tumble down the walls of Jericho with her shy, girlish ways. At the tender age of eleven, she was twice the actress of many a rising Hollywood starlet, this the result of intensive therapy designed to help heal her emotional wounds.

"You promised," Bridget said. "You told me we would see your horse race today." When Patrick didn't relent, she tried coaxing him. "She even has a good chance of winning."

He had to remind himself that even with the consent of the two men with whom he shared guardianship of the young girl, Jack Merlin and Russ Ian, it was he who had the final say. And promise or no promise, he knew the outing to be unwise.

"There'll be other races."

"But you promised!"

One look at Bridget's carefully timed pout gave him second thoughts, but they were quickly squashed. To make the ultimately stupid mistake of underestimating the people it was rumored were trying to locate Bridget could get her killed.

"We're not going," he said firmly, watching as Bridget turned away from him and gave her attention to the filly. The horse did have a good chance of winning today. He hated to miss the race or to break his promise to Bridget, but her safety was more important than his pride.

He sighed softly and turned to watch Bridget. She was talking to the horse as she stroked its sleek coat with her hand. Her red-and-white-check shirt was tucked into the blue jeans that hugged her slender legs and ended inside red cowboy boots. Wisps of dark hair had escaped her once neat French braid and were dangling in her green eyes.

He couldn't bear the thought that he might lose her, too, that those men might actually find her and kill her. She was all he had left.

"Bridget?"

The despair in his voice startled her and stilled her hand. Bridget looked over at him, then quietly walked toward him, the hay-covered stable floor beneath her feet muffling any sounds. Her hand slipped trustingly onto his open palm, his strong fingers curling around hers reassuring. But she could tell something was seriously wrong. Patrick was brimming with tension.

Slowly, that same fear she'd known the night her parents were murdered began to consume her. What was wrong? She had never seen him this worried, almost frightened. Why wouldn't he look her in the eye?

Patrick crouched down beside her, gently brushing the loose strands of dark hair out of her face. He was the one responsible for her. He had to see the pitfalls for both of them. For a moment he had almost forgotten that.

"I love you," he whispered softly into her ear.

She nodded and Patrick picked his little girl up, hugging her tightly before setting her astride the filly. The horse whickered softly, then was still, quieted by Bridget's calming touch upon her smooth, sleek neck.

Her chin was resting on the horse's mane, hands gripping each side of its strong neck for support. There was total trust in her eyes as she looked at him; Bridget believed in him, and why shouldn't she? He'd gotten her safely out of trouble before and now he was going to do it again or die trying.

"Patrick?" Bridget whispered. "I love you, too."

He plucked her off the horse, holding her close again as he tried to decide how much he should tell her.

She wrapped her arms around his neck, her legs encircling his waist. "Tell me what's wrong?"

Bridget's small heart was pounding against his chest and he felt tremors running through her. He cursed the fear and adrenaline coursing through his own veins, knowing he was communicating his worry to her.

Rubbing his chin across the side of her head, he murmured softly, "We think the men who killed your parents know about you. I'm going to find them, but in the meantime you'll have to stay on the move with Russ and Kathleen."

She nodded, burying her face in his neck and hugging him tighter. "I'll be real good."

"I know you will, sweetheart." He held her for a moment longer, savoring her sweetness, then set her down.

"Patrick?"

"Yes?"

"Will I ever be able to stop running?"

Rourke sighed, hearing the longing in her voice. A tumult of emotions washed over him. Love. Fear. A burning desire to make everything right. And some of that very same longing, for an end to turmoil, a sense of place at last. He was determined to provide, for her, that peace that was forever denied him.

"Yes, honey," Patrick assured her. "Someday soon. But right now we need to leave."

Texas

TWO DAYS LATER, Rourke walked into a crowded coffee shop and sat down in a padded booth. The man sitting across from him was one of the few people he trusted completely. As usual, his navy-blue suit and white shirt fit him to perfection, the maroon paisley tie matching the kerchief in his pocket.

In his faded blue jeans and brown leather bomber jacket, Patrick felt like a ruffian in comparison. That suited him just fine. He was feeling pretty rough today.

"Bridget okay?" Patrick asked.

Jack Merlin poured a cup of tea for him. "She's fine. Perky as ever, according to Russ."

"Good," Patrick said, running a hand through his dark hair. "I still can't believe I even considered taking her to the horse races. How stupid! When I told Russ what I had almost done, he didn't even yell at me."

Their friend Russ Ian didn't believe in mincing words. And at times he seemed to think the louder he yelled the clearer his meaning became. Silence on his part was an admission of guilt. Jack felt the same. They were both glad it had fallen on Patrick to face Bridget's pleading eyes, break the promise he had made to her and then give her the news of this latest threat that made it necessary for her to go on the run. Again.

"You weren't the only one being stupid. Stop beating yourself up over it and be thankful something happened to bring us to our senses!" Jack told him sharply. Then he sighed and forced himself to calm down. This had all of them on edge. "You didn't say much over the phone. Just who was the woman who found you in Iowa?" he asked.

Patrick slouched down in the booth. "Annie Sawyer. I worked with her once."

His answer and defensive posture aroused Jack's curiosity. "What was she doing there?"

"Looking for me. She has orders to stop me from killing the men we're after," Patrick replied.

Even though the loud clatter in the coffee shop covered their conversation, Jack kept his voice low as he leaned over the battered tabletop. "What! Exactly who is she? How did she find out about this?"

"She works for your government," Patrick replied with a shrug. "And I'm not sure how much they know about what's going on, or how they came by the information. I do know they aren't telling Annie very much of anything. That bothers me." He smiled bitterly. "It bothers her, too."

"And me." Completely baffled, Jack leaned back and began fiddling with a spoon. "You don't suppose the United States government knows the identities of the men who killed Bridget's parents, do you?"

"No. I'd guess that's why they've sicced Annie on me." Patrick looked at Jack evenly. "I imagine they want us to locate these men and then quietly turn them over for questioning."

Jack plunked the spoon he'd been holding into his cup of now-cold tea. "Then they have to be involved in something big, something the government would be interested in. Drugs, arms dealing, smuggling, espionage." He shook his head. "Who knows? The possibilities are endless. It could be anything!"

"I agree. I made some phone calls to various contacts, but it was useless. Whatever they're wanted for, it's being kept very quiet."

Jack mulled this over. "And you're going to be walking smack into the middle of it, Patrick. Not good. I'll give Julie a call. You can meet in the usual way."

"Okay. I'll have ample opportunity to find out things from Annie, too," Patrick told him. "From what I can tell, she isn't about to leave me alone. The man who trains some of my horses informed me she showed up at the stables looking for me yesterday."

"Sounds like a resourceful lady."

"She is," Patrick agreed with noticeable rancor. "And I suppose that should make me happy. If she hadn't surprised me in Iowa like she did, I might have gone blithely on and taken Bridget to that race. And since a couple of goons showed up there looking for me, it seems I owe Annie a debt of gratitude."

"Well, I for one am relieved that you're going to have help," Jack pointed out. "We can use it on this one."

Patrick made a face. "Don't remind me. But I can't trust anyone, Jack. You know that." Rourke tried to conjure up vile thoughts about the woman in question, thoughts that had come easily to him less than seventy-two hours ago. All he could think of now, however, was that Annie had been the one who'd stopped him from making a stupid mistake. That, and her feminine charms were memorable. "She could still be more trouble than she's worth."

Jack gave Patrick a sharp look, obviously wondering if Annie Sawyer was getting under Patrick's skin. Jack knew him too well to think he'd admit it if she was. But if he wanted to know more about their relationship, this wasn't the time to find out. They had more pressing matters to discuss.

"I have the last location of Orren Hagen for you," Jack said, responding to Patrick's determined expression.

"Where is he?" Patrick asked, leaning forward. So far, Orren Hagen was their only link to the men after Bridget.

Jack handed him a folded piece of paper. "The village is in Northern Ireland," he announced quietly. "I should have an exact address for you tomorrow.

Their eyes met for a brief moment before Patrick looked away. His friend was well aware of the anguish this trip would cause him. He was going to have to face the past whether he wanted to or not. Bridget's life was at stake.

Patrick unfolded the piece of paper and read the name of the town. Then he placed the paper in the ashtray, flicked his lighter and watched as the specially treated paper was instantly reduced to fine ash.

"Any flights out today?"

"I've booked you on one this afternoon to New York City, tomorrow into London." Jack pulled an envelope out of his inside suit-coat pocket and handed it over. "From there you can choose your own route."

Patrick slipped the envelope into the pocket of his leather jacket. "Thanks. I'll try to check in with you as often as possible. And Russ and you both know how and where to leave messages if you need me."

Someone had to stay in one place, act as a coordinator for the three of them. Jack was good at that and he hadn't objected to taking that role. He had a wife to protect now.

"How's your ace reporter?"

Jack's expression softened. "Cassie's fine. She's up to her nose investigating a doctor who's never been before a review board in spite of numerous complaints against him."

"The guy doesn't stand a chance against her skills." Rourke managed a small smile. "Just look what she managed to do to you."

Cassie O'Connor had been determined and skillful enough to keep digging until she had come up with enough on Jack Merlin to blackmail him into helping her on what

had turned out to be the biggest story—and most dangerous escapade—of her career to date.

"She is good," Jack said with a chuckle. Though he
hadn't found it funny at the time, he could laugh about the
matter now. Especially since, along the way, the two of them
had also fallen in love. "When you come up with names, let
me know. Between us we'll find out everything about
them."

"I will." Patrick sipped his tea. "I've spent the last two
days leaving an obvious trail in order to lead anyone who
might be following me away from Bridget."

"Good. The more confusion you make out there, the
better. Russ will be constantly on the move with her. He
knows what to do."

All three men were good at hiding out, a natural result of
their previous trade. Stealing from thieves was a risky business, but quite profitable as long as one stayed several steps
ahead. Still, Jack was worried.

"But watch out for yourself, too," he told Patrick gruffly.
"We don't know what's going on. To use one of Bridget's
favorite words, our past is hardly pristine, either. Could be
someone's playing both ends against the middle on this one.
And I don't think I have to remind you that you're not in-
vincible."

"No." Patrick's expression was sour. "That was recently
made crystal clear to all of us."

There was another pressing problem they had to deal
with, one from their own past that wouldn't go away.
Rourke and Jack shared a common tragedy, the death of
their families at the hands of one horribly despicable man
many years ago.

Recently, that man had outwitted them again and was still
alive. If they didn't get him first, he'd get all three of them,
and perhaps Bridget as well. That, they had all vowed,
would never, ever happen.

"Anything on Flynn?" Jack asked.

"No." Patrick frowned. "The only lead I had was that flight to London he supposedly took, but it was a waste of time. No one reliable saw him." He sighed disgustedly. "I've contacted every source I have, but no one's seen or heard from him in the last month."

Jack waved off the approaching waitress. "I don't have anything on him, either." He looked at Patrick. "It's possible Flynn set you up, got you over to London and then followed you back here."

"The thought did cross my mind," Patrick admitted. "I was careful, just not careful enough. After all," he added bitterly, "an amateur like Annie Sawyer found me."

Jack sighed. The woman was getting to Patrick, all right, but Jack doubted she'd be prepared for the anger she would find inside him. "Maybe you're not giving her enough credit."

"More likely I'm not giving Flynn enough," Patrick replied with disgust.

"Keep a weather eye out and remember that if he does show up, it'll be when you least expect it. Ireland is familiar territory to both of you," Jack reminded him.

"Unfamiliar now, it's been years for me. And Bridget is my first priority."

"Just watch your backside," Jack warned him. "Don't get so involved in tracking down those men that you forget that Flynn might be after *you*. You're no good to anyone if you don't make your first priority staying alive."

Chapter Three

Iowa

"Are you with him?"

Annie Sawyer scowled at the voice on the phone. "Why do you want to know?"

"Because it's your job, Sawyer. That's why," Bruce Holloway reminded her sharply. "We want those men alive."

Bruce always got on her nerves, and she couldn't resist taunting him a bit. He was a desk man, had never worked out in the field and had no desire to give up the cushy comforts of his plush family home.

"If you think you can do a better job, Bruce, why don't you come keep him company yourself?"

He ignored her. "You have no jurisdiction to work in the States," he reminded her needlessly.

"I'm on vacation," she answered, the proper response delivered with a very improper amount of ice in her voice. It wasn't her imagination. Bruce was out to make trouble for her. Her having fended off his amorous attentions years ago still bothered him. Well, he would rot before she ever went out with him again. "Do you have anything of substance to tell me? Or did you call just to hear your own pompous voice?"

"How dare you talk to your—"

Annie pushed the white button down, cutting him off. Bruce was indeed her superior, had been for the past five months, but she didn't care. She wasn't working with him on this particular job, and if she had her way she'd never have to report to him again.

Everyone knew what an inept jerk he was, but getting him transferred to another department wasn't going to be easy. No one wanted him. And the higher-ups were afraid to touch him because of his family's political influence and wealth.

The phone rang again. She let it jangle on her nerves for fifteen times before answering. "Yes?"

"I hope I didn't interrupt something quite important or stimulating?"

The formal, clipped English brought with it instant recognition. A man she knew and trusted was on the other end of the line. Annie pictured him sitting in his elegant office, graying hair cropped short around his lined face, his clothes always comfortable, tweeds and wool, and his ubiquitous, well-used pipe close at hand. Even though he was an American by birth, he had been educated in Great Britain and was always very proper in manner. Even when his tone of voice hinted that he might have caught her in a liaison with the opposite sex.

"Gerald, I haven't been that lucky in a very long time."

"I can only assume you fail to take advantage of your opportunities. How is your friend?"

"Gone, as you well know."

Gerald chuckled at her wry tone. "He flew into Houston this morning, disappeared for a few hours and will land in New York City this evening. Future destination, London."

"Figures."

Though they'd tracked him for the last two days, Annie hadn't bothered running after him until last night. It had been too easy. From Kentucky he'd completely disappeared, only to emerge in South Dakota, and from there back to Iowa. She knew Rourke had been laying a false trail for anyone following him and upon arrival at his motel last night, she hadn't been surprised to find him long gone.

"Chin up, Annie," Gerald told her.

"I'll try. Oh, Gerald, minutes before you called I was talking to Bruce."

"What!" The expletives floating in the air were colorful and lively. "Excuse the outburst, Annie. I'm going to wring that little twit's neck."

Annie grinned. "What a lovely thought. Please do."

"But not before I find out who told him your location." He sounded troubled. Before Annie could ask why, however, he continued briskly. "Which will soon alter, by the by. There's a ticket waiting for you at the airport. Your flight leaves in forty-five minutes."

"Wait! Don't hang up, Gerald. Nothing's changed since I last spoke with you. I still want answers. Why do you want these men? How did you link Patrick Rourke to them? At least give me a name to work with."

A long silence passed before he spoke. "We don't have any names. I'm not at liberty to reveal more than that. Keep me posted and do be careful."

Annie listened to the buzzing tone in her ear for a moment, finding it hard to believe such a gentleman as Gerald would hang up on her. Nor could she believe what he'd said.

No names? What was going on? She knew there was only one way she was going to find out. After taking one last look around the motel room, she grabbed her blue flight bag and headed for the airport.

New York

ROURKE SLOWED DOWN, the relative quietness of this street pleasant after the noisy, overcrowded, garishly neon-bedecked area of Times Square. A heavyset man dressed in

gray sweats emerged from a shallow doorway and fell into
step beside him.

"You're not going to like this, Rourke."

"Then say it fast."

"There's nothing in the computers."

"There has to be something, Julie."

The big man shook his head. "Not necessarily. Some of
the older agents still play things very close, never file any
reports until an operation is over with. Even then, a lot
never makes it into files of any kind. You know that."

"What about Bridget or her parents?" Rourke asked,
restraining pace. Julie couldn't talk if he walked too quickly.

"Not a thing. But Flynn's another story. Him they have
extensive files on. Miles of 'em."

They crossed the street in silence, walking around a crowd
of people going in the opposite direction. "Send it all to
Jack." Rourke glanced at him. "Tonight, Julie."

"Yeah, yeah. I know. And anything else I discover later
on you might be interested in. Nice doing business with you.
At least you guys pay well."

At the next corner they moved off in opposite directions.
Patrick was worried. Julie had access to just about every
computer out there, and he'd found nothing. Was Annie's
boss running an independent operation? She'd indicated she
was going to demand a few answers, so maybe by now she
had something. Either way, he had the funny feeling he'd be
seeing her soon, whether he wanted to or not.

Rourke paused in front of a large display window on Fifth
Avenue, noting the name of the store. The aquamarine cot-
ton shorts and vest displayed in the window were perfect for
Bridget. He'd buy the coordinating plaid blouse, too.

A ghost of a smile softened his features as he thought of
the girl as she'd looked running across the meadow the other
day, black pigtails flying, her laughter infectious. It amazed
him how quickly she had gotten over his announcement that
there were men after her.

Quite a change from the time when he'd found her hiding in her bedroom from the men she'd seen shoot her parents a short time before. She'd clung to him then, a total stranger, and refused to let him go. He'd gotten her out of Ireland that very same night, taking her to Jack and Russ for safekeeping. Then he'd gone back to find out what had happened.

Bridget should have been staying with friends that night five years ago, but her parents had picked her up earlier than planned when their business trip was cut short. It was not, Rourke discovered, a very savory trade they were involved in. They had been active in the never-ending troubles in Northern Ireland and their business trips were used as a cover for their various activities on that cause.

After weeks of tedious checking, Rourke had come up with a possible name for only one of the four men responsible for their deaths. Orren Hagen. But in those weeks, he'd also made sure that virtually everyone in the village believed Bridget was now living with distant relatives, some seventy miles away.

Against his better judgment, he'd let the matter drop, accepting the logic Jack and Russ had used to convince him. It was best for the child not to stir up trouble, she'd been through enough. Let everyone continue to believe she had seen nothing.

The logic had proved sound until just over three months ago when rumors of inquiries into her present whereabouts began in Ireland. Very quietly and discreetly, they began investigating those rumors, but the source proved impossible to track down. While in London searching for Flynn, Rourke took the opportunity to dig deeper, even going so far as to ask a few of his contacts about the elusive Orren Hagen. But again, information had been slow to turn up.

Until now. Now they had a location to go with Orren Hagen's name. It was up to Rourke to take advantage of it, and remove this threat to Bridget once and for all.

Patrick suddenly became aware that he'd gotten lost in a world of his own thoughts—and that two policemen were staring directly at him. He nodded at them and continued briskly on his way. The cops had probably thought he was going to rob the place. Maybe once upon a time he might have, but never just for clothes. There had always been a purpose for stealing before: to save innocent lives.

Even now, he knew of a few miscreants with ill-gotten gains in their possession, tempting targets he could steal back for the reward. But those thieves could rest easy. There was already more than enough money in his account to fund the search for the men after Bridget.

He headed back to his hotel, contemplating the task ahead of him. It wasn't going to be easy to find out the identity of the four men after all this time. They had managed to keep their identities secret for years. What were they protecting? Why was the government interested in them? Why were they risking exposure now?

The questions continued to nag at him, as did the possible answers. They were desperate, greedy men; if one fell, they all fell. That was why they protected each other so carefully. But there had to be a weak link and this time he was going to find it.

Rourke slipped into his room, locking the hotel door behind him. Two lamps were on, bathing the room in a rosy glow. With a wry smile lifting the corners of his mouth, he quietly walked over to the built-in minibar and picked up a bottle of Irish whiskey. There was a note beneath it.

"Your taste in rooms is definitely improving. Keep up the good work."

Patrick poured a shot of whiskey into a glass, then sat down, putting his feet up on the coffee table. As he sipped the golden liquor, he gazed across the room at the bed, where a slender form slept peacefully beneath a cream-colored quilted comforter. This was becoming a habit.

He didn't want a habit like her in his life. It was in Annie's nature to be persistent, not only in her job but in everything she did. That was a fine, admirable quality, except when it came to her persistent curiosity. Before she'd almost gotten him killed, she'd nearly driven him nuts when they were forced to spend three days together cooped up in the same motel room. Not even his sternnest looks had put her off what she seemed to view as her duty to find things out about him and his past.

Annie Sawyer reminded him of a cat sometimes, curious but painfully patient, waiting for just the right moment to pounce. Thinking of her that way made him feel like a mouse, a role he wasn't accustomed to playing and didn't like one bit. So what was he going to do with her?

Chapter Four

Ireland

Brady Adair was a man who didn't dwell on past mistakes. He learned from them and moved on, more than happy to deal with anybody who got in his way. At this moment, however, without anyone to focus his anger on, he was not happy.

Not happy at all.

Sighing heavily, he gestured with his cigar, his brogue thick as he spoke. "Anything on this Rourke character?"

"They tracked him to Iowa."

Brady's eyes went wide. "Damn! He isn't working for—"

"Your brother? Anything's possible," Colin Farrell interjected, rather enjoying his partner's discomfiture. "But I don't believe so."

"Then what was he doing there?"

"They don't know. Other than the motel owner, he didn't talk to any of the people they interviewed, which was nearly the whole town of six hundred and one people. He was a stranger, just passing through. They know he paid cash for the room and he shared it with a woman. The woman arrived and left in her own car. She didn't speak to anyone they're aware of, either."

"Who is she?"

The slender, dark-haired man relaxing in the chair across the desk from Brady didn't answer him or meet his gaze. Instead, he carefully brushed a piece of lint from his dark trousers.

Brady thumped the desk violently. "They haven't found out *her* name yet, either? What in blazes am I paying them for, Farrell? You expect me to believe he flew all the way from London to Iowa for a one-night stand? Bull!"

The ruddy hue of anger on Brady's face didn't bother Farrell. He'd worked with the man for too many years to be intimidated by his bluster. "They're working on finding out her identity. And it doesn't look good. Her car rental was charged to the United States government."

"What?" Well-developed furrows deepened between his bushy red eyebrows. Brady didn't like the implications at all. "They're the last people we need involved in this mess." His black eyes narrowed shrewdly. "Could she really be just an old flame?"

Farrell nodded his head. "Doubtful, but again, anything is possible. From what we've been able to piece together so far, Patrick Rourke is a loner. He picks and chooses who he works for, completely free-lance. He likes risky assignments."

"Family?"

"None left," Farrell replied. "It is quite conceivable he knows this woman from a past job and is having an ongoing affair with her."

Brady mulled the idea over in his mind. "I don't buy that theory." He pounded his desk again, the pens and paper atop it jumping off the unmarred mahogany surface. "It's too coincidental. Iowa. Government agents. Bah! Find out who she is and get a description of her out to our people. I want to know what she's up to. Men like Rourke don't opt for lasting relationships."

"People change."

Brady ignored him. "What about his friends?"

"It takes time. Patrick Rourke has never worked a nine-to-five job in his life. Tracing his past movements will be difficult, maybe even impossible. Evidently, he has more than one identity and they haven't uncovered details on any of them."

This wasn't what Brady wanted to hear. "And Orren Hagen?"

"No sign of him at all."

Brady closed his eyes and leaned back in his chair, feeling on the verge of an apoplectic fit. They had to nip this in the bud, eliminate any potential problems. There weren't many. But this supposedly dangerous man named Patrick Rourke, who looked as if he might be nothing more than another pesky hired snoop, was poking his nose where it didn't belong. All this trouble, and for what? A man whose usefulness was now over. It didn't make sense.

Brady opened his eyes and glared at his partner. Farrell seemed to be taking all this much too calmly. He always did, and it irritated Brady no end. "Orren Hagen knows too much. He can identify us, Farrell. Our entire future is at stake here. If our involvement gets out, our cover will be blown. We'd be ruined!"

Farrell simply studied his carefully manicured nails as if he hadn't a care in the world. "No, Brady," he corrected mildly. "What we'd be is stone-cold dead."

New York

THE SOFT MURMUR OF HIS VOICE woke her up. Annie rolled over, her sleepy eyes zeroing in on him through the brilliant sunlight filling the room. Rourke was talking to someone on the phone, his tone so low she couldn't understand a word.

Refreshed from a good night's sleep, she stretched, then kicked back the covers and stood up, her fingers automatically combing through her curls as she followed her nose toward a more important priority than Patrick and his clandestine conversation. The smell of strong, fresh-brewed coffee was calling out her name, begging her to imbibe.

Rourke was on hold now and his eyes followed her as she found the coffee—and pounced on it. Her legs really weren't that bad. The more he saw of them naked, the more he liked them. She was sipping at the hot steamy brew, both hands holding the dainty china cup. Her wrists were quite delicate looking, belying the strength in her arms.

"I've never met another woman who gets such a blissful, satisfied look on her face from coffee," he said, setting the phone receiver down.

"We all have our vices." She gestured with her empty cup before setting it down. "Thank you for remembering." Rourke was sitting in an overstuffed chair by an antique desk, his pot of tea close by. A white shirt was tucked into his everpresent jeans, his feet bare.

"It was the least I could do," he said, acknowledging her thanks with a nod as she pulled a fluffy golden croissant apart. She looked so damned young, her face scrubbed clean of makeup and flushed from sleep.

"The very least," Annie agreed. "Want one?" She tossed a croissant across the room before he could reply. "They're excellent."

Rourke caught the bread before it hit him smack in the face. "Your aim is still good."

"There wasn't room for improvement." She sat down by the room-service cart and refilled her cup. This morning, his steady gaze upon her unnerved her. She wasn't at her best in the mornings.

He bit into the airy bread, savoring the buttery flavor. "I can't remember. Is it three or four cups before you become human?"

He'd ordered coffee for her more in self-defense than for any other reason. She'd seemed like such a sweet person until the second day they'd worked together. Annie, without her coffee in the morning, was a monster.

She looked at him disdainfully. "Two, generally, but around a sourpuss like you, Rourke, it takes at least four." Her retort brought a glimmer of light to his gray eyes. "I thought you'd be happier to see me this time, human or not. If I hadn't been harassing you, you'd never have known about the others who came looking for you in Kentucky."

"If you're looking for abject gratitude, forget it. You can leave anytime, Sawyer. I didn't invite you to my party."

"No, you didn't." He was needling her on purpose and she was falling for it far too easily. "But consider it crashed. When do we leave for Ireland?"

Rourke chuckled dryly. So the little cat had learned to change her spots quickly in the last few years. He'd have to remember that. "Tomorrow."

Like the false trail he'd left that any moron could follow, his reply came too easily. She didn't believe for an instant this battle was over. Some people were just naturally good liars, and Patrick Rourke was one of them.

He ignored her disdainful expression. "Do you want the last croissant?" he asked, helping himself to more tea.

Annie tossed it at him. "You'd better have it this time." He caught it easily and took a bite. "You're going to need all your strength if you plan to keep running away from me. That's your real plan, isn't it?"

"Who knows?" He shrugged. "I'm not worried, but you should be. What did you find out about the men I'm after?"

"More than one government wants them." She'd known this from the start. But like any good gambler, she kept a tight hold on her chips.

Rourke leaned back in his chair. "Why?"

"I don't know. And stop looking at me like that," she demanded. "I really don't."

"What else?"

Annie paused, considering her options. Then she replied, "They don't have any names."

"Do you believe that?" Rourke asked.

"Yes. It fits. Why else would they have me chasing after you?

"Why else, indeed." He stared at her. "Well, I suggest you keep trying to find out more. If you're going to keep getting in my way, you might as well be useful."

"I already have been, Rourke, and I'm not going to let you forget it, either." Annie stood up, keeping a tight rein on the triumph she felt inside. "Let me splash some water on my face, then I'll see what else I can find out."

When she came back out of the bathroom, he was gone, just as she'd expected. Desperately in need of more coffee, she went to the room-service cart and lifted the pot to pour herself another cup.

Beneath the coffee pot was a hastily scrawled note. As she read it, her black mood lifted in a way no amount of caffeine could equal. "You've improved, Annie. I'd tell you to keep up the good work, but that goes without saying, because if you don't, you won't make our meeting. Three days, home ground. Names don't change there much."

Annie smiled, then laughed out loud. Rourke's note spoke volumes to her, in more ways than one. She would never forget any of the personal information she'd dragged out of him six years ago, not after fighting so hard for every little tidbit. She'd make the meeting, all right.

Even better than figuring out his code, however, was the knowledge he had bothered to leave it for her in the first place. It was a sign, an offering of the sort only Patrick would make, the first inkling that he might be willing to trust her. But first she had to live up to his challenge.

Chapter Five

London

Gerald shifted in the wing chair, not at all pleased with the proceedings. With his high level of rank, he rarely found his decisions being questioned or overruled.

"Use Annie Sawyer." It was a direct order from his superior, Charles Johnson. A slender, gray-haired, dapperly dressed man in his early sixties, he didn't look like the cold, calculating head of the European office.

"She's out of her depth," Gerald protested. "Her expertise is in putting people or events together, not in tracking—or running away from—unlawful citizens."

"The point is moot. These men have never left a trail that could lead to them. A live trail, that is. Until now."

"But—"

Charles held up his hand, stopping him. "We've been certain before that they were about to be caught, Gerald, but each surefire lead fizzled, and each time the people we sent in ended up dead with nary a clue as to who killed them." He folded his hands atop his desk and stared pointedly at Gerald. "We cannot let this chance slip by us. According to your own information, Patrick Rourke is after the same people we are. He doesn't care if he finds them dead or alive. We do. They're our only link to finding the others."

"All the more reason to use someone capable of stopping him," Gerald insisted.

"There isn't anyone. Annie has worked with him before. Her persistence and persuasiveness may be just what we need. You said it yourself. Rourke has already proven himself quite capable of losing anyone watching him."

"He can lose her, too," Gerald reminded him.

"True, but she's the only one with a chance to convince him to let us in on the hunt. If Annie isn't working with Rourke, we won't have a chance of capturing these criminals. Years of work and questions could go unanswered forever.''

Gerald did not like having his own words thrown back at him. "Human life means nothing to these men."

"Their past actions have shown that, but you know our policy. Any agent is expendable if their death will flush out the men we're after and allow us finally to put an end to their violence." He raised his pencil-thin gray eyebrows. "Are you losing your touch, old boy?"

"No." The coldness of his own words bothered Gerald, as did his guilt, proof it was time to get out of this business. He'd lost his objectivity. The ability to feel such personal loyalty was a detriment in their line of work. "I'm simply concerned."

"Is there something you aren't telling me, Gerald?"

"Of course not," Gerald lied smoothly.

Perhaps he wasn't as detached as he used to be, but he could still look out for number one. Telling details of a certain incident in his past could jeopardize his pension, and he was close to retirement, too dangerous a time to be dealing with the repercussions of past mistakes. He wasn't willing to go that far, even for Annie.

"Then I take it you've no further objections?"

"None," Gerald replied quietly.

He stood up and took his leave, deep in thought. Patrick Rourke wasn't a cold-blooded killer. But he was dangerous. Who knew what lay dormant in such a man until he was pushed too far. It didn't seem as if Rourke could be pushed any further than he had been in the past, but how could they be sure?

When Gerald entered his office, he found Bruce Holloway leaning over his desk, reading the papers scattered about. "Find out anything useful?" Gerald asked tersely.

Bruce jerked upright and stepped back, sitting down in a chair facing the desk. "You wanted to see me?"

"Indeed I did." Gerald sat behind the cluttered desk, eyeing the other man with unconcealed distrust. Was his secretary losing his marbles? He knew better than to let Bruce inside Gerald's private office alone. "Why did you call Annie in Iowa?"

Folding his hands, Bruce leaned back, completely at ease. "I have to keep tabs on the people under me."

"She may be working within your area of jurisdiction, but she is not currently under your control. This operation has been taken out of your hands and I won't tolerate any interference. Do I make myself clear?"

"As crystal, sir. Anything else?"

Bruce Holloway was cocky, obnoxious and inept. The product of too much money and pretty-boy good looks, he was a constant irritant to Gerald. Since Ireland was normally his bailiwick, that irritation would undoubtedly get worse as this operation progressed. Gerald frowned at the thought.

"How did you find out her location?" he asked.

"I heard your secretary making reservations."

The intercom on his desk beeped, then a voice announced, "Annie, line one." Gerald reached for the phone, but stopped with his hand resting on the curving black receiver. "That will be all, Bruce. I'll talk to you later."

Bruce got to his feet and left the office. Gerald waited until the door clicked shut. "What went wrong?" he asked impatiently. "You didn't call in as arranged."

Even over the phone, with all the distance between them and a rather dubious connection at that, Annie could still tell Gerald was seriously peeved. Tough cookies. After a bumpy transatlantic flight, a bizarre game of cat and mouse at the Dublin airport, and then a mad dash to make her bus, she wasn't exactly in the mood to apologize.

Annie pressed a tissue to her cheek, dabbing up the droplets of water dripping from her hair. The Irish mist had coated her as she'd walked from the depot to the phone booth. She was tired and confused. And now Gerald had the nerve to be upset with her for not calling in sooner?

"What went wrong?" Annie repeated incredulously. "You tell me! Did you order a team to tail me in Dublin?"

"Of course not. Why would you assume they're ours? Did you recognize them?" Gerald asked.

"No, but they certainly recognized me, and I'm hardly what you'd call a high-profile field operative, now am I?"

"Describe them."

"Average height and build, dark hair, your basic, non-descript, don't-stand-out-in-any-crowd type of tail."

Gerald ignored her sarcasm. "Any ideas on who they were?"

"No. Maybe Bruce is sticking his nose in again. Find out, will you? I don't need the added grief."

"I intend to." Gerald paused. "I'm not sure I like the way this is shaping up. It still might be best to pull you out of there."

Annie struggled to keep her temper under control. There was no way she would let Gerald pull her out now. Rourke needed help, and she wanted, needed, to be there for him this time. Besides, she didn't like the way things were shaping up, either. It wasn't like Gerald to hem and haw like this.

"What else haven't you told me?" Annie asked calmly.

"A bloody lot!"

She sighed, leaned back against the wall of the phone booth and waited for him to continue. More than anyone else, Gerald had taught her the usefulness of being patient.

Finally he said, "We believe the men Rourke and you are after know the identities of the masterminds behind a string of violent international crimes." He listed various unsolved cases over the years. "We know they've dealt in the sale of arms, too."

"How did you make the connection?" she asked.

"I can't reveal that information."

Annie snorted. "So this is all conjecture?"

"No, it's based on facts gathered over the years. Now listen. One of our contacts reported seeing Rourke in Limerick. You'd best get on your way there. And remember, check in when you do locate him. Keep me informed."

"That's all you're going to tell me?" Her suspicions increased. "Gerald, I know you pretty well. Why are you withholding facts from me?"

"It's for your own safety."

"Thanks a lot! I do hope I don't die wondering what the facts were," she retorted.

"Annie! Wait, don't hang up. Where are you now?"

"I'm in An Uaimh."

"Excuse me?"

She refrained from yelling. "Otherwise known as Navan," she announced, then promptly hung up on him.

Annie glared at the pay phone. She would never understand the inner workings of the agency. Though she had a high-level security clearance and they trusted her with other people's lives, they wouldn't tell her diddly squat about the men she and Rourke were tracking down. That worried her, as did those two tails she had had to lose on the way here. What was going on?

Everyone involved in this mess had to know that eventually Rourke would end up in Ireland, so it wouldn't have surprised Annie one bit to find someone other than her tailing him. But who, besides Gerald and a select number of others, knew about *her*? If Bruce hadn't had her followed, who had? Someone else from her own company? Why? And why was Gerald being so uncooperative?

Right now she didn't have time to worry about that. She knew Gerald's tip about Limerick was a wild-goose chase; Rourke might, indeed, have been there, but he wasn't likely to be there still. Since it was also possible whoever had reported the sighting wanted her to go there for reasons unknown, Annie decided not to risk playing that game. In order to meet Rourke's challenge, she had a game of her own to play. She had to prove herself worthy of his trust.

Fortunately, Navan was a small town. Everyone knew their neighbors and their problems. Secrets were hard to keep in a town this size, she knew that for a fact, having come from one not much bigger than this.

Even with the small influx of tourists right now, a stranger passing through all alone would be noticed. Which suited her just fine. She was going to take a page from Rourke's book and leave an easily followed trail. Then she would disappear.

Chapter Six

Rourke hunched his shoulders, burying his hands in his jacket pockets to keep warm as he waited in the barn for Derry to show up. His brief trip into Northern Ireland to check out the address Jack Merlin had given him had been a waste of time. Orren Hagen had indeed lived there recently, but a family occupied the apartment now and they had no idea of where he had gone, nor had anyone else in the neighborhood.

Since then, Rourke had repeatedly traversed the Irish countryside with the aim of confusing and losing anyone following him. Maybe he'd lost Annie Sawyer, too.

Rourke chuckled softly. "Right. And pigs will fly," he muttered to himself. He didn't trust her, but he was gaining a grudging respect for her abilities. That was the trouble. She should have been here by now.

He didn't want anyone to know about his meeting, therefore he supposed her tardiness had only made the job easier. But he'd expected her to be on time. If Annie was going to insist on hanging around, Rourke would have to make sure she did it on his terms.

The sound of an approaching vehicle pierced the shadowed silence of the musty old barn. Rourke stayed near the rear exit, waiting and watching as the lone occupant of the truck got out. Only then did his melodious whistle fill the still, damp, evening air.

The man dropped the sack he was carrying and spun around. Rourke watched as he pursed his lips, struggling for a moment before answering with a short low-pitched whistle of his own.

"You've a good memory, Derry."

"Patrick!"

Rourke stepped forward into a slit of gray moonlight that was streaming in through a crack in the wood planking. "You were expecting leprechauns?"

He didn't laugh. Neither did Patrick. The concern and worry on Derry's face was understandable. Derry knew Patrick would only be here if he needed help again, if something was seriously wrong.

"What happened?" Derry finally asked.

"Nothing. Yet."

Derry's body visibly sagged with relief. "Then let me fetch the bottle I keep hidden out here first."

"Dee still on you about your drinking?" Patrick asked, studying his lifelong friend as he plucked a bottle from a hiding spot in the wall. He hadn't changed: dark hair cut close around a narrow boyish face; his body still slender and wiry on a five-five frame.

Derry turned over two wooden crates near the door, then sat down on one and brushed his sleeve across the mouth of the bottle. "Some things never change in my life, and Dee heads the list. To me good, loving wife," he said, holding the bottle up in a mock salute before taking a healthy swallow and passing it to Rourke.

As much as Derry groused about her, Rourke knew he loved his wife and would do whatever was necessary to protect her and their children. Nor would Rourke endanger them. That was one troubling aspect of using his old friend like this.

Rourke took a big swallow from the bottle, the heat and strength of the liquor hitting him like lightning. Potent stuff, this homemade brew; it brought back too many memories. He sighed and passed the bottle back to Derry. "Hard to come by out of Ireland."

"Something worth coming home for?"

"Yes, but that's not why I'm here. Remember the little girl you helped me get out of the country?" Rourke asked. The other man nodded. "Someone's after her."

Derry leaned forward. "Who? Why?"

"I don't know those answers yet." Bitterness crept into his voice. "But it's why I'm in Ireland, though I swore I'd never come back here after getting Bridget out."

Derry put a hand on his friend's shoulder, his voice somber as he spoke. "Someday, Patrick, you'll have to make your peace with this land. Or your life will always be as it is now."

"And how's that?"

"Empty."

"I have Bridget," Rourke objected.

"No, you share her with Jack and Russ." Derry shook his head sadly. "You've nothing of your own to love. You won't admit it to yourself, but you've always been a man who needs to be needed. Else why would you have been doing the things you've done the last few years." He read the surprise in Patrick's eyes. "I keep in touch with the others. It's you who cuts himself off."

"Irishmen do love to give advice."

Derry grinned at him, exaggerating his brogue as he spoke. "We do like the sound of our own voices, they be so charming. And don't forget, you're as Irish as a peat bog yourself, you old sod. By birth, and no denyin' it. You may be able to hide your brogue, but you can't forsake your heritage. It still haunts you."

It was hard to be angry with Derry. They'd known each other since grade school, been best man at each other's weddings. Rourke knew he meant well. "I need a favor."

"Name it."

"I need someone you'd trust with your own family's safety to help me with this. You know that to protect Bridget, we quit looking for Orren Hagen. Now I need to know if he's alive, and if so, where he is."

Derry hesitated for a moment. "I'll do it myself," he told Rourke soberly. "I already know what needs to be done."

"No! I don't know who or what I'm up against and I'll not take the chance of involving you or your family." He tried to soften his harsh words with an explanation. "I can't allow it, Derry. Flynn is still running loose."

"I know. He's here in Ireland," Derry said softly. "I don't know where, but my source is reliable."

Rourke nodded. "I suspected as much, and it's all the more reason for you to stay totally out of this."

Though Derry tried not to let it show, Rourke knew he was relieved by this decision. Derry had helped to track Flynn before and knew the destruction the man had wrought in the past. And, though Derry had left that life behind him years ago, Rourke knew he stayed in touch with others who were still involved.

"I've just the man," Derry said. "His name's Casey. I'll set up a meet for tomorrow night, same time, here."

Patrick shook his head vehemently. "No. I don't want you connected to this. Make it the crumbling ruins of that place up the coast, late tonight."

"Suits the occasion, and you, as well. You always did like the remnants of that old stone castle," Derry said, grimacing. "It'll be as you wish. I'll arrange it for tonight." He rubbed his hands together. "Now, why don't you come up to the house for a bite of supper."

Rourke took another sip of the whiskey, letting the brew warm his chilled bones. "Did your wife ever learn how to keep a secret?"

"That one? Never!" They grinned at each other in shared remembrances of a carefree time so long ago, when keeping secrets hadn't mattered. "The earth'll crack open and swallow us all first, and no mistake."

"Then I'll have to beg off this time, I'm afraid," Rourke said, standing up and handing the bottle back to Derry. "And I don't want to see any sign of you up on the cliff, either, or I'll tell Dee where you hide your bottle."

"Some friend you are, threatening to take away a man's first pleasure," Derry groused.

Patrick arched a dark eyebrow high. "I can remember a time when that came second."

"Still does," Derry replied, grinning widely. "Dee is still hankering after a girl, not satisfied with those four boys. Baby's due in two months."

"I hope it's a girl then," Patrick said. He turned and started to walk away, then paused and looked back over his shoulder. "Thank you, Derry."

"Any time. Our prayers are with you, Patrick. They always have been."

Rourke slipped out the back and walked briskly across the fields, his hands shoved into the pockets of his leather jacket. Seeing Derry again brought back even more memories, and he felt stinging tears struggling to escape from his eyes, but he held them back, quelled them as he had so many times in the past. His own son would have been—

No. He would not dwell on what might have been.

He had to live for today, right now. He hadn't been given the chance to save his own child, but he could save Bridget. Realizing he'd been squeezing his eyes shut tightly, Rourke slowly opened them. For the first time since his arrival, he let himself enjoy the beauty of his homeland. For it was beautiful, even on this gray rainy day.

Lush green fields; flowers growing wild and abundantly in the meadows; the tall wet grass whipping against his pant legs as he strode toward the sea. He stood for a precious moment and watched the water flowing up onto the beach, foamy curving white lines of bubbles popping and drifting back into the ocean.

At last, Rourke untethered the horse he'd hidden nearby and rode back down the beach, the wet sea air forcing him to seek shelter without delay.

THE COTTAGE WAS WARM and snug, remarkably up-to-date inside while its exterior blended unobtrusively with the bleak surrounding countryside. But the man who had sought temporary refuge there took precious little comfort from the cozy dwelling—or anything else, for that matter.

There was a crackling fire beyond the hearth, but the flames didn't burn half as hot as his anger. Food was close at hand, but none of it could sate his hunger for complete and total victory. Good strong ale was there aplenty, too, but it was like water compared to the heady brew he sought.

Vengeance. Of that he would drink his fill. Soon.

The phone beside him rang. A thin, cruel smile formed itself upon his lips as he reached out his hand to answer it. He hardly missed the absent little finger on that hand. On occasion it ached, phantom pain, but he paid that no mind.

Pain, after all, was his stock in trade. He'd made a good living inflicting it on others. Death, despair and pure, sweet pain. As he pressed the phone receiver to his ear, Flynn's smile grew broad.

"Well?"

"He's in Ireland."

"Is he now?" The four-fingered hand squeezed the receiver even tighter. "You're positive?"

"Yes. Saw him myself."

Flynn forced down the excitement welling within him. It wasn't going to be that easy. "Just a moment."

He got up from his chair by the fire and crossed the snug, sparsely furnished parlor, quietly closing a door that let onto one of the cottage's two small bedrooms. This was a private conversation, not for anyone else's ears, not even his oh-so-cooperative houseguest.

Returning to his seat, Flynn asked, "Where is he?"

"I don't know," the man on the phone replied. "He got away from me. But I've put out the word. Your price is right. It won't be long until someone comes up with Patrick Rourke's location."

"Call me as soon as you get word."

Flynn grimaced as he hung up, the light of the fire glinting in his hazel eyes. Patience was not his strong suit. He was warm, dry, well fed and relatively safe in this remote place, but it was still a hideout, one he had been forced into against his will, and that galled him to the point of a murderous rage.

There was no doubt who would be the victim of that rage. Patrick Rourke. Not only had Rourke and his friends botched the deal Flynn had so carefully arranged in Houston, preventing him from getting hold of a top-secret electronics schematic he'd intended to sell, but then he had added insult to injury by taking from him the very jewelry Flynn had stolen in order to pay back a debt he owed.

The people he owed had expected payment on time. Rourke was not the only one looking for him. Unfortunately, Flynn didn't have a few spare million to pay them with. If they caught up with him now, they would most certainly kill him.

In fact, from recent information he'd received, even coming up with their money might not save him. That was a particularly strange turn of events, one Flynn intended to get to the bottom of as soon as he'd dealt with Rourke.

None of this, however, could be done openly.

Which meant he had to stay in hiding and use others to do the dirty deeds. It was the way he usually worked, of course, but in the past it had always been his choice. Now, he didn't have any other option and he didn't like it one bit. There were evil portents on the wind.

Unable to sit still, he went to the window and looked out at the roiling sea far below. It suited his mood, wild and unsettled. There was something mysterious going on beneath the surface of that troubled water, just as there was something happening around him that he couldn't quite put a finger on.

But he would figure it out. Oh, yes. At that very moment, even as he smiled at his own wild-eyed reflection, dozens of puppets were dancing to his tune. Like a spider in the middle of a large, intricate web, Flynn felt every small vibration on the silk of his dominion. He must interpret each one carefully, weigh the options, then make his move.

Using a tip he had gotten that very night, he might be able to put together another deal to pay the money he owed. If that was not enough, he would pay in violence. Nothing was going to stop him from going after Rourke. He needed a plan, and for that he needed more information. That in turn would take time.

Anger and impatience welled up inside him, but he forced them down. He'd been foiled twice already. He couldn't afford mistakes. Allowing himself to be spotted in London had brought Rourke on the run, smack into the middle of a trap. Unfortunately, the so-called friends to whom Flynn owed all that money had learned of his location as well and had sent men to demand immediate payment—or to collect his head on a plate. He'd fled, his trap for Rourke unsprung.

His own men had then followed Rourke back across the Atlantic. Through his myriad sources, Flynn had discovered that Rourke owned race horses and that one of them would be running at a track in Kentucky. Another trap was set there. But something—or someone—had spooked Rourke and he'd never showed. A bizarre flurry of activity ensued, obvious trails that led nowhere. Worse, two-legged bloodhounds other than his own were found sniffing about.

Flynn hadn't liked the feel of it. He'd recalled his men and gone to ground. Thus he found himself in this cottage, stewing in his own bile.

Now Rourke was in Ireland. Very obliging of him. But something didn't feel right about that, either. Flynn returned to his seat by the fire. Staring into the flames, a grim smile again played at the corners of his mouth, as the nebulous fog of his thoughts coalesced into an idea.

It was more a dark dream than a plan, but it pleased him and would help fill the restless hours and days that lay ahead. He would need patience. And more information. But at the end of the bloody road of vengeance he saw so clearly in his mind's eye, Flynn could also see the destiny he had always known would be his someday. Total victory.

ROURKE LEFT THE HORSE with the inn owner's son and headed upstairs to change before he ate. He was wet through to the skin. The sight of Annie Sawyer relaxing on his bed surprised him.

Doing his best to ignore the relief he felt at knowing she was all right, he growled, "You're late."

"I had my reasons."

"They'd better be good ones. Comfortable?" he asked with heavy sarcasm as he closed the door behind him.

"Lovely. It's a charming room."

Unable to sustain his anger, his lips twitched at her reply, almost a smile. "That's exactly why I chose it." He grabbed his dry clothes and headed for the bathroom.

"Please don't jump out the window."

"Now why would I do that?" He looked back at her, surprised by her perception. The thought had crossed his mind. Seeing her again was making him think twice about using her, especially since he now had confirmation that

Flynn was in Ireland. "You're not that rotten a dinner date."

Annie stuck her tongue out at his retreating back and stood up, straightening her sweater. She ran a brush through her hair, pulling a few strands down as wispy bangs, brushing the rest behind her unadorned ears.

"How did you get a key to the room?" He was leaning against the door jamb, dressed in dry jeans now and a crisp white linen shirt, his black hair still damp but freshly combed.

"I'll tell you after we're eating," Annie replied. "I missed lunch."

Rourke nodded and followed her down the staircase and into the small dining room. The inn had a warm, homey feeling Annie found quite comfortable. But the way Rourke was staring at her made her uneasy.

"I know you're having second thoughts about my being here, Rourke, but you can forget them. I'm not going to go away. You invited me. Remember? And now that I am here you won't be able to lose me. I'll just keep popping up like a pesky critter you can't get rid of."

Rourke leaned back in his chair, studying the woman sitting across from him. The soft, creamy sweater looked good on her. But "pesky critter" was still an apt label.

"What story did you use to get a key to my room?"

"Surprise! You're my fiancé."

Rourke raised his eyebrows. "Cheeky. Why are you late?"

"I was tailed out of Dublin, but I lost them."

Her confidence did little to reassure him. "You're sure about that, are you?"

"Positive. Anyone following me is down the coast over a hundred miles away. I followed your example and left an easily read trail." His look of interest encouraged her to continue. "I went from one small village to the next looking for my wandering fiancé. You have amnesia, poor dear.

The people along the way were extremely helpful and friendly.''

"Who knows you're here at the inn?"

"No one. I haven't called in my location since Navan."

He continued to look at her, gray eyes assessing and evaluating. "I want you to do something for me tonight."

She looked at him warily. "What?"

"Use that same story around this village. Make sure everyone knows I've suffered a relapse and taken off. Say you think I'm heading for Kilkenny. Then go there yourself."

"That's at least two hours away!"

Patrick frowned. "I thought you wanted to help?"

"Running off on wild-goose chases isn't helping."

"Yes, it is. This step is very important." He chuckled. "Besides, you should feel complimented. I like your tactics enough to use them."

Annie looked away. His sincerity was obvious, but as usual, he didn't seem in the mood to offer any explanation for what he was doing. She knew she was going to do as he asked, so why was she even questioning him on this?

Because she knew Patrick didn't really trust her, that's why. Well, she didn't really trust him, either, so they were even. Annie sighed. This wasn't exactly what she'd hoped for in the way of equal footing.

"How do you want to work this?" she asked.

"After dinner I'll go up to the room first."

"That'll look odd, don't you think?"

"Good point. Here." He handed her a tourist guide he'd found on the table when they'd sat down. "Study this, like you're planning tomorrow's itinerary or something. Give me twenty minutes, then come up. Make a big scene."

Annie leaned back in her chair and crossed her arms. "All right. Who are you meeting tonight?"

"No one you know," Patrick replied, unable to contain a wry smile. Her tracking skills weren't the only thing that had improved. She had developed a pretty fine-tuned set of instincts, as well. "Did you find out anything more from your boss?"

She frowned. "Some. He believes the men you're looking for can identify the masterminds behind a string of violent crimes. They also deal in weapons." Annie repeated the list of tragedies Gerald had given her. "Not one of those was ever claimed by any group. Some of them, like the bombing of that airline terminal a few years back, were even denounced quite vocally by those accused of the action."

Rourke knew from personal experience that such things did happen. The bombing that had killed his family in Northern Ireland had nothing to do with the troubles there, though people naturally assumed it had. It had been a personal vendetta carried out by a few men—"nonaligned terrorists" the authorities smugly called them—who were actually nothing more than criminals, with Flynn as their leader.

"Where are we going to meet tomorrow?"

Annie's question brought him back to the present. "Let's make it Dublin." He gave her the name of a hotel there, then added, "But we'll meet at the cathedral."

"Be there or I'll find you again, Rourke."

"I don't doubt you will," he muttered under his breath.

Dinner was served, giving them both something else to think about. It wasn't too difficult to chat and act as if they were engaged. But in fact, other than superficially, Rourke supposed they didn't really know each other at all. That was fine with him. At the moment, the only thing he wanted to know about Annie was that she'd do as she was told.

Chapter Seven

"Where is Patrick Rourke?"

Colin Farrell sipped his drink. "We don't know. The man is quite adept at losing our trackers."

"He *is* still in Ireland?" Brady Adair asked, his patience long gone.

"Yes, and we know the general area, but our source did not know his exact location."

Brady slammed his fist down on the top of the desk. "Find him! And kill him! Eliminate him right away!"

"That's not a good idea at this time," Farrell cautioned.

"And why not?"

"If we capture Rourke, we can force him to tell us what he knows. Then we can arrange an unfortunate accident for him."

"Hmm," Brady hummed thoughtfully, warming to the idea. "That might prove interesting. What about the woman?"

"Annie Sawyer. She does work for the U.S. government. And she's in Ireland, too." Farrell glanced at a piece of paper before him. "According to the last report, she's spending the night in Kilkenny."

"Why is she here? What's she after?"

"Her motives are still unclear."

"Perhaps we're jumping at shadows. Given Rourke's murky past, maybe she's hunting him," Brady suggested.

Farrell straightened the sheets of paper on the desk, making sure they were perfectly in line. He liked the way this business had changed over the years. Reports from the field, fresh off the fax machine.

"I don't think so," he said. "They spent the night together in Iowa, you'll recall. And I have recently received word from an informant that confirms there is some sort of bond between them. As for her involvement, however, our source hasn't come through on that yet. For the moment, we'll have to assume she's working with Rourke to find Hagen."

"That's all we need! Maybe we should get rid of her."

This situation was warping Brady's usually methodical thinking process, making him rash and careless. But Farrell remained calm. Always. He appreciated efficient things. Such as fax machines. Well-made weapons. And people who knew how to use them when the time was right.

"No. She may lead us to Rourke," Farrell reminded him. "And if they do have a close relationship of some kind, that could prove useful to us, as well. Besides, even if we arranged an accident, we would end up with a tedious investigation from her government. We need to watch both of them and see what they're up to before we take any action. Don't you agree?"

Scowling, Brady replied, "What we need to do is find out why she's here and why her government is involved!"

"Perhaps they know more than we think."

"Don't feed me that garbage. You were right the first time—it has to be Hagen." He looked at Farrell. "We'd better find out what else he's been up to. His shenanigans could bring us even more trouble."

Farrell nodded. "I have already requested a report. It should be in tomorrow or the next day."

"Good. I don't suppose there's anything new on *his* whereabouts, either?" Brady asked sarcastically.

"Hagen seems to have disappeared completely. It would be nice to think he'd done us the favor of dying, but I doubt it very much."

"As do I." Brady leaned back in his chair. "I don't like it. Orren Hagen may be tough as nails, but he isn't that smart. Someone has to be helping him."

"I agree. But as you say, we know Hagen. He'll make a mistake and show himself." Farrell's smile was cold. "When he does, we'll be ready."

Brady jumped to his feet. "We'd better be!" he bellowed.

"Don't get so excited, Brady. I'm taking care of it."

"See that you do."

Farrell straightened his papers again. Brady paced, stricken by the unfairness of it all. With his partner's meticulous attention to detail and his own methodical approach to a business that had heretofore been ruled by idiots and anarchists, they'd built an empire. Now that empire shuddered like a house of cards. And for what?

"Run for political office," Brady groused. "Why would anyone want to do that?"

"It's a different kind of power," Farrell replied.

"Money is the only real power."

His partner shrugged. "You expect me to disagree? But if we keep our heads, he might even prove useful in the long haul. His kind of power can be purchased. We've done it before."

"Bah!" Brady exclaimed, still pacing. "I wouldn't give him the time of day. This whole situation is entirely his fault. Can you believe it? My own brother putting detectives on me, afraid I might taint his chances of getting a cabinet appointment. And now he's hired even more snoops because the first ones couldn't find anything. So much for brotherly love." He looked at Farrell. "Well, the last laugh will be mine. They aren't going to find anything on me."

"I agree. Once we clean up this one loose end, those detectives won't be able to find anything except a highly successful businessman."

"One tiny mistake and now it's coming back to haunt us." Brady stopped pacing, having worked off the worst of his frustration. "It might be wise to cancel our next project."

Farrell stood. It was good to see Brady thinking again. But he said, "Let's give it a few more days, see what happens. By then, it could all be over."

A GENTLE BREEZE RUFFLED the damp strands of grass near Annie's face, tickling her cheek. She was wedged facedown into a narrow culvert just below the rounding curve of a hill. This position gave her a good view of the area, and the slant of the land provided needed cover.

Who was Rourke meeting tonight?

Earlier this evening she had done as he asked, using her rental car to get to Kilkenny. After spreading her story and renting a room, she had changed her appearance and caught the next bus headed toward Balbriggan on Ireland's east coast, spending the travel time studying a detailed tourist guide.

Rourke had challenged her memory with the cryptic note he'd left her in New York, and she had met that challenge, tracking him to what he'd once called "home ground." Though she doubted it had been his intention, he had also caused her to remember other things, bits and pieces she'd managed to drag out of him on previous occasions. Gaelic quirks aside, this was indeed a place where names didn't change much. And he'd told her about some of them in passing, locations where he had spent—or perhaps misspent—his youth.

Maybe he had actually needed her to go to Kilkenny as a ruse. Or maybe he had just wanted her out of the way. Whichever, he was meeting someone tonight and Annie wanted to know who. Knowing that Rourke had a penchant for out-of-the-way spots, and considering his seemingly innate sense of the dramatic, she was betting on this crumbling ruin as his choice.

It looked like her bet was paying off. Someone dressed in dark clothing was inching across the opposite edge of the low hill. She adjusted her miniature infrared binoculars to bring her target into clearer focus. A crescent moon gave her all the light she needed, though the night was quite gloomy, with heavy clouds moving across the area.

Annie studied him as he slowly approached the ruins. He stayed in a crouched position, a fisherman's hat covering his head, his patrician nose and narrow face in deep shadow.

When he moved in her direction, Annie tucked her head down, trying to become part of the dark landscape. She concentrated on the sounds of his movements, visualizing his path as he came closer, his shoes barely making a sound on the grassy hillside as he neared her hiding spot. He was almost on top of her when he stopped. Annie held her breath and lay perfectly still.

It seemed an eternity before he turned away and moved off to her left. A short time later, she looked up to find him still perusing the area. Cautious man.

Eventually he took refuge behind one of the bigger boulders and sat down, his hands hanging loosely between drawn up knees. Annie waited with him, frequently scanning the surrounding area for signs of movement.

It was midnight when another dark-clad figure came crawling around the far side of the stone where the man sat. This new arrival almost had him from behind when he suddenly rolled away, out of reach.

"Casey?"

She recognized Rourke's voice, watched as both men stood up and brushed themselves off. Through her binoculars she could see that Rourke was talking but he was speaking so softly she couldn't hear what he said.

Without making a sound, she eased her body out of the narrow, sodden culvert and started crawling toward them, using the fallen stones of the ruin as cover. As she got closer, their voices became clearer.

"I need you to find Lunn Kendrick," Rourke was saying. "He shouldn't be that hard to track down, but he's skittish and plays dirty, so be careful."

"How do we communicate?"

"Face-to-face or not at all, for now. Contact Derry only if you have to. We'll meet again in two days, Dublin cathedral," Rourke told him. "I'll be watching for you."

In the solid blackness of her hiding place, Annie arched her eyebrows. The cathedral was where she was supposed to rendezvous with Rourke tomorrow, or rather, later today, since it was now after midnight. Was Rourke planning to invite her to his next meeting with this man? Fat chance. More likely he would have another supposedly important errand for her.

Annie didn't care what he wanted. She'd be there, either by his side or in hiding like she was now. Who was this stranger named Casey? Who was Lunn Kendrick? She strained her ears, listening, hoping for more tidbits.

Suddenly, a movement off to the left caught her eye. Someone else had joined this clandestine party, and from the stealthy way he was creeping up on them, Annie didn't think he had an invitation, either. The distance between her and Rourke was too far. There was no way to quietly warn him without making herself a moving target.

The name Orren Hagen and the address Casey was giving Rourke barely registered as Annie sought deeper cover behind the huge stone. Putting two fingers into her mouth, she let loose with a chilling, shrill whistle.

There was a terse exclamation of surprise, followed by a flurry of movement. Moments later, she cautiously peered around the rock, binoculars raised to the last positions of the men. They were gone. She quickly scanned the area, finding no movement. The quiet was unnerving. She felt like a duck out in the middle of a pond with nowhere to hide.

Then a dull, thudding sound rippled through the eerie silence of the ruins. A body hitting the ground? Adrenaline rushed through her. Rourke! Stretching out flat on the grass, she began inching forward, angling carefully through the rocks.

Without warning a hand clamped over her mouth and the full weight of a body rolled on top of her, squashing her into the damp ground. Annie fought instinctively, sinking her sharp teeth into the hand over her mouth as she tried to kick and punch the person attacking her.

"Pesky critter?" The words came out as a groan.

Relief coursed through her, her heart racing like a charging bull. "Damn you, Rourke!"

"I thought so."

Rourke moved off of her, but she could still feel the heat of his body alongside her. There was no mistaking the anger on his face as they glared at each other, almost nose to nose, eyes level. A few strands of hair had fallen across his brow, his black turtleneck adding to his menacing air. Annie was suddenly glad she'd bit him.

"What are you doing here?" he demanded.

She grinned. "Looking for you."

Rourke rolled onto his back and stared up at the heavy, dark clouds drifting in from the sea. "Well, you certainly found me." He massaged his hand and grimaced. "I do hope you've had your shots."

"I'll give you a shot, you—"

"Hush!"

"What are we waiting for?"

"A signal," Rourke replied.

Shortly thereafter, a soft whistling filled the air, drawing closer to them. Rourke stood and helped Annie up as a man approached. He stopped a few feet in front of them, a ski mask in one hand, his own fisherman's hat in the other.

His lightly freckled face was manly and handsome, though the tufts of short red hair sticking out on his head in a ring where his hat had been gave him an almost boyish appearance. The distrust gleaming in his eyes was all angry adult male, however, and directed at Annie Sawyer.

"You know her?"

"Unfortunately," Rourke answered.

Casey looked at him. "The guy says he's working as a backup." He jerked his thumb at Annie. "For her."

Rourke kept his eyes on Casey. "Who gave him his orders?"

"Somebody named Bruce Holloway."

"Blast it!" Annie exclaimed. Now both men were looking at her suspiciously. "It's okay. Bruce isn't a threat. Just a big pain in the rump with delusions of omnipotence." She and Gerald were in for a shouting match. "Where is this guy?"

"Out cold, down the hill a ways to your left."

"Don't worry about him," Rourke told her. "He'll survive." He turned to Casey. "Two days, Dublin."

"I'll be there." Casey nodded and headed toward the opposite side of the cliff, leaving the way he had arrived.

"Let's get out of here." Rourke took off without waiting for her, his stride long and fast. It took him a moment to realize Annie wasn't following him.

"I said let's go!" he whispered harshly.

She continued down the hill at a left angle. "I want to get a look at this guy."

"Why?"

"To see if he's one of the men I spotted in Dublin."

Rourke hesitated, then changed direction to follow her. When he caught up, she was down on her knees, rolling the man over on his back. "Recognize him?"

Annie pulled a pencil-thin flashlight out of her shirt pocket and aimed it at the man's face. "No, do you?"

Kneeling down beside her, Rourke studied the man. He had dark hair, pock-marked ruddy cheeks and bushy eyebrows. "Yes. I saw him come out of the local pub late this evening." He checked the man's pockets and found a driver's license. "Kenneth Blair. Recognize the name?"

"No."

Rourke sat back on his heels. "You reported our location."

Offended by his accusation, Annie lashed back, "I did not! I didn't know you were going to be here. It was sheer guesswork on my part." Educated guesswork, of course, but she wasn't in the mood for explanations. "Who else did *you* tell? And who's Derry?"

"I told no one," Rourke glared at her. "And I trust Derry with my life. He would never betray me."

She almost scoffed at his naïveté, then thought better of it. For Patrick Rourke to trust anyone was a monumental occasion. He wouldn't put such faith in this Derry character without very good reason.

"There are other possibilities," Annie finally told him, breaking the silence of their mutual glares. "Either this Casey guy leaked the location, or one of us was followed."

Rourke stood up without comment and held his hand out to her. Annie grabbed it, letting him pull her up. They walked in silence from the cliffs toward the road. Rourke was scowling. Had someone followed him to Derry's? To be on the safe side, he was going to have to contact Derry and warn him.

"Wait here a minute," Annie said.

Rourke watched as she crossed the dirt road to a large rock. She leaned over and pulled her bag out from behind it. "Luggage and all," he noted with a dour smile as she rejoined him. He took the bag from her. "I guess I should be thankful you travel light. Where are you planning on staying?"

"With you."

"Silly question." Rourke sighed and flung her blue flight bag over his shoulder. The tall, green grass brushed against their jeans with a raspy sound as they made their way across the field. "I have lovely accommodations lined up for this evening," he informed her as they headed in the direction of the horse he had waiting nearby. "If you're partial to barns, that is."

Chapter Eight

It had been a gray, oppressive dawn, but now the cloud cover was burning off, revealing increasing patches of clear blue sky. An omen if ever there was one. Flynn smiled and turned from the parlor window, then walked into the kitchen, where he took a seat at an old but serviceable table in the middle of the cheerful little room.

His breakfast was spread out before him, ham and eggs. He ignored it. At the moment his appetite was for other things. "Did you take care of it?" he asked.

"Naturally," the large, muscular man opposite him replied, cutting into a thick ham steak with obvious anticipation. "Everything's set up. No worries."

"There are always worries, you fool."

The man shoved a big hunk of ham into his mouth, talking at the same time. "I suppose. Say, this ham is really good! Mind if I take some to my brother?"

"Take the whole thing for all I care!" Flynn struggled to control his temper. His dining companion's easygoing manner irritated him no end. "Just make sure you stay on top of this operation."

Another man came into the kitchen, poured himself a cup of tea and took a seat at the table. "Smells good," he said, then began to eat.

Flynn stared at him. "These men you hired," he said. "Are they reliable?" He didn't like having to use or depend on people he hadn't chosen himself. Trusting other people wasn't how one stayed alive.

"Sure." His mouth full, the dark-haired man mumbled adamantly. He took an enormous gulp of tea before adding, "I've used one of them before. He's good at his job."

"He'd better be," Flynn said. "Or he won't come out of this alive. You relayed my orders exactly?"

The man nodded again. "I read it just like you wrote it," he replied. Then he proceeded to attack his eggs with gusto.

"Good."

If Flynn's sources were correct, one of his fondest dreams was about to come true. He had wanted to be there to witness Rourke's undoing, but it wasn't a wise move. Too many people were looking for him. The satisfaction of knowing Rourke was gone from his life forever would have to be enough.

Flynn sliced his ham steak into thirds, smiling at the way the sharp knife cut through the meat. Three pieces. Easily managed. He continued to slice and cut and devour, chewing and grinding until one of the pieces was gone. The thought pleased him immensely.

One down, two to go. If all went well on his road of vengeance, in a few weeks he'd be a free man. Of course, he would have to get rid of the other two, Jack Merlin and Russ Ian. But again, if all went as planned, he'd have the cash to do that, too. The deal he was in the process of setting up would provide him with what was required to pay off all his debts—including those he intended to repay in blood.

And to think, with just a few quick moves at the right moment, he might even be in a position to gain control of a highly successful business at the same time.

Maybe his gluttonous companion was right after all. No worries. But not because of idiotic optimism or misplaced trust. Flynn wasn't too worried because of who and what he was. As always, if this particular plan didn't work out, Lian Francis Dougall had another waiting in the wings.

The big man glanced at Flynn, misinterpreting his blissful expression. "I told you it was good ham," he said.

"Sweet," Flynn agreed. He cut another bite and chewed it slowly, smiling at his guest. "As sweet as revenge."

WAS HE GOING TO FOLLOW HER? There was only one way to find out. Annie finished her cup of coffee before leaving the small restaurant. It was turning into a clear, beautiful day.

She had awoken this morning, before sunup, to find Rourke gone. His terse note had not appeased her. Wait there until he returned? Right. Like she was one of the horses that had shared their sleeping accommodations last night or something. Annie didn't know if he was worried about her safety or if he was just still trying to keep her out of the way. It didn't matter. She left him an equally terse note and went out. Rourke would not be happy. That was fine with her.

Right now she had problems of her own. Why was one of Bruce Holloway's agents at the meeting last night and how had he found them? She needed to find out what was going on. This kind of interference wasn't just annoying, it could jeopardize her relationship with Rourke. Annie was determined that if anyone was going to irritate him, it would be her, not her superiors, even if the motive was nothing more than misguided concern on Gerald's part.

Annie strolled down the deserted sidewalk, taking her time, pausing occasionally to look at a window display in one of the closed shops. Every now and then she'd glance casually over her shoulder. Just fishing, in the parlance of her trade. It was working. The man from last night was following her.

At the next alleyway she turned the corner, playing the tourist following her nose. Then she broke into a run, her black, rubber-soled shoes making little noise as she raced past a red-brick building. At last she came to a U-shaped delivery area and ducked out of sight.

From her flight bag she pulled out an unfamiliar but effective snub-nosed revolver Gerald had arranged for her to recover from a secure location upon her arrival in Ireland. Now she'd see if her fish rose to the bait.

He came pounding down the alleyway, the echo of his heavy footfalls pinpointing his position. What kind of help was the Company hiring these days?

He sprinted past her. "Going somewhere?" Annie asked. She cocked her gun for emphasis, stopping him in mid-stride.

"Hey! Take it easy!"

"Shut up," she said mildly. "Keep your back to me and step inside my office here."

"I—I can explain," he offered, backing up a few steps.

"Come in further." Annie didn't want anyone to see them in the alley and interrupt them while she was questioning the man. "Now, stop right there."

The guy was panting like a racehorse. His forest-green sweater was tight enough around his expanding middle to show he wasn't carrying a gun there. Evidently an unarmed tail, a local by the look of him, probably with more interest in the job as a source of income than any particular dedication. Still, she was cautious.

"So. Bruce sent you?"

He started to turn toward her as he spoke, gasping, his voice heavily accented. "Aye! We're on the same side, see? We can talk this out."

"Don't turn around. Put your hands on top of your head."

"Satisfied?" he asked after complying with her order.

Annie eased her bag to the ground, then stepped forward, pressing her gun into his lower spine as she patted him down. Assured that he didn't possess a weapon, she moved back to the brick wall, wanting to get distance between them.

"Okay, you can lower your hands."

"Finally." He pulled his sweater back into place and turned around. "Watch that thing, lassie!"

"*You* watch it." He was definitely the same man from last night, pock-marked face, dark hair, midforties. And now he was sporting an egg-sized bump on the side of his forehead. "Why were you following me?"

He grinned, showing crooked teeth. "It's my job."

"What are you after?"

"Information."

Losing patience with him, Annie said, "Would you like a little blood to go with that bump? I'm an excellent shot. What part of you should I start with?"

"A mite bloodthirsty, aren't you?"

"Mean, too. You'll find out if you don't answer my questions," she warned. "What are your orders?"

Annie knew the determination in her hazel eyes made almost as strong an argument as the gun in her hand. It seemed he thought so, too.

"I'm to keep an eye on you, help out if I'm needed."

She studied him. At the ruin last night, in the dark, she hadn't recognized him. The light of day confirmed it. He wasn't one of those she'd spotted following her before. Still, with all the strange goings-on, there was no harm in asking.

"Were you following me in Dublin?"

"No. I picked up your trail in Navan. You ran me a merry chase before finally giving me the slip," he admitted.

She could tell it galled him to admit she had lost him, and Annie couldn't suppress a smile at the man's chagrin. "How did you find us last night?"

"It wasn't easy, lass, and that's sure. After I lost you I checked in with Bruce. He gave me Rourke's last location, in Limerick, and through a few of my own contacts I managed to find him. It was him I followed to the stones."

Rourke was not going to like this piece of information. Annie, on the other hand, found it rather amusing in spite of the implications. Maybe this guy could provide a few other missing pieces. "Who did Rourke see yesterday?"

"I don't know. I lost him when he took off on a horse."

She frowned and made a threatening gesture with the revolver. "Just a second, bub. You just said it was Rourke you followed to the meet last night!"

"Aye! Relax, will you? It was him, in the end." He shrugged. "It's been a real job, this one! I find you, I lose you. I find Rourke, then lose him! So I buy your feint and drive to Kilkenny, but it was no go, so I came back here." The man took a deep breath then blew it out, shaking his head. "Lo and behold, there's Rourke! Almost missed him, too. But there's not much out the way he headed. Once I knew his destination, I hung way back so he wouldn't spot me."

Curious. Convoluted enough to be true. But Annie wasn't satisfied. "Why is Bruce Holloway involved?"

The man looked at her, puzzled. "Why wouldn't he be? This is his territory, after all."

Great! The guy didn't know this operation had been taken away from Bruce. There might well be others out there with the same lack of information. And, knowing Bruce, he was going to do everything possible to make sure he botched it up for her, if only by stupidly blundering on where he wasn't wanted or needed. She squeezed her eyes shut, but quickly opened them.

"What did you overhear last night?"

"They're meeting again in two days in Dublin. In the meantime, they're looking for Orren Hagen and Lunn Kendrick. Did you get the address for Hagen?"

His quick answers made her uneasy. "It's just occurred to me how cooperative you're being. Why?"

He shrugged. "First of all, lass, you've got a gun. Second, you're the main operative and I'm backup. And like I told you, we're on the same side. I work for Bruce, too."

Annie waved the gun at him. "Get out of here." He didn't move. "I'm serious. Take a hike."

She watched him walk back up to the street. Why was Bruce interfering? Was he simply overstepping his bounds because Gerald had pulled rank on him? Or was something else going on? If Gerald was playing his cards close to his vest like he said, how had Bruce gotten the information on their locations?

A nagging suspicion began crowding her thoughts. It was time for Gerald to supply some answers. Annie left the alley in the opposite direction from her supposed backup and went in search of a phone booth, found one, then waited impatiently for her connection to be put through. Phone service in Ireland tended to be capricious at best and never failed to be at its worst when one was in a hurry.

"Gerald here."

Annie didn't waste time with pleasantries. "How did Bruce get my location at Navan?"

After a short silence he said, "I don't know."

"Find out! Somehow Bruce also got a line on Rourke and gave it to one of his agents here." Brusquely, Annie explained what happened last night and this morning. "I'm not blowing smoke, Gerald. Find out how Bruce got that information and stop him!"

"I intend to, as soon as he gets in," Gerald promised.

Annie fumed in silence for a moment, trying to form the question that was uppermost on her mind in a way that wouldn't make Gerald too mad. He was, after all, her boss. She didn't want him to overreact and pull her out. Besides, she needed his support. No matter what was going on, Gerald was her main pipeline to the Company information network.

At last she decided on a concerned, businesslike tone and asked, "Do we have a leak in our department?"

Gerald was just as businesslike in his curt reply. "I'm not at liberty to discuss that."

His snooty British voice annoyed her, but Annie knew no amount of pressing would gain her an answer now. Even if he knew the allegation to be true, it was against policy for him to reveal anything to a subordinate. But it had been worth a try.

"All right. New subject. I need some input. Do you have someone who goes by the name Casey working in Ireland?"

"Not that I'm aware of, no. But if he's a freelancer, like Rourke, we'll probably have some sort of information on him. What do you know about him?"

Annie listed his features. "That's all I have other than his name, and that might be first or last. Just Casey."

"I'll start running it through the computers right away."

"Don't put your pencil down. I need information on the following other people as well. The first is Lunn Kendrick. I'm guessing he's someone Rourke knows from the old days. The second is Orren Hagen. This is the address we have for him," she said, rattling off the location she'd overheard Rourke giving Casey last night.

She paused, listening to the puffing of Gerald's pipe over the phone line. It was vaguely reassuring, the sound of Gerald at work. Annie cursed herself for her earlier tirade. No matter what was happening, she had to keep cool.

"Any questions on what I gave you?" she inquired.

"Who's Orren Hagen?" Gerald asked.

"I think he may be the key to the men you're after."

"Hmm. Anything else?"

Where did she start? "Did you find out if it was Bruce's men who were following me when I arrived in Ireland?"

"Bruce swears they weren't."

"But the one I accosted this morning was," she informed him. "His name's Kenneth Blair."

Gerald sighed. "Yes. I recognize that name. He does work for us. We've people all over the Emerald Isle."

"All the more reason that you have got to keep Bruce from interfering!" Annie sighed, too. "I'm sorry for behaving like this, Gerald. But how am I supposed to gain Rourke's trust if it appears that you don't trust me?"

"I do trust you, Annie. Look..." His voice trailed off, then in a warmer tone he said, "I'll put a gag on Bruce if I have to."

She smiled. "A nice tourniquet around his neck might work," Annie suggested. "After you find out how he got his information."

"Perhaps I'll use a tourniquet to get that, too."

"One of his fussy school ties would be appropriate. If that doesn't offend your sensibilities." Annie heard him chuckle, and that put her at ease. Gerald was on top of things, and Bruce was such a wimp, violence wouldn't be necessary. "Hagen's place should be our next stop. After that, we're returning to Dublin," she informed him, giving him the name and address of the hotel Rourke had mentioned in case he had to leave a message for her.

"Be careful and keep in touch," Gerald ordered.

The street was still pretty well deserted when Annie left the phone booth. She walked to the end of the block, intending to head back to the barn when she changed her mind and turned around. Why bother? Rourke was probably in town.

If she hadn't just vacated the phone kiosk herself, she probably wouldn't have even noticed that it was already in use again. As it was, however, it struck her as strange. She hadn't noticed anyone waiting. Her shadow, perhaps?

As she neared the booth, Annie saw that it wasn't Bruce's man at all. This one had red hair. Little tufts of it stuck out in a ring around his head, as if he'd just taken off a hat. Casey! Her eyes widened and she ducked behind a lamppost, wishing she was even more slender than she was.

Annie waited until he turned his back to her, then she ran to a flowering bush near the booth and crouched down behind it. Luckily, the shop behind her had yet to open for the day. But it wouldn't be long now. If someone came out, maybe she'd tell them she was playing hide-and-seek with some of the children who seemed to pop up everywhere in Ireland.

Whatever, it was impossible to look inconspicuous, so she settled for hiding from the man in the booth—and praying no one passed by. It couldn't hurt. One prayer had already been answered. He'd left the kiosk door ajar.

"Don't worry," the redhead was saying. "I'm closer than ever. Adair will get his money's worth."

It *was* Casey! But what was he talking about? Who was Adair? And more importantly, who was he reporting to?

"Don't worry," Casey repeated. "I'll keep you posted. Yes, I said! I'll check in daily."

He hung up the phone and banged out of the kiosk, muttering under his breath. Annie waited until he was out of sight before coming out from behind the bush. What was going on? How many people was Casey working for?

She turned and walked slowly down the sidewalk, almost in a daze. She'd slept well in the old barn Rourke had taken her to; the smells of livestock had reminded her of home. But it had been a busy couple of hours. Too many questions and not enough answers. Her head was spinning. What she needed was some more coffee to help clear her mind.

At last, the town was waking up. As she made her way back to the small restaurant for another dose of confusion-dispelling caffeine, she saw a couple of people walking on the opposite side of the street. She even saw an occasional car driving past.

But Annie never saw the hand that grabbed her from behind, jerking her back into a deserted alleyway.

Chapter Nine

Annie's flight bag slipped down her arm, hitting her in the legs and making her stumble. Strong fingers dug into her shoulders, holding her upright as she was shoved back into an alcove and up against a wooden door. She looked up, finding herself pinned by a pair of stormy gray eyes.

"Woman! I was.... Where have you been?"

"Rourke." Annie breathed a sigh of relief. "Here in town. And you?"

His lips were clamped into a thin line. "Trying to find us transportation. Didn't I tell you to stay put?"

"And why didn't you wake me and tell me what you were up to?" Annie countered.

He squeezed her shoulders gently, almost massaging them before he let go. "I thought you'd still be asleep when I returned."

"I got cold."

Rourke sighed heavily, relaxing the tight muscles of his face. She wasn't hallucinating; he was actually worried about her. Annie hadn't meant to worry him. Then again, maybe she had. She couldn't deny his concern touched her.

He shoved his hands into the pockets of his brown leather jacket, contemplating her face and struggling for some sort of control over his anger. So she'd gotten cold, had she? Not as cold as he'd half expected to find her.

Rourke cut the thought off. But other disturbing thoughts quickly filled the void. Such as how he had felt this morning when he'd awakened to find Annie wrapped around him spoon fashion. Her soft, warm body had felt good. Too good. Easing away from her on their straw bed hadn't helped, for within minutes she'd wrapped herself around him again.

Sleep had eluded him from then on. The soft curves of her body pressing into his brought desires leaping to the surface. He'd kept ignoring them until he no longer could, then he had left. He couldn't afford to let himself get involved with her.

"Let's get out of here. A bus leaves for Dublin in the next half hour. We can pick up a car there."

Annie walked beside him as they headed for the bus stop. Her comment about being cold had revealed plenty, both about her own feelings and the reaction to them she'd seen clearly in his eyes. But Rourke wasn't ready to commit himself to anything, not even an affair. That was all right with her, at least for now. To be honest, she wasn't too sure of her own feelings either.

It was a short, pleasant walk to the bus stop, the morning sun warm upon their faces. When they arrived they sat down on a wooden bench to wait. After a moment of silence, Annie asked, "Are we headed for Orren Hagen's place?"

"Yes." He glanced at her. "What were you doing in town?"

"Talking to the agent from last night."

"Who was he tailing?"

It wasn't a casual question. She could tell by the tension in his body that this was important to Rourke. "Me at first, but I lost him. Then he picked up on you. He lost you when you took off on a horse yesterday."

"How did he find us at the ruins?"

Annie told him how the agent had followed her to Kilkenny, before coming back. "He followed you to the meet with Casey last night and he overheard everything, including where your next meeting will be."

Rourke leaned back, his arm stretched out along the top of the wooden bench behind her. Like it or not, Annie was proving to be quite useful. "It can be changed." He glanced at her, sensing there was more. "Go on."

She shrugged. "That's it." It was work enough to gain Rourke's trust. There was no way she was going to tell him there might possibly be a leak in her own department. He would run from her as if she had the plague—and rightly so, she supposed. Also, so far her suspicions of Casey were just that, suspicions without any proof.

At this time she didn't even want to voice her concerns about Casey. It was obvious Rourke trusted him, perhaps because of their mutual connection with Derry, and he'd already made it quite clear how he felt about her doubting Derry. Besides, while it was true Casey had known their location, and could have betrayed it, the fact of the matter was Rourke had been followed.

Or had he? Just how reliable could information from one of Bruce's men be? While she was pondering this dilemma, Rourke stood up, breaking her train of thought.

"Where are you going?" Annie asked.

"To a phone. I'm going to leave a message for Casey."

Annie stuck right beside him while he spoke to Derry, changing the meeting place from the cathedral to the hotel. Then they went back and caught the bus to Dublin. Since they made it in the nick of time, and no one came running after, she felt sure they would have lost a tail had there been one. In Dublin they picked up a rental car and headed north to the Hagen farm, just outside of Monaghen, by a circuitous route that would have had Annie completely befuddled if she hadn't been reading the map. By then she was certain they'd lost anyone who might have been following them along the way. Still, she kept both her eyes open.

One for possible trouble, and the other on Rourke.

He parked behind a cluster of bushes and they walked over uneven ground back to the two lane road, approaching the place with caution. There had been an uneasy silence between them all the way there, but now she felt compelled to speak, even if it was pushing her luck.

"Let's do this my way," Annie told him. "I'm much better at coaxing things out of people. You stay in the background, to make sure no uninvited guests take us by surprise, and wait for me. Agreed?"

Rourke looked up the narrow dirt road before them. There was a shed on the right, then the road wandered around the small white cottage to a red barn set back off to one side.

"Hagen is dangerous, and he could be one of the killers."

"I know that, but as a woman I have a much better chance of getting inside that cottage and taking him by surprise."

The house appeared empty from a distance. "Agreed."

"Good. I'll take the house and barn, you check out the surrounding area and that shed.

Rourke nodded. "Yell if you get into trouble."

"You'd better believe it."

Annie strolled up the brick-lined path to the front door like an expected visitor. The lion-head knocker made plenty of noise when she banged it, but no one answered.

There were windows on each side of the door and she chose one, pressing her forehead against the cool glass to peer in. The sheer white curtains hid nothing. Inside, the place was neat, clean and empty. She tried the polished brass doorknob, but it didn't budge.

A well-trodden dirt path led to the back door and, even though Annie found it unlocked, she didn't go inside. First, she needed to check out the barn. If no one was on the premises, there would be time to search the place later.

Her nose wrinkled up as she entered the old building from the rear door. "Definitely smells like a barn," she told the two sleek, dark horses quartered within. "Hi, guys. Don't mind me." The horses snorted and shuffled in reply, following her movements with brown, watchful eyes. "Starved for company I'll bet, being stuck way out here. Where's your owner?"

"Right behind you."

Annie twirled around. Pointed right between her eyes were twin holes of doom—the business end of a double-barreled shotgun, close enough to touch her nose. She arched her eyebrows and swallowed carefully, waiting for him to speak.

He gestured sharply with the gun. "State your business."

"Are you Mr. Hagen?" She had expected someone younger and bigger, not a thin, tall old man. His face was deeply lined with wrinkles, and a shock of thick white hair offset his sunken pale blue eyes.

"Who's asking?"

"Annie Sawyer."

"You'd be looking for my grandson, I expect. The boy ain't here. What'd he do, get you in trouble?"

She looked at him, confused. "Excuse me?"

"Are ye with child?"

"No," Annie replied, shaking her head for emphasis.

"Lucky for you. He's a good for nothing. You're better off without him."

"Could you tell me where I might find him?"

His pale eyes narrowed and Annie knew he was assessing her, trying to decide what she was really after. "Why?"

She took a wild chance. "He owes me."

"Boy owes lots of people. It'll be hard to collect."

Annie tilted her chin up, her expression defiant. "I'm still going to try."

"You seem like a determined thing, you just might at that." He looked at her curiously. "Where are you from?"

"America." She had hoped the soft twanging of a Southern accent would make him curious. "West Virginia."

Hagen nodded and at last lowered the shotgun. "Hill country. Want to come in for a cup of tea?"

"Do you have coffee?"

"Tea's it."

Annie smiled at him, not put off by his gruffness. "Then tea it shall be." She glanced at him as they walked toward the cottage in the afternoon sun. "Fresh cream?"

"Aye." He glanced at her, a twinkle in his faded blue eyes. "Have a sweet tooth, do you?" Annie nodded. "Got just the thing for you. Widow down the road won't leave me alone. But she's a good cook."

Annie followed him inside, feeling only a small amount of remorse. Though she was here to do a job, she was still deceiving what appeared to be a nice old man. He obviously had a rotten kid for a grandson, one who had brought trouble his way before. Well, for the next hour or so, maybe she could make his life more enjoyable and gain some useful information in the process.

Outside, Rourke watched from a distance as Annie entered the cottage with the old man, chatting and laughing. He shook his head. She really was something. It was hard not to respect someone who could talk her way past a codger with a shotgun. When he snuck up and peeked in a window, he saw her sitting at the kitchen table, sipping tea and eating some kind of cake. The old man sitting across from her was at least thirty or forty years older than the Hagen they were looking for. His father or grandfather, perhaps.

Quietly, Rourke turned from the window and made his way to the barn. He would have to wait the tea party out and hope Annie came up with something useful.

But first he was going to take another walk around. He had spotted a pile of cigarette butts not far from the road near a ravine. Someone was keeping tabs on this place. That meant he and Annie weren't the only ones to come here looking for Hagen.

Maybe the others had found him. If they were still here, Rourke sure couldn't figure out where they were hiding.

Cautiously, he entered the old-fashioned barn, but found it empty except for the horses occupying two of the stalls. Three other stalls along the opposite wall were clean. To the right, a wooden ladder led up to the hay loft.

Rourke climbed up, checked the loft thoroughly and then stretched out a soft pile of hay. He might as well make himself comfortable. He had a good view of the house from here, and he'd hear anyone approaching long before they arrived. And, with the way Annie talked, he knew he could be in for a long wait.

It was nearly an hour later when Annie emerged from the house, full of tea and cream cake. She hoped Rourke hadn't gotten too bored; she'd certainly been well entertained herself. Maybe it hadn't been such a good idea to leave him alone this long after all. If he'd run off on her again, she'd strangle him with her bare hands!

While standing in the middle of the yard, contemplating that not entirely unpleasant thought, she became aware of some kind of commotion taking place in the barn. Old man Hagen's horses were very restless, clearly upset about something. As she headed that way, she could also hear scuffling noises coming from inside. The hairs on the back of her neck stood on end. Annie ran to the door to see what was going on.

Just as quickly, she ducked back out of sight. There was a full-tilt brawl going on in the barn. She crouched down beside the door, breathing shallowly as she looked around for a weapon. Her gun weighed heavily in her jacket pocket, but she'd only use that as a last resort.

There was a pitchfork leaning against the wall near her. Its handle was weathered, rough beneath her hand, but solid. Annie clutched it firmly and peered around the edge of the door. Four men were engaged in hand-to-hand combat, literally beating each other to a bloody pulp. And not one of them was Patrick Rourke.

They were too intent on killing each other to notice her, and Annie decided to keep it that way. She winced as punch after punch was thrown, landing with jarring precision. Suddenly, the silver flash of steel arcing through the air brought one fight to a quick and final end. Goose bumps covered her at the sight of that wicked knife.

Where was Rourke? What had happened to him?

Finally there was only one man left standing and he was staggering slightly as he shook his head, obviously trying to clear it. Pitchfork in hand, Annie rushed at him while he was still disoriented, jabbing the end of the handle hard into his stomach. He folded in two over the blow and she swung again, this time whacking him on the back of his skull with her best baseball swing.

He crumpled like a falling toy soldier, floundering for a moment before tumbling to the dirt floor with one tiny grunt. Annie jabbed his rear with her trusty pitchfork; he was out cold.

Not bad, Sawyer. She jabbed another one of the men before she realized there was no need. Where the heck was Rourke? Why didn't he give her a signal? Annie licked her lips, deciding to whistle the tune they had used years ago.

She'd only managed a small peep when the screeching of hinges behind her stopped her cold. Startled, Annie instinctively swung the handle of the pitchfork in an arc as she spun around, connecting solidly with someone emerging from one of the horse stalls behind her. He lurched forward, clutching his arm and cursing.

"What are you trying to do, Sawyer? Kill me?"

"Rourke, you idiot!" Annie yelled. "I might have done just that! I thought you were one of them!"

He glared at her. "You could have given me a signal."

"I whistled!"

"You call that a whistle?"

"At least I tried!" she shot back. "Why didn't you give me one, instead of sneaking up behind me like that?"

She was right, of course, but her insulting tone didn't sit well with him. "I thought I was coming to your aid, you silly twit!"

"*My* aid? I came out here to help *you,* you jackass!"

"I can take care of myself."

"So can I, Rourke. If you don't believe it, just try me!"

"Don't tempt me," he ground out through clenched teeth.

Maybe it was his smug expression. Or the way he kept leaving her behind, treating her as if she were an annoyance instead of the asset she had already proven herself to be. It seemed that no matter how professional she was, Patrick Rourke refused to think of her as anything more than a pesky schoolgirl who was always underfoot.

It hurt that Rourke didn't believe in her ability to help him, that he doubted her skills. And all because of her actions years ago. Well, he still had a lot to learn about the new Annie Sawyer!

She raised the handle of the pitchfork and held it against his arm. "This is about where we left off, I believe. Let's find out what would have happened if you *had* been one of the bad guys."

Rourke laughed. "You're joking! Here? Now?"

"Why not? Old man Hagen's taking his nap, and those guys are either dead or down for the count," she told him, indicating the men with a jerk of her head. Then she smiled wickedly. "Besides, this won't take long."

"Maybe it is about time I taught you a lesson."

No doubt about it, Rourke was fast. In a blur of movement, he grabbed the handle of the pitchfork and pulled, jerking her off balance. But Annie was just as quick.

Rather than fight for control, she allowed him to pull her forward, then suddenly released her grip. The pitchfork went flying and Rourke stumbled backward a few feet, into the open doorway of the horse stall. Annie tucked her head down and rolled, tumbling across the short distance between them and catching him right in the knees. He went over backward, landing in a pile of hay with a startled grunt. She picked herself up and immediately leapt on top of him, knocking even more wind out of him.

The force of her landing loosened the top of the hay pile and it came cascading down in a dusty heap, burying them both. Coughing, Rourke tried to roll out from under it, but she wouldn't let him. He felt as if a wildcat had climbed into the pile of hay and was clawing at him, pouncing on him, pummeling him with a flurry of arms and legs. Every time he thought he was free, she grabbed him again, fighting desperately to keep him from gaining the upper hand.

Finally, Annie got a good hold on him and brought her knee up swiftly between his thighs. Rourke managed to deflect the blow, but he wasn't about to give her another shot. He drew a coughing, gasping breath and yelled.

"Dammit, Sawyer! Let up!"

"Not until you say it!"

"Okay! Uncle!"

She stopped her frantic assault and struggled up through the sea of fragrant hay, grinning triumphantly. Rourke wasn't taking any chances. He quickly rolled on top of her, his body pressing heavily into hers, holding her down with his weight.

"Hey!" Annie complained. "You gave up!"

"That I did and not ashamed to admit it," Rourke assured her. "Boy! Do you fight dirty!"

"My brothers were good teachers."

"All right. So maybe you can defend yourself," he said, still gasping for breath.

"Maybe?" She moved her knee against the inside of his thigh. "Care to try for two falls out of three?"

"No." Her movements beneath him were rapidly putting Rourke in a mood to do anything but fight. He reached out and brushed some hay off her forehead. He gazed into her eyes, frowning. "What am I going to do with you, Annie?"

"Start treating me with some respect, for one thing."

"But I do respect you," he said. "I have an abiding respect for anyone who can cause as much trouble as you."

"Rourke," she said quite sweetly, "you can shove—"

He clamped his hand down over her lips, but it didn't stop the flow of her words, only muffled them. "I do believe that's anatomically impossible."

Annie stopped her graphic tirade and glowered at him. When he took his hand away she said, "You would know."

"You just don't give up, do you?"

"You're right. I don't." Annie tried to roll him aside, but he wouldn't budge. "Do you intend to continue squashing me until those guys wake up? You weigh a ton."

Rourke pushed himself up on his elbows, removing most of his weight. "Is that better?"

"Not really." His jean-clad hips were still pushing intimately against hers, securely holding her captive, his fingers casually combing through her hair. She wasn't sure she liked the stirrings he aroused inside of her. "Would you move? I'd like to get up."

"You can. After you tell me what you wheedled out of the old man inside the cottage."

"Not now! What about those goons over there?"

He glanced over at the bodies. A couple of them had knives sticking out of them. "Nice try, but as you pointed out earlier, at least two of them are dead. What did you find out, Annie?"

Lord, he was an exasperating man. She knew how to get him off of her, she just wasn't sure she wanted to hurt him any more. Besides, it wasn't that unpleasant to have him stay. In fact, now that they'd blown off some of the steam that had been building up between them, Annie felt her anger dissipating.

But that didn't mean she was ready for the feelings that were taking its place. It was safer to stay angry.

She sighed loudly. "The old guy knows nothing of the whereabouts of his rotten grandson."

"Come on, Annie. We may not have worked together in a long time, but I can still tell when you're holding back," he said, his eyes narrowing. "The old guy must have some idea where Hagen might be hiding?"

Annie nodded reluctantly. He wasn't going to like her answer. "In Belfast."

Rourke got up without a word and turned his back on her, the desire he'd felt stirring within him gone. She rose and started to walk over to one of the men.

"I'll check them. You find some rope." He was no longer in a teasing mood. "We don't need much," he told her, feeling for another pulse. "Three of them are dead."

A thorough search of the men turned up five guns, six knives, a couple of lead-shot-filled saps and a knuckle duster, as well as plenty of cash, but no identification. Rourke dragged the one still breathing across the dirt floor to the main entrance of the barn. Then he wiped the sweat from his brow and stared at the bodies.

Who had they worked for? Since torture wasn't his style, the chances of getting the one left alive to talk was nil. Besides, these men were hired guns and probably didn't even know who was paying them.

"What exactly were you doing in this stall, anyway?" Annie asked, closing the squeaky door and retrieving the pitchfork from where it had landed.

Rourke didn't look at her. "I was in the loft when they came in. The hay doors up there wouldn't budge, so I slipped down into the stall from above." He cleared his throat. "It was my only choice."

Annie kept her smile to herself. They both knew it would have been smarter to stay out of the stalls. She handed Rourke some rope and pointed to the assorted pile of weaponry on the floor. "Gee. A paranoid lot, weren't they? Is that all you found on them?"

"Some cash. We'll give it to the old man to make up for the mess we're leaving him with."

While Rourke tied up the lone survivor, Annie knelt and pulled a red cloth from her back pocket. She unloaded the guns and wiped them off. Since the men were all wearing gloves, the only fingerprints would be hers and Rourke's. The local authorities would eventually be notified, and Annie didn't fancy explaining to them what part she and Rourke had played in this fracas, at least not until they'd accomplished their mission. After cleaning the rest of the items, she placed them in a rusted bucket filled with water that she had carried over.

"Were they after you or Orren Hagen, do you suppose?"

Rourke shrugged, his black hair flopping down across his brow. "By now, probably both." He stood up, his fingers automatically combing his hair back into place as he checked the area once more, making sure there was nothing their captive could use to break free. "Since they attacked each other, it's obvious they're working for different employers. Or were. It also explains why they didn't know I was in the barn. They were too busy keeping track of each other."

Something was bothering Annie, and she decided to risk voicing it. "Don't you find it strange that Casey gave you this address?" Annie asked.

"No. If Casey found this address so quickly, then other people have it, too. Like I said, by now word is out that we're looking for Hagen. And don't forget, your backup agent from last night overheard us talking about this place."

That had occurred to her, but she didn't have as much reason to suspect him of wrongdoing as she did Casey. Then again, perhaps his affiliation with Bruce was reason enough. She'd assumed Bruce was simply being a jerk. If, however, there really was a leak in the agency and he was it, that assumption could get her killed. Again, too many questions, not enough answers. Annie knew she would have to get some, and fast.

"What's that hanging out of your jacket pocket?" Rourke asked suddenly.

"It's of Orren Hagen." She pulled the folded photograph out and handed it to him. "I found it in the cottage."

Rourke smoothed out the creases in the photo. Standing next to the old man was a younger version in his late twenties. They looked alike, except for the hair. The elder's was white, the other's dark brown. They had the same tall, thin frame and pale blue eyes, but the younger's held unbridled defiance.

"He wrote the address in Belfast on the back," she added.

"Good work," Rourke said. "Let's get out of here."

A green tackle box sat on a wide ledge by the door, and Rourke placed the wad of cash inside. The old man would find it tomorrow or the next day when he went fishing.

After securing the door, Rourke dragged the unconscious man a short distance and tied him to a post. Annie walked toward the house, carrying her bucket.

"Where are you going?"

She turned around but kept walking, backward. "To be on the safe side, we can't very well leave this stuff in the barn, now can we? Old man Hagen will have to feed the horses later, after his nap. When he finds this bucket full of deadly paraphernalia on his porch, the men in the barn won't come as such a surprise to him."

Her condescending tone irked Patrick, but he watched quietly as she leaned over, avoiding the noisy wooden steps, and set the bucket on the front porch. Then she straightened and headed to the other end of the house.

"Now where are you going?" he demanded irritably.

She held up the red cloth. "Just in case someone else does find the guns first, I'm going to put the bullets in an empty planter I saw around the side."

Rourke watched her round the corner. Maybe she was better than he'd given her credit for, but the fight had begun in earnest now and Annie could get hurt. Rourke didn't bother to analyze his reasoning. All he knew was that now more than ever, he didn't want to see her injured.

Unfortunately, he also had the uneasy feeling that from now on, she'd be even harder to get rid of than before.

Annie returned and came striding past him, full of purpose, her walk still confident and flowing. "Well? Are you coming?"

He sighed and went after her, watching her saunter along ahead of him. She had a loose-limbed grace to her movements that he found appealing. Maybe that was the problem. She was just too pretty and full of life to be allowed in harm's way. People such as himself, ragged around the edges, were much better suited to it.

"Where to?" he asked as he fell in step beside her.

"The one place you don't want to go back to. Belfast."

"I don't suppose you'd consider—"

"Don't even think about it, Rourke," Annie interrupted.

They piled into the car, Rourke at the wheel, and headed north. He was even quieter than he had been on the trip out, but she could tell he was trying to think of some way to convince her to stay behind.

Would the man never learn? He didn't have to protect her. She had just proven how capable she was of taking care of herself! And she could take care of him, too. He was going to check out that address, in a dangerous part of Belfast. He needed backup. Not that he'd ever admit it. How could a person with such skills in some areas be such an idiot in others?

Annie was instantly suspicious when he pulled into the first filling station they came across. "Why are we stopping here?" she asked.

"To get gas," Rourke replied irritably. "What else?"

She looked pointedly at the dashboard gauge. "But we still have over half a tank."

"We're going over the border, Annie. Not, I might add, by the short, normal route past the checkpoints, unless you'd like to go to prison for that gun you're toting?"

"Oh."

"So if it's all right with you, I'm going to fill up here while we have the chance. Any more questions?"

"All right! No need to get snippy!"

Rourke scowled at her. "By the way, I don't want you slowing me down, either. Do you mind?"

"Excuse me?" she asked, puzzled.

"All that tea you drank with old man Hagen."

Annie scowled back at him, grabbed her bag and stepped out of the car, slamming the door behind herself. As an afterthought, she reached in through the window and pulled the keys out of the ignition.

"Why, Annie! Don't you trust me?"

"I'll trust you when you start trusting me," Annie returned, jangling the keys in front of his face. "And not a second before then, Patrick Rourke."

Rourke watched her stroll off toward the rest rooms, smiling to himself. He patted the pocket of his coat that held the extra set of keys he'd asked for at the rental firm. Then he got out of the car and hurried inside to have a quick word with the station attendant, who was puzzled but happy to oblige, taking the money Rourke gave him.

Annie undoubtedly had plenty of cash, but paying for transportation back to Dublin was the least he could do. After all, he was abandoning her. Again. This time, however, it was making him feel extremely guilty.

He jumped back in the car and sped off, almost expecting Annie to come dashing after him. But his ploy had worked. He had enough gas to get him where he was going in the little sedan. If it held together. As he turned off the main road onto a rutted country lane, it made some unusual thumping noises. Rourke knocked on the wood-trimmed dash for luck and drove on, heading north.

Chapter Ten

Patrick Rourke was a tricky, conniving jerk. The only thing he hadn't lied about was the route he was going to take across the border. Unfortunately. He hadn't hit one check point, which was good, but he did manage to hit every last rut, pothole and bump along the way. Annie knew because she had a bruise for each one of them. It was a wonder he hadn't gotten a flat tire.

Too bad he hadn't. The look on his face when he opened the trunk would have been priceless. She supposed she'd just have to settle for the black eye she intended to give him when she rejoined him. Had he really thought her dumb enough to fall for that ploy at the gas station?

But she could plan and savor her revenge later. Right now she had other things to worry about. Annie moved slowly, staying in the shadows of the buildings as she looked for the address where Hagen was supposed to be staying. The streets were barren, like a ghost town at high noon, right before an old-west shoot-out.

That wasn't surprising considering the dangerous reputation this section of town had earned from past incidents. And though the turmoil and strife had lessened recently, it wasn't gone. The yellow signs along this street were there to prevent car bombings; parking vehicles of any kind in the marked zones was not permitted at any time.

And for as far as she could see in either direction, the two-lane street before her was posted with yellow signs.

Annie stepped back into the shadows of a shop entrance, looking across the street at the address the old man had given her.

The cool night air was pure, untainted by the smell of explosives or smoke; what she saw was an old wound. The block of shops had undoubtedly been blown apart by a bomb.

It was rare for the remnants to be left standing. Few walls remained completely intact in the block of one-story shops, and there weren't any windows or doors left in the structure. Jagged black streaks resembling lightning bolts stained all the openings, evidence of what must have been a horrendous fire.

Even at night she could read the words sprayed in white paint on the crumbling walls, the opinions of two bitterly dissenting sides. Neither position seemed to justify such destruction.

To each side of the shops were more two-lane roads, also marked with yellow signs. Annie crossed the dark street, looking around as she approached one end of the crumbling structure. Ignoring the many posted warnings to keep out, she stepped past what was left of a doorway and stopped.

Pale moonlight poured into the roofless maze of rooms, revealing bricks, rubble and shattered glass. No way could she walk through that undetected. Walking along the outside would be safer. Only an occasional honking horn could be heard off in the distance, otherwise all was quiet. Too quiet, even for two in the morning.

She was in the middle of the block when a familiar sound made her freeze. Someone had just struck a match against stone. Then he coughed. If her calculations were correct, he was nearby, maybe one room over to the inside.

Had old man Hagen set them up?

There was only one way to find out. Annie moved quickly to the next opening in the structure, entering cautiously, gun in hand. Each step she took was carefully placed amongst the brick and rubble, the moonlight illuminating a path through the shadowy inner rooms.

The red glow of the cigarette gave his position away. He was standing in a corner of the next room, protected on all sides by thick walls, a gun held ready in his other hand.

To confront him head-on would be foolish. She'd have to come up with another plan. Stepping backward, she heard the loud crackle of glass beneath her foot—as did he. Immediately she sank to the ground, her back against a wall. The almost silent zing of a bullet hit where her head had just been, a lump of mortar falling into her curly hair.

Annie grabbed a piece of brick and hurled it into the room behind her. It made a thunking sound as it landed on debris, and more noise as it rolled off. She stayed put, betting that he was going to double back by crawling through a jagged opening she had seen in the other room.

Moving quietly, she picked up a narrow piece of wood, balancing it precariously on chunks of rock so that it lay across the entrance beside her, a couple inches off the floor. A puff of wind would be enough to send it falling, such as that caused by anyone stepping near it.

In a crouched position, she walked to the other opening and pulled a coil of very thin wire out of her jacket pocket. After hooking the wire around an exposed beam, she stretched it across the opening a foot off the ground, pulled it taut and wrapped it around another beam on the opposite side. Another long piece of wood, placed below the wire, completed her plan. It should give her the diversion she needed.

Her opponent was good, giving nothing away until he encountered the traps she had set. When his movements at the first entrance made noise, he retreated and approached the next. This time he tried to step cautiously over the board in his path. As he did so, his foot got caught by the wire, bringing Annie on the run from her hiding place nearby.

Unable to catch his balance, he floundered, and Annie helped him on his way, grabbing hold of the front of his jacket. She jerked hard with one hand and brought the butt of her gun down on the side of his head with her other.

He slumped forward and she struggled with his weight, finally managing to lower him to the ground without too much noise. She felt for his pulse, finding it strong.

With precise, fast movements, she pried his fingers off his silencer-equipped pistol and tied his hands together with wire. A quick search of his pockets produced nothing useful. While wiring his feet together she studied him. It wasn't Hagen. His face didn't come close to matching the photograph she had gotten from the old man. Nor was it one of the men who had followed her in Dublin. Annie was beginning to feel like Little Red Riding Hood in a forest full of wolves.

She put his gun in her pocket. Was he working alone? Probably not. It seemed everybody in this case was working in cooperative pairs, except for her and Rourke. That would have to change. And just where was Rourke, anyway? Going outside again, she moved quickly, skirting the edge of the building and heading for the opposite end.

Once back inside, the soft murmur of a voice drew her like a magnet. Two men were in a small inner room, but all she could see was the backs of their heads. Annie inched her way forward, this time being more careful of where she placed her feet. She paused in the shadows to listen.

"Not talking, eh?" a thickly brogued voice asked.

The man speaking was jabbing his gun into someone's skull, thumping it like a ripe melon. "Put your hands on top of your head." He waited for his captive to do as he had ordered, then stepped back a few feet, out of reach. "Now turn around real slow."

The other man turned around. Annie's eyes went wide.

"Looks like I found who I'm looking for," the man with the gun said, very pleased with himself. "You can say your last prayers, Patrick Rourke. It's time to meet your maker."

"Oh, I don't think so darlin'," Annie drawled, stepping into the room and placing her gun behind his ear. "No sudden moves or you'll be hearing a very loud bang. Of course, if you'd rather, the gun in my other hand is equipped with a silencer."

Rourke watched the smile drain from the man's face. "I wouldn't tempt the lady if I were you," he told his captor. "I have a funny feeling she's in a very antimale mood right now."

"Actually, my mood just improved. Being right does that for me. But later we're going to have a serious talk about the way you drive." She thumped the man in the head. "As for you, toss the gun across the room," Annie ordered. When he hesitated, she jabbed him again, leaving him in no doubt her second weapon existed. "Now, or you'll find out what a nice gun your partner had." He complied, his heavy revolver clattering on a pile of rubble.

"See?" Annie smiled at Rourke over the man's shoulder. "I'm feeling pretty charitable. Your turn, I believe."

"Assume a spread-eagle position against that wall." Rourke frisked him, finding a hunting knife and a backup gun strapped to one leg. "Take your shirt off."

When the man hesitated, Annie cocked her gun. He quickly stripped off his shirt. Rourke sliced it into strips with the knife and tied him up, leaving him sitting atop a pile of rubble in the middle of the room. A puddle of pale moonlight illuminated his face, which was now as white as his undershirt. He was watching Rourke.

"Nice knife," Rourke murmured, running his finger along the flashing eight-inch blade. "Who sent you?"

The man stared at him mutely.

"I don't really need this knife," Rourke said, squatting down on his heels in front of their captive. "Do I, friend? What kind of record do you have?"

Still no answer.

"We're wasting time," Annie said with irritation, following Rourke's lead. "Let's get out of here, call the police and let them deal with him."

Rourke smiled coldly. "I'll bet the police would love to get their hands on you." He set the tip of the blade on a piece of stone in front of the man and dragged it across the rough surface, creating a jagged white line. "Or is there some other group even more interested in you? I'll bet they'd have you talking in no time."

Eyes on the knife, the man gulped, his Adam's apple bobbing. Beads of sweat popped out on his forehead. But he still refused to say a word. Obviously there was someone he feared even more than his enemies, Rourke or the police.

"One last chance," Rourke told him, "or we turn you over. Who hired you?"

He licked his lips. "How do I know you won't turn me over anyway?"

"You don't," Rourke told him. He grinned, but it was totally without humor. "You'll just have to trust us."

The cold hardness on Rourke's face worried Annie. He was barely holding his temper in check. "This is a waste of time. Let's go."

"I agree," Rourke said, scraping another jagged white line across the stone. "Have fun with whoever gets you first."

"Wait! All right!" the man cried. "It was Flynn."

Rourke's grip tightened on the knife handle, but he didn't stand up. "Where is he?"

"I don't know! I was hired by phone, never saw anyone!"

That fit. It was the way Flynn liked to work. "Then how did you know it was Flynn paying you?"

"I was to make sure that you . . ." His voice trailed off.

Rourke nodded, his expression grim. "You were to make sure I knew before you killed me," he finished for him. The man looked away. It was answer enough. Rourke stood up, glancing at Annie. "Let's go."

Annie was stunned. She'd read the latest files on Rourke. She knew his enemy Flynn wasn't dead, but why hadn't anyone told her he was in Ireland right now? Rourke didn't seem surprised. She was willing to bet Bruce wouldn't be, either. And what about Gerald?

"You can't just leave me here!" The man on the rubble pile was rocking back and forth, frantic. "He'll kill me for blowing this ambush."

Rourke grabbed Annie by the elbow and practically dragged her out of the room. "Run!" he ordered. "Flynn's a demon for back up plans."

They sprinted out of the shattered building, across the street and down the long block. Annie had built up such momentum that she practically knocked Rourke down when he stopped suddenly in front of her.

"Damn!"

"Now what's the matter?" Annie asked. Then she followed his gaze and figured it out for herself. Two policemen had rounded a corner and were heading right for them.

"Not what we need," Rourke said quietly.

The weapons they both carried were highly illegal in this country and would land them in jail. Even Annie's boss would have trouble getting them out of this one. Rourke looked around desperately, but there was no escape. They'd been spotted.

Annie suddenly leaned against Rourke and raised one knee, rubbing it up and down the inside of his thigh. At the same time she began toying with his belt buckle.

Then, in the most unusual Irish accent Rourke had ever heard, she said loudly, "You won't be late for work this time. I promise."

"Annie, what are you doing?" Rourke ground out.

"Oh, don't be like that. Be sweet!"

Flashlight beams swept their faces. Annie winked and smiled at the two young policemen staring at them. Her fingers, having slid down below Patrick's belt buckle, were making slow, demanding circles across the rough denim fabric of his pants.

Rourke groaned, but she doubted it was with arousal. At least not yet. She made bigger circles. "Why so stubborn? This won't take long. I promise I'll be quick," she whispered loudly, gazing up at Rourke like a wistful lover.

As the policemen came closer and their powerful flashlights clearly illuminated this amorous tableau, they started to chuckle. Rourke's face turned bright red with embarrassment. Though a man of great self-control, there were certain reactions even he couldn't suppress. Annie was getting to him, and he was rising to the occasion.

Annie grabbed one of his hands with both of hers and began pulling Rourke in the direction the policemen had come from. "Five minutes," she cajoled. "That's all I'll need tonight." Her accent may have been odd, but there was no mistaking the breathless promise in her voice. "We have time, if only you'd hurry."

The policemen laughed and turned off their flashlights. "I should be so lucky," one murmured as the pair moved past and headed down a side street.

"And me," the other agreed.

Rourke and Annie hurried down the block. "I guess we must have looked sufficiently in need," she told him when they'd rounded the next corner. "Sorry if I embarrassed you."

"No you're not."

."You're right, I enjoyed myself immensely." She smiled at·him, adrenaline rushing through her, making her feel alive and excited. Maybe it hadn't all been an act. "We'll have to do it again sometime."

Rourke glanced at her, noticing the flush of color over her cheekbones. She was serious! "Annie, you're amazing."

"About time you noticed." They arrived at the car. "I suppose I'll let you drive, since you know the area. But I think I'll keep this set of keys for a while longer," she informed him. "And I am *not* riding in the trunk."

"Just get in the car, will you?"

"Where to now?" Annie asked as she settled into her seat.

Rourke was careful not to speed, but not dawdling, either. He found the way to the main road leading up the coast without mishap. "I know a place we can spend the night."

"With beds, I hope. I think I'm developing hay fever."

Rourke glanced over at her. "Annie, I—" He stopped, unsure of what to say. How did he thank her for saving his life, for taking dangerous chances, for caring enough to come after him? Mere words, he knew, would not suffice.

It wasn't going to be easy to rely upon her; she had failed him before. But that was a long time ago. This time she had been there when he needed her, had proven that she was indeed dependable when push came to shove. She had earned more than a simple thank-you. She had earned his trust.

Annie was gazing at him curiously. "Yes...?" she prompted.

"I..." Why couldn't he say it? He didn't understand how there could be so much between them and yet really nothing at all. Or was he kidding himself? "Look," he continued gruffly, "what you did was dangerous. Your accent needs work. And you can't follow orders worth a hoot."

She chuckled softly. "Lucky for you. Right?"

"You're not going to leave me alone, are you?"

"Nope. You're stuck. We're in this together, no matter how many times I have to save your butt."

Apparently he could trust her to do anything, except let him face the danger of what lay ahead by himself. But he couldn't rationalize his way out of it this time. She had saved him. "I guess I was lucky," he finally admitted. "And I owe part of that luck to you."

As begrudging as his words were, she savored every nuance. His saying them meant a lot to her. In his own way he was telling her he had accepted her as an equal, not just as someone temporarily useful and easily discarded. It was a small victory, but one she would treasure.

After a long silence, she spoke. "I still can't believe I was fooled by old man Hagen. He set us up."

"It wasn't your fault. It may not even be his. You know Flynn's background. He may have lied to the old man and counted on him to pass the lie along as truth. Or he could have threatened to kill him, or someone he cares about." Rourke glanced at her. "You did know Flynn was alive, didn't you?"

"Of course."

She also knew Rourke was right. Where Flynn was involved, all bets were off. Those he couldn't deceive, buy off or threaten, he murdered. In this instance, however, there was yet another possibility, one she hoped wasn't true for Rourke's sake.

No matter how many times he reassured her, the suspicion wouldn't go away. Casey was reporting to someone. For all they knew, that someone could be Flynn.

"I realize this is a touchy subject," Annie said, "and believe me, I'm as tired of thinking about it as you are of hearing it. But Casey could have sold us out, too, Rourke."

"Not a chance."

"Flynn's influence is wide. You know that."

"Forget it, Annie."

His fervent trust of Casey galled her, almost to the point of making her tell him about the phone call she'd overheard Casey making. But Rourke's faith in the man was so complete he'd either shrug it off or come up with some explanation, and a rational, believable one at that.

She'd as soon keep her suspicions to herself until she came up with facts so plain he couldn't ignore them. By morning, Gerald should have more on Casey and his previous activities, maybe even something that would verify Rourke's trust in him. Annie hoped so. That would leave her with one less problem. It was bad enough to suspect that the very information network she had been using might be working against her in some way, without worrying about Rourke's teammates, too.

Unfortunately, after tonight, an even bigger and more dangerous problem loomed on the horizon.

"Growing up on a farm, I learned to watch where I put my feet," Annie said. "But I'm beginning to get the feeling I stepped into something really nasty this time. That's what you'd been doing before I caught up with you in Iowa, wasn't it? You'd been over here, looking for Flynn."

"Not here. He'd been spotted in London." His hands tightened on the steering wheel. "Supposedly. Who knows? He may have had a surprise party planned for me there, too, just like the one tonight. If so, something scared him off long before he could spring it on me."

"Like what?"

It was a very good question. Unfortunately, Rourke didn't have an answer. "How should I know? The only thing I'm sure of is that he's up to his old tricks again. And this time I'm going to put a stop to it. Permanently."

His face was grim, an expression marked by deadly intent. Annie was well aware of why his hatred for Flynn ran so deep. That was the other reason she wasn't going to go away. She wanted to help him through this assignment, as he had helped her through the one they'd shared before, but she also longed to help him get over the sorrow inside him.

Annie wasn't entirely sure why she felt so strongly about it. But until he got over the loss of his family, he wouldn't be whole. And she wanted him to be whole, as in love with life as she was herself. Maybe when that happened she could fully explore the other feelings for him she had inside her. Maybe...

"Patrick," she said softly, "let someone else deal with him." Her fingers tugged on the sleeve of his leather jacket. "You're too close to the situation. Let it go."

"I can't! And it's none of your business, Annie."

He was staring straight ahead, refusing to look at her. "Right now *you* are my business," she told him.

"That's your choice." Trusting her was one thing. It was entirely another to accept responsibility for her. "You've read Flynn's file, so you know there's only one reason for him to come out of hiding. He's broke. In the past he made his living creating and setting up bombs to kill people. I am not going to let him do that again."

She knew what he said was true, and that it wasn't the whole story. There was vengeance in his gray eyes, and a pain that ran straight down into his soul. "Stopping Flynn isn't going to help you, Patrick. It didn't before, when you thought him dead, and it won't now."

"Stay out of what doesn't concern you, Annie."

His voice, cruel and harsh, hurt like the lash of a whip. Still, she had to try.

"When is it going to end for you, Patrick? After you get Flynn?" When he didn't answer, Annie answered for him. "I don't think so. You'll find another cause, another man, another reason to hold on to all that anger you carry around with you. It won't stop until you let the past go, until you stop running away."

"Enough!" He didn't know if he'd ever be able to let go, either, but he didn't need her probing at his pain. "Quit meddling, Annie. I'm not going to tell you again."

Annie decided she probably had pushed him far enough for now. But she wouldn't quit. She'd chip away at the wall around him bit by bit until some daylight shone through, exposing the truth. Then she'd force him to look at it.

When he had calmed down, Annie approached the matter from a different angle. "Why do you think Flynn chose this particular time to make a run at you?" she asked.

"I don't know," Patrick replied, frowning. "We're poking our noses into a lot of dark corners in this search for Hagen. As I said, Flynn's broke and maybe there's something going on in one of those corners he doesn't want me stumbling onto. Knowing him as I do, however, I think it's probably nothing more than the fact that I'm here. He's an opportunist. And I'm on his turf, making a convenient target of myself."

"I know a bit about Flynn, too," Annie reminded him. "And even though he's fond of working by proxy, so to speak, I find it strange he's not willing to risk the pleasure of taking care of you in person."

"That is strange. But whatever plan he's hatching in that twisted brain of his, I'm not going to let him stop me from doing what I came here to do."

She could tell by the set of his jaw that Patrick was deadly serious. "Then I suggest we forget about Flynn for the moment and concentrate on the job at hand."

"Bridget is always my first priority."

"I know." Annie touched him on the shoulder. His love for the little girl was a point of hope in his life. But a single point was not enough, and Annie knew it. "That's a start."

"Annie..."

"Okay! You can't blame me for trying."

"Yes I can. And I do. You just refuse to listen."

This time Annie just laughed at his belligerent tone. "Get used to it. Stubbornness is one of my finer qualities."

Rourke pulled off the main road, parking the car behind a large farmhouse. He turned to her. "Not all of my reasons for wanting to get Flynn concern the past, Annie. One of them is about the future, Bridget's future."

"Flynn knows about her?" she asked, surprised.

"He knows *of* her, probably not much more than that," Patrick replied. "But it's enough. He knows that she is important to Jack Merlin, Russ Ian and me. Maybe all of this didn't make it into the file you read. You're aware of the incident in Houston, the one that gave Flynn his cash-flow problem in the first place?"

"I'm with you so far," she said.

"Well, as usual, Flynn had people everywhere, watching, doing his dirty work. Somehow, they got wind of the fact that we had a small girl under our protection. Flynn tried to have her kidnapped. He failed, but now that he knows about her, we never know when he might try again."

"To use as bait to get the three of you?"

"Yes," Rourke replied. "Or just to kill her."

Annie shuddered. "But why?"

"To punish us for meddling in his affairs. To avenge his brother's death, which he thinks we caused, when in fact it was a bomb Flynn designed and set that killed him." The man was responsible for so much needless death. Patrick leaned back against the car seat, suddenly exhausted. "And, of course, he hates us for hounding him. Flynn doesn't like to hide, so much so that he cut off his own finger in an attempt to make us think he was dead."

"I knew most of that," Annie told him. "But not about the kidnapping attempt. It's not in the files."

He sighed. "Good. The fewer files with Bridget's name in them the better as far as I'm concerned. It was probably some obscure, supposedly top-secret file that led your boss to make a connection between Bridget, the men I'm after and these supposed masterminds he wants you to find. Right?"

Patrick was staring at her. Annie shrugged. "He said he couldn't reveal how the connection was made," she admitted.

"Some boss you've got there."

"He is being something of a pain." Annie was hardly in the mood to stick up for Gerald at the moment. "I appreciate you telling me all this, Patrick."

"It was something I thought you should know. Flynn is a sick man, Annie. He is as much a danger to Bridget as the men we're after are. Maybe more. Eventually, I'll stop him, too."

With that he yawned elaborately and got out of the car. Obviously, he considered the subject closed. Annie didn't but she was tired, too. She followed him inside.

Chapter Eleven

The old couple in the farmhouse knew Rourke and asked no questions. The room he and Annie were given was simply furnished with white linen curtains, a wooden dresser with matching nightstands and a double bed. Annie hid a sly smile at that. What she did let him see was her generous nature, by letting him have the bathroom first in spite of the stiff muscles she had thanks to her ride in the trunk. Of course, she also warned him that if he used all the hot water, she would probably shoot him.

"Stay here often?" Annie asked, coming back into their room after a short bath. The polished hardwood floors were cool beneath her bare feet.

"Not recently," he murmured.

Patrick had stretched out on the double bed, leaning back on pillows he'd piled against the headboard. He was barefooted but still dressed, his black jeans and shirt uncustomarily wrinkled. A thin, oversize book sat on his stomach, and he was thoroughly engrossed.

Her blue flight bag on the bed was wide open, its contents in disarray. "Find what you were looking for?"

"I ate one of your chocolate bars."

He looked up at her. A riot of thin, damp curls skimmed her shoulders, her fuchsia T-shirt barely covered her thighs. When she leaned sideways to set the bag on the floor, a long stretch of smooth leg drew his eyes. He could still feel an echo of her hands on him, from earlier when she had teased him in front of the policemen.

With a nod of her head, Annie indicated the book he'd purloined from her bag. "Find it interesting?" she asked, sitting down on the bed, her legs curled beside her.

Patrick was looking at the copyright. "You wrote this?"

He sounded baffled, and Annie had to laugh. It was a children's book, all about people in France and how their culture differed from that in America, how different customs helped shape their lives and thought processes.

"No, my sister did," she replied. "That's our third one." Annie stretched her legs out, crossing them at the ankles and leaning back on her elbows. "The Company needed a cover for me so that I could travel freely, asking questions and seeing people I wouldn't otherwise have access to. My older sister came up with the idea. I make sketches, take photographs and tape everything." Annie grinned. "And then I plunk all of it on her lap to piece together."

"This is interesting," he murmured, reading a page.

"That's the general idea," she returned dryly.

Rourke closed the book and set it aside. "What exactly do you do? For the Company, I mean."

"I arrange meetings, help certain underground movements flourish. Sometimes I help get people out of countries they don't want to be in, or set up situations where escape is possible. I also act as a courier, on occasion. Whatever."

He kept his eyes on her face. "You like your job?"

"It's very fulfilling." Annie rubbed the nubbly weave of the bedspread between her fingers. Her curiosity was winning. "Did you ever stay here with your wife?"

"Here comes the inquisition." Rourke groaned and closed his eyes, giving in to the inevitable. Her free-style, rapid-fire method of interrogation was as effective as it was annoying. He knew from past experience that Annie was not going to leave him alone until he answered her questions, if not today, then tomorrow. "Yes, my wife and I stayed here. She has family in this area. Satisfied?"

"No. Was it hard to go back to Belfast?"

She could see the conflicting emotions chasing across his face. The bombed out building in Belfast had to have brought back memories of the death of his wife and child in that same city.

Patrick was trying to conjure up their faces. Each day it got harder for him to do so, but it was harder still to let their memories go. "It wasn't as bad as I thought it would be."

"You've been widowed a long time. Why haven't you ever married again?"

"Why haven't you married?" he shot back.

"Who says I'm not?"

His eyes flew open and he looked at her. She was grinning. He shook his head. "I didn't think so. No man in his right mind would want to take you on for life."

"A few have wanted to," she informed him, "but I didn't want them. They were sane." The sad bleakness in his gray eyes seemed to lessen with her teasing. "They all wanted me to quit traveling, find something dull and boring to write about or not work at all." She paused, then continued with a shrug of her shoulders. "Not one of them knew what I actually did for a living, of course. They would never have understood."

His gaze wandered along her smooth legs to the hem of her T-shirt, then upward to her breasts. The strong yearnings of desire didn't surprise him. He'd wanted her before. But he hadn't given in then, either.

"We need to get some sleep," he said.

In one graceful movement, Annie curled toward him, rising up on her knees. Leaning over him, she placed her hands on either side of his head. "I agree."

She gazed into his surprised eyes, her mouth hovering over his. Gently her lips brushed his, then she deepened the kiss as his mouth opened. Her tongue touched his, dancing, teasing him as she let no other part of their bodies touch. Then slowly she backed away and stood up.

He hadn't resisted her. It was a start. This time he wasn't going to walk out of her life without her knowing why he got to her as no other man ever had. Was there something between them, or was it just jumbled feelings because he had once saved her career—and her life? She pulled the covers back and slid in as Rourke turned out the light.

"What next?" Annie asked, stretching under the covers. "The meeting with Casey tomorrow?"

Rourke muttered an affirmative.

"And then what?"

"We take it as it comes."

Had she heard right? "We?"

"Changed your mind?" he asked.

"No."

Annie lay still for awhile, listening to the night sounds of the farm house. Rourke, too, seemed unable to fall asleep. She could tell by his breathing that he was awake. What was he thinking, she wondered? His thoughts would be worth a lot more than a penny to her, but she didn't think he'd part with them for any amount.

"Patrick," she whispered a short while later. "Do us both a favor. Take your clothes off and get comfortable." Annie giggled softly. "I promise not to attack you in your sleep." When he'd done as she asked and slipped back into bed beside her, she added, "At least not tonight."

FLYNN LOOKED AT THE MAN who had arranged the ambush for him. The fear in his eyes didn't make up for his failure, but it was nonetheless gratifying. It was good for a puppet to fear his master. "So. This pair failed, as well."

"Yes. But one of them was able to describe Rourke and the woman in detail."

If the traps had been properly set no one would have escaped. This was the price he paid for using people he hadn't checked out personally. But that was why each of his plans had backups; if the first part failed or malfunctioned, the second part got them.

Usually. This was the second dose of bad news in twenty-four hours, proving that the man standing before him was a poor judge of hired guns. The two he'd chosen for the ambush at the farm had not only failed to accomplish their task, they'd gotten killed, as well. Flynn had planned for that possibility, of course, by making sure that their first duty upon arriving at the farm was to convince the old man to send Rourke to the building where the backup trap had been arranged. Now that, too, had failed. Flynn was tempted to kill this idiot just to relieve his frustration, but the man could still be useful.

"I'm not very happy with you, my friend," Flynn told him. "Is this how you repay my kindness. With failure?"

"Maybe I'm not properly motivated," he said. "Why are we wasting time? We've bigger fish to fry than these two."

Flynn sipped his whiskey, staring at the man and trying to resist the urge to carve him up on the spot. He was not going to spend the rest of his life in hiding. Patrick Rourke and the others had to be eliminated in order for him to be free. In a way, however, this fool was right—for the moment, anyway.

"'Bigger fish to fry,'" Flynn repeated. "An appropriate turn of phrase. Very well. It is about time we thought about putting those particular wheels in motion. Perhaps you can atone for your failures, as well." He smiled. "You can accompany our two associates on the operation."

"Me! That's not—"

"Shut up! If you want motivation, here it is."

The man looked at the gun in Flynn's hand. Flynn was not the best shot in the word; bombs were his forte. But at this distance he wouldn't miss.

"You *will* go," Flynn continued. "To personally make sure we succeed. Or I will personally hunt you down and put a bullet in your brain." His smile had broadened into an evil grin. "Am I making myself clear?"

He nodded. "Yes, Flynn."

"That's better. Now get out of my sight."

When the other man left the room, Flynn put his gun away and sat down by the fire. It had felt good to hold a life in his hands at close range, like the old days in Northern Ireland, the place where his career had begun.

Flynn laughed out loud. To think that once upon a time he had actually been an idealist, believing in the cause and what they were trying to achieve. That was before he had learned there was money to be made, lots of it, in doing things from a distance. If you were good.

He *was* good. The fees he'd earned over the years spoke of his brilliance, his daring. It really was a shame his skills were not going to be put to more of a test as he eliminated his current opponents. Perhaps soon he would be using them to their fullest once more. After Rourke, the woman and any others who stood in his way were all dead.

But it would take time, planning and patience. In the meanwhile, there were still other options available to him, other sources he could tap. He picked up the phone. "If at first you don't succeed, try, try again." Flynn chuckled as he waited for his call to be connected. With a little haggling, maybe he could get two tries for the price of one.

THE NEXT DAY'S DRIVE BACK to Dublin was uneventful, and much more comfortable as far as Annie was concerned. When they arrived, Rourke parked two blocks away from the hotel. "It will be safer if we enter the hotel separately," he said. "I'll check in first, then go find us another car."

"Fine," Annie agreed. "I need to pick up a few things."

"Casey should be here in two hours. We'll meet then."

Annie watched him walk away before heading for the nearest phone. Gerald had some explaining to do. The more she thought about the things he was keeping from her, the madder she became.

Annie waited impatiently for her call to go through. "Why didn't you tell me Flynn might be in Ireland, Gerald?" she demanded when the connection was finally made.

"I—I didn't want to worry you."

The uncertainty in his voice pleased Annie. It gave her a kind of perverse pleasure to know she had shaken him. "Well, I'm worried now, believe me. And not just because of Flynn. I'm wondering when something else you didn't want me to worry about might jump up and bite me."

He sighed. "Your anger is justified, Annie, but in some areas my hands are tied. As for Flynn, you were made aware of the blood feud he has with Rourke."

"True, but you should have told me he might pop up."

"I didn't know how much of a factor Flynn would be in this," Gerald returned. "Or if he was even in Ireland."

"Oh, he's here. Or at least some of his henchmen are. A couple of them tried to kill us last night in Belfast."

"Explain!" Gerald ordered. "In detail!"

Her report concerning the events at Hagen's place and their excursion to Belfast was detailed, but concise. When she finished, Annie gently rubbed her forehead, trying to ease the furrows her frown was causing.

"Rourke was looking for Flynn before all this started," she informed him. "He'll now redouble his efforts."

"This is to be expected."

Her frown lines deepened. What kind of game was Gerald playing? "Well, I would have been expecting it, too, if I'd had all the details to begin with!"

"I do apologize, Annie. We aren't completely up to date on Flynn's whereabouts. But you must realize, he isn't an easy man to track."

Her head was pounding, making her yearn for a cup of coffee and some aspirin. For all her bravado last night, she hadn't slept well with Rourke so close beside her. "All right. What do you have on Casey?"

"Nothing. The name and physical description are still being run through the computer."

Annie's patience was wearing thin. "Don't your local contacts know anything about him?"

"We're working on it, but these things take time," Gerald reminded her. "What else have you found out?"

She couldn't resist a little jab. "Why don't you ask Bruce Holloway? He seems to know more about what I'm up to than I do myself." The only reply she got was static crackling across the phone lines. Annie sighed. "Sorry, Gerald. I'm understandably on edge. Did you talk to Bruce?"

"He called in sick yesterday."

"Something serious, I hope," Annie remarked.

"Apparently not. I checked. He wasn't at home."

Her headache throbbed. Did Bruce have a new woman friend, or was he up to no good? Either way, she pretty much had to depend on Gerald to find out. That meant more waiting. And he might decide to keep that from her, as well.

"Anything on Hagen?"

"A small-time criminal, no permanent address," Gerald replied. "The same for Lunn Kendrick. In his case, though, he has a very wealthy father who buys him out of trouble."

"Okay. Now I have another name for you. Adair."

"Doesn't ring a bell. I'll run it through right away."

"Great. I'll be in touch."

Annie hung up the receiver and looked at her watch. Gerald hadn't been of much help. Was he being uncooperative, or was she expecting too much? She'd worked in data retrieval herself for a time, and was therefore aware of the enormous amount of information that was now being sifted on her behalf.

Still, it was becoming increasingly clear to her that something strange was going on in her agency. Maybe not evil, but certainly something obstructive and, in her present situation, that could amount to the same thing. It was high time she covered her own backside.

She would have to tap into another source. To do so, however, had its dangers. The person Annie had in mind was trustworthy, or at least as much as could be expected from a man whose talents were for sale. Of course, she had an edge; if he ratted on her, she'd rat on him. But as big and convoluted as this operation was, who could tell what might happen? Another source was also another window of vulnerability. To say nothing of what would happen to her should Gerald find her stepping out of bounds.

Indecision slowed her, but not for long. She soon dialed another number, again waiting impatiently until the call went through. Luck was with her. He answered.

"Yes."

"Julie, dear, I need—"

"Dammit, Annie! I've told you not to call me here!"

Annie laughed softly. "So many times that I lost track long ago, Julie. What are friends for if not to irritate?"

"Are you trying to get me into trouble?"

"I wouldn't do that to you! I need your resources. Besides, I know you keep this line clean."

He grumbled a few highly unflattering descriptions of her possible lineage, then sighed. "All right. I'll do you a favor if you'll do me one. Spare me the blackmail routine this time. Just tell me what you want."

"You're a spoilsport, Julie. No fun at all."

Early in her career Annie had discovered that Julie, though otherwise a dedicated public servant such as herself, sold information out of the government computer network under his control—as well as any other network he could wheedle, connive or hack his way into.

Rather than turn him in, she had blackmailed him over the years whenever she needed information, particularly information that, like now, her own agency hadn't been able to readily supply. More than once what Jules Harcourt had come up with had saved her life.

"Ready for some names?" Annie asked.

"Hang on for a second." Even through the static on the phone lines she could hear his chair squeaking as he moved his considerable bulk around. That and his photographic memory were legendary in the Company. "Okay. Shoot."

"These are all in Ireland," she began, then gave him the names of Orren Hagen, Lunn Kendrick, the mysterious Casey and unknown quantity Adair, spelling each of them in turn. "With Adair, try a global search, see if there are ties to Ireland. And I'm particularly interested in Casey. Those names I need yesterday."

"Natch. Have you ever asked for anything tomorrow?"

"You know me so well, Julie. There's another name. Flynn. That's an alias. His real name—"

"I know what his real name is," Julie interrupted sharply. "What the hell are you doing investigating him?"

Annie knew his gruff manner to be concern, and found it rather touching. "He's intruding on my current assignment," she explained. "When you go through his file, look for specific addresses in Ireland where he might be hiding."

"That's already been done."

"It's what?" she exclaimed. "Why? Who?" Julie didn't answer her. "Was it Patrick Rourke? It's okay to tell me, I'm working with him on this."

"It is not okay and you know better than to ask, Annie. But I will tell you there isn't a place in Flynn's file that exists any longer, except for the one where he spent the last few years, off and on, and that isn't in Ireland. It's an island in the Caribbean."

"Is he there now?"

"No, it's been under surveillance but he hasn't shown up."

She congratulated herself for deciding to call Julie. He hadn't even begun to dig for her, and already she felt better informed. Still confused, of course, but that was often the case for an agent in the field. Maybe he could help clear up one more aspect of that confusion.

"Julie, is there a leak in my department?"

His reply was quick and to the point. "Possibly, but it hasn't been confirmed or narrowed to one person. It also could be simple office jockeying for position. You know the routine, make the other guy look bad at promotion time."

"Lovely. And I'm caught in the middle. Keep an ear cocked for any scuttlebutt, Julie. I'll be in touch. Bye."

Annie looked at her watch again. If she hurried, she should have time to get some coffee, buy the things she needed and still make the meeting on time.

As it worked out, she breezed into the hotel without a minute to spare. "The key to Patrick Shaunessy's room, please," she told the man at the desk. That was the name Rourke had told her he would be using. The clerk eyed her suspiciously. "He's expecting me," she added. "I'm his wife."

"May I see some identification?"

Annie handed him her international driver's license. The short, gray-haired man studied the photograph, looking up at her and then back at the license a few times. Finally, he shoved a white registration card in front of her, muttering under his breath.

"Is something wrong?" she asked.

"I need your signature."

She signed the card and exchanged it for her license and a room key. "Thank you," she said, then turned toward the elevator. *What a strange little man.*

The number engraved on the brass key led her to a room that had a Do Not Disturb sign hanging from the knob, probably Rourke's handiwork. Annie inserted the key and pushed the door wide open. She hesitated for a moment, some inner alarm going off. But it came too late.

"Get in here." The voice was gravelly, with a thick brogue, and the person to whom it belonged was obviously the impatient type. "Come in or I'll shoot you right between the eyes."

He didn't leave her much choice. She entered the room, her bag knocking the Do Not Disturb sign off as she closed the door. In the far corner, to her left, a man was sitting in an armchair, the big, chrome-plated automatic in his beefy hand pointing right at her. He was built like a weight lifter, with a thick neck, huge arms and legs. Definitely not someone she would have forgotten had she ever seen him before.

"Drop the bag," he ordered.

Annie set it down by the door. "Who are you? What are you doing here?"

"Waiting for Patrick Rourke."

The room had been torn apart. Pictures hung crookedly on the walls, white sheets were lumped in a pile on the gold carpet, the mattress had been slit open and was hanging half off the bed. All the dresser drawers had been pulled out and dumped on the floor as well. The phone was off the hook.

"Find what you were looking for?" Annie asked.

"Shut up and take a seat."

She walked around the bed to the window and sat down on the narrow sill to look outside. From so far up people looked like miniatures. Annie pressed her nose against the glass. They didn't get any bigger.

"Get away from that window."

She rose slowly, pondering her situation. Had Casey set them up? Who else had known they were going to be using this hotel? Annie bleakly ticked suspects off in her mind: Casey, Derry, Gerald, probably Bruce Holloway as well the way things were shaping up. This operation had sprung a few leaks, all right, but the possibilities were so numerous they made her head spin.

"You need some help finding a seat?" the man rasped. He patted his lap. "Got one for you right here."

The leering look on his face made her stomach heave. "No, thank you." There wasn't another chair in the room so she perched on top of a low wooden dresser, staying far away from the bed. "Who do you work for?" she asked.

"Look, missy, I didn't say you could talk. And there are lots of ways to shut you up," he told her, waving his gun and leering at her, "without using this."

Annie swallowed thickly and looked away, deciding that perhaps this was one occasion when silence would be golden. Of all the times to be late, why did Patrick pick this one?

Chapter Twelve

The delay troubled Rourke. Casey should have arrived by now. He walked up to the reception desk, hoping that perhaps a message had come for him while he had been out arranging for the car. When he opened his mouth to ask, the clerk cut him off with a wave of his hand.

"I'll be with you in a moment."

The sharp, rude tone of the old man shocked Rourke. What was going on? He waited while the young couple at the desk finished filling out a form and received their room key.

"My messages?" Rourke asked.

"Only one. Direct from the management. This is a fine old Irish hotel, sir, not some...some parlor of delight!" he spluttered, staunch disapproval dripping from his every word. "You and your mistress will have to leave. Immediately!"

"My what? What are you talking about?" Rourke asked. "I don't have a mistress."

The man tapped a registration card with his index finger. "No? Well, if the young lady waiting for you in your room isn't your mistress, who is she?" He sneered. "Your niece? She certainly isn't your wife! You lied to me, sir!"

Rourke read the name beneath his, Annie Sawyer, written right next to her license number. He smiled, trying to lighten the situation. "Is that all?"

"Don't mock me, young man. This is not the Côte d'Azur, and even there I would not run the sort of establishment you seem to be looking for. Elsewhere in town this may be common, even accepted. But not here." The little man leaned over the counter. "Worse, you lied. There are laws concerning the honest treatment of innkeepers. I—"

"Let me explain!" Rourke interrupted. "She's an American, you see, and it's quite usual for them to keep their own names."

The clerk rocked back on his heels and pointed at the gold band around his left ring finger. "And not wear wedding rings, too, you'll be telling me next. I repeat, this is a respectable hotel, not a place for illicit trysts!"

"But I—"

"No! I want no more of your lies!"

Throughout this tirade, the man had been gesturing wildly, with an occasional nervous glance toward the office door to his left. Rourke looked that way and saw what he imagined was the cause of the clerk's histrionics—and perhaps his exaggerated moral outrage as well. A very large woman, undoubtedly the little man's wife, was glaring at Rourke in that special way some females reserved for rakes, bounders, drunkards and other assorted masculine pond slime.

Sensing his goose was already cooked, Rourke still gave it one more try. "This is all quite innocent, I assure you. The woman and I are business partners, you see," he explained, talking directly to the man's wife now. "We arranged to meet an associate here in your fine hotel, and to be honest, we just couldn't see the expense of two rooms." Rourke gave her his most winning smile. "We'll only be here a short while."

"Business? Monkey business, more likely!" the woman bellowed. "A short while of hanky-panky! And on the cheap! Bah! I'm calling the constable! I want you out of here now!"

She turned around and grabbed the phone. Rourke heard the ding of a bell announcing the arrival of the elevator. He dashed to catch it, cursing under his breath. He thought the police would most probably find the whole crazy situation hilarious—except for the alias he'd used and the several other apparently genuine passports in his possession. They wouldn't find the weapons he and Annie had one bit funny, either.

Everything could be explained, eventually, and with a great deal of assistance from Annie's boss. But it would take time they didn't have, and such an interrogation might blow their entire operation out of the water.

Rourke wouldn't stand for that. They would have to move fast to get out of there before the police arrived.

He waited impatiently for the aging elevator to climb to his floor. "The stairs would have been faster!" he groused, then went striding down the hallway the instant the elevator doors creaked opened.

But Rourke slowed down as he approached his room. The Do Not Disturb sign he'd left hanging on the door knob was now on the floor. It was a small thing, but he'd saved his own life more than once by noticing even smaller clues.

As a test, he slipped his key into the dead bolt lock and twisted it slowly. The door was already unlocked. Annie might have bumped the sign, but she never failed to lock a hotel room door. Quietly, he moved to the left of the door jamb and waited, knowing the sound of his key turning in the lock would have been enough to alert anyone inside.

The door opened a crack. Rourke tensed, fists clenched, his eyes glued to that widening crack. Then Annie stuck her head out the door. She looked up and down the long hallway, ignoring him.

"I don't see anyone out here," Annie said, but she was signaling him, holding one finger up. One man.

Rourke pointed at her with his own index finger, curling the rest into his palm, his thumb cocked. The man inside could see her head, so rather than nod, she copied Rourke's gesture, mimicking a gun.

"You're sure?" a gravelly voice behind her asked.

"Positive. No. Wait a minute." Annie leaned further out the doorway. "I think someone is hiding at the end of the corridor, near the stairwell."

"Get back in here!" gravel voice ordered.

Rourke mouthed one silent word. Run!

Annie heard the metallic click of a gun cocking right behind her. She looked at Rourke and raised her eyebrows.

The man repeated his order, with added emphasis. "Get back in here *now!* Or you'll be leaving your brains outside!"

Rourke repeated his silent mime. Run!

Annie took a hesitant step backward, then plunged through the door, slamming it shut behind her. With only a faint *pop* and the sound of splintering wood, a bullet came through the door and whizzed past her head, missing by inches, making her run even faster. Rourke joined her and together they sprinted down the hallway.

Behind them, the door banged open. Another bullet slammed into the carpet near their feet. Rourke almost fell on top of Annie as they dashed through the exit at the end of the hall.

"What do we do now?" Annie asked.

"Try not to fall!" Rourke replied.

They took the stairs two at a time, past the door on the fourth floor, then around the landing and down the next flight, gaining speed as they passed the third, spiraling downward.

"Who was he?"

After another two flights it was getting hard to talk and breathe at the same time. "Didn't give his name," Annie said, panting as they rounded the last landing, "but he wants you."

"Doesn't everybody?" They practically smacked into the last door, marked with a big *G* for Ground. "Wait," Rourke told her as she reached for the knob. The pair stood still, listening for the sound of footsteps following them.

There weren't any. "He took the elevator," Annie said.

Rourke nodded. "Catch your breath before we walk out there." He scowled at her. "We don't need to bring any more attention to ourselves."

"What if he's already waiting for us?"

"Are you kidding? That elevator is too old."

Annie peeked out the small rectangle of glass set into the door at eye level, scanning the hotel lobby. She cursed. "It must go down faster than it goes up."

"What?"

"See the guy sitting on the sofa near the entrance, in the navy-blue suit? He's the one from upstairs."

Rourke's face was touching hers as they peered through the small window. "Can't be! That guy was there when I came into the hotel." Rourke leaned back against the wall, arms crossed over his chest. "Take another look."

"I am!" The elevator arrived. Another man got off, identical to the one on the sofa. "But I don't believe my eyes. Twins!"

"Their poor mother," Rourke muttered. "What's happening?"

"They're talking. I wonder who their tailor is? You can't even see the bulge of a gun under my guy's suit and it's a big chrome-plated job. Suppose his brother has one, too?"

Rourke couldn't believe her. They were running for their lives and she was impressed by their tailoring and choice of armament. "Why don't you go ask them?

Annie made a wry face. "Why are you so testy, anyway? I'm the one he was holding hostage."

"You—"

"Cripes!" she yelped. "One of them is coming this way."

"Where's the other one?"

"Heading back to the elevator."

"Great." He grabbed her arm again and pulled her toward the stairs. "Take a deep breath and start climbing."

"Of course," Annie muttered. "The only logical choice. But where are we climbing to?"

"Back to our room."

She missed a step. "What?"

"Keep moving. Would you expect us to go back there?"

"No, because the idea is insane. If someone noticed the gunshots, the police will be on their way here."

"They've already been called." He glowered at her as they jogged up the stairs side by side. "The old man thought I was having an affair. You picked a fine time to play the emancipated lady and sign in under your own name."

"I had to," Annie returned. "I'm not the person of a thousand identities you are. He asked for my license first."

"What'd you do? Behave suspiciously or something?"

Annie scowled back at him. "Are you telling me I look like the sort of woman who visits strange men in hotels?"

"That's not what I—"

"This is more your fault than mine," she interjected. "The only thing suspicious about me was my lack of a ring."

"He did mention it," Rourke admitted. "But I don't see how that makes it my fault."

"Simple." They were both huffing and puffing now. But Annie still managed to sound indignant. "It was your idea to take one room. And even a pretend wife needs a pretend wedding ring to match the one her pretend husband still wears. You were undone by being cheap."

"I am not cheap!"

"You made me ride to Belfast in the trunk of your car."

"That was your idea!" Rourke objected.

She grinned. "For which you will be eternally grateful."

"Sometimes, Annie..." His face was red with more than the exertion of the climb. "All right. Let's just say we've been victimized by a suspicious old busybody and leave it at that, shall we?"

"Whatever you say, Patrick."

They stopped on the fifth-floor landing and peered out the rectangular window while listening for noises from down below. Silence.

"Let's go." They ran to the room, finding the door wide open. Rourke surveyed the mess. "I'm glad I didn't pay for this room with a credit card," he muttered.

Annie chortled. "Cheap, cheap!"

"You'd better be practicing your bird calls, Sawyer."

"Don't get mad at me," she told him, stepping over a lamp to get her bag. "It was like this when I arrived."

"Come on, let's get out of here. If the state of this room has been reported, we'll be in even more trouble if the police catch us. They should be arriving any minute now."

He didn't have to convince her; she was more than ready to leave. Back inside the stairwell, Annie set her bag down on the linoleum floor and began rifling through the contents.

"I know it's in here," she muttered, searching methodically through the bag. "There you are." She held a slim black case up for inspection while stuffing her jacket back into the bag with her other hand. "Let's go."

"At least we're getting our exercise," he said, descending the stairs beside her. They stopped at the door to the next floor, opened it and looked up and down the corridor. No one was in sight. They continued to the next floor. Rourke pointed to the black case she held. "What is that, anyway?"

"Government-issue lock-picking kit."

Rourke groaned. "That's just dandy. False names, guns, a torn up room and now burglary tools. We may as well stand against this wall and wait for the firing squad."

"Oh, quit griping. Since the emergency exits have alarms, you choose the floor and the room, I'll get the door open."

"I want out of this hotel, not in it. Once they see that mess they'll do a room-to-room search to find us."

She kept her voice at a whisper. "The cops are coming in the front, the innkeeper's office is toward the back and we've got two big, ugly brothers somewhere in between. What do you suggest we do? Make ourselves invisible?"

"I take it you have a plan?"

"Get inside a room and go out the window."

They were approaching the third-floor landing. "I thought you were afraid of heights?"

"Not anymore. I took up skydiving—the kill-you-or-cure-you method." Annie opened the door a crack and looked down the hallway. "We know where one of them is," she told him, easing the door shut. "Let's go down two more. If we fall one flight, less should break at that distance."

"How confidence inspiring."

Suddenly, Annie twirled around in front of him, her hands sliding around his neck and pulling him toward her.

"Kiss me," she demanded.

"Excuse me?"

"Shut up and kiss me, you fool!"

Then Rourke heard the voices, too. "Oh, no," he muttered. "Not again." But he obeyed, his lips covering her warm, open mouth without hesitation. As he did so, two constables climbed up the stairs toward them. Rourke diligently applied himself.

Their tongues touched, almost making Annie forget where they were and the danger surrounding them. A wonderful warmth spread through her and she quivered as his arms tightened around her, deepening the kiss. Was this for effect, or was Patrick getting carried away, too? Her fingers slid into his hair as she leaned against his hips.

"Ach!" one of the men exclaimed when he saw them. "For a respectable place, there's a lot of tomfoolery about!"

"And old enough to know better," the other agreed. "Here now! Shame on you two! Carrying on like that in a public place." The pair ignored the constable's chiding. "You'd better be gone when we get back!" he warned.

"What floor are we heading for?" his partner asked.

"Fifth. Wouldn't you know. They should get that darn elevator fixed. Breaks down regular."

Annie pulled back as the belabored, disapproving voices filtered into her mind. "Honey, stop," she whispered, loud enough for the men to hear as they rounded the next curve of stairs. "We have to meet my parents for lunch and they'll be mad if we're late again."

Her head was resting against his chest and the rapid, uneven pounding of his heart flowed into her. They were both breathing heavily, and it had nothing to do with their excursions up and down the stairs. He was as touched by that kiss as she had been.

Rourke let the silky softness of her hair caress his throat as they waited for the men to move out of sight. Cops and bad guys he could handle; this was serious trouble. If she hadn't pulled back, he would have gone a lot further than the situation called for.

Even now his hands itched to slide up under her sweater and feel the sleek smoothness of her creamy skin, to glide up toward her breasts and let their weight fill his hands. But this was hardly the time or place.

"Curious chemical, adrenaline," he observed.

Annie nodded her head in agreement. "I'll say."

"Let's go before someone else comes along. You never seemed like the repetitious type to me."

"Only when I happen to like what I'm repeating."

They made it to the first floor without encountering anyone else. Rourke chose a room and knocked. When no one answered, Annie went to work with her tools. She was quite skillful, opening the door in a matter of seconds.

Annie went in first, then backed out quickly, stumbling over his feet in her haste to close the door. "Cripes," she muttered. "Trust you to pick one where somebody's taking a shower. Do I have to do everything myself?"

She went two doors down on the same side of the building and knocked loudly. No answer. This time she pressed her ear against the door. As she did so, it suddenly opened.

"Who the heck are you?" a deep voice inquired.

Annie straightened and came face-to-face with a burly young man. He wasn't wearing a shirt. Nor was the girl standing behind him. Neither of them seemed very pleased to see her. "I—I'm so sorry. We must have the wrong room."

"Perverts!" The door was slammed shut in her face.

"Well!" Annie whirled around. "Some people have no manners at all in difficult situations."

Rourke couldn't keep the chuckle building inside him from pouring forth into hearty laughter. Only Annie Sawyer would expect politeness out of a man who had just discovered her listening at his keyhole. "I guess there are worse things than being called a pervert," he told her, enjoying the outraged expression on her face.

"I'm glad you find it funny." Her piqued tone only made him laugh harder. "Quit that! We have to get out of this hotel, unless you want to spend the night in jail explaining all this."

"Annie, dearest," he said, still chuckling softly, "we couldn't explain this in a month of Sundays, and it'd take twice that long to live it down." Rourke took her arm and continued on to the next door. "Third time's the charm."

They waited a full extra minute after knocking on this door. Then Annie got them inside. The room was indeed empty. "Why couldn't you have picked this one first?"

"Why didn't you?" he shot right back, briskly making absolutely sure the place was unoccupied. When he opened the curtains, the room was flooded with a hazy gray light. Tiny droplets of water spotted the window. "It's starting to rain. Maybe that'll work in our favor."

"Any police cars?" Annie asked.

This side of the building faced a quiet side street. "No. Hey, where are you going? Our exit is this way."

"Back in a minute," she replied, heading for the bathroom. "My mother always told us to never pass up a chance to go. And with you around, I've developed an even greater aversion to public rest rooms than I already had."

Rourke shook his head and leaned out the window. Luck was with them, but just barely. There wasn't much of a ledge to stand on and they were going to have to lean pretty far to the right to grab hold of the metal downspout. If they missed it, the landing would be hard, either cement or dirt.

Annie returned. "Have a plan?" she asked.

"It's very complicated. We're going to slide down the rain gutter and hope it holds." He was still smiling. "Or you can practice your skydiving. Want to go first?"

"Yes. You're heavier than I am. Your weight might rip the gutter away from the wall, and I learned at the age of six that a sheet doesn't make a very good parachute."

He held out his hand. "Give me the bag, I'll drop it to you after you're down."

She gauged the distance, then stepped out on the ledge. For a moment it felt like she was falling, then she caught hold of the cold metal gutter and hugged it for dear life. Her tennis shoes screeched as she slid down a bit. A drop of rain splashed in her eye and she cursed, blinking to clear her vision. But at least the downspout wasn't slick. Yet.

"Hurry up," Rourke ordered. "You stand out like a sore thumb. Better yet, make that a red bug on a white wall."

Annie stuck her tongue out at him, then started down again. The backs of her hands were rubbed raw from the rough, whitewashed brick by the time she made it to the ground. Her bag hit the dirt beside her, making her jump. She looked up and saw that Rourke was scurrying down the pipe with amazing speed and efficiency, though the downspout groaned under him.

"You've done that before," Annie accused.

"Many times." She arched her eyebrows. "As a child!" he informed her. "Honestly! The opinion you must have of me! Come on, I have a green sedan parked around this corner." He led the way, moving to the edge of the building.

Rourke peeked around the corner. "Damn," he muttered, stepping back and flattening himself against the wall.

"Police?"

He nodded, his expression grim. "And the innkeeper's wife, undoubtedly describing us both in great detail. I'll bet she's enjoying it, too, the nosy cow. We'll have to try and . . ." Rourke trailed off, staring at Annie. "Oh, Lord. What are you doing now?" he demanded

Annie was kneeling on the ground, her bag open, various articles scattered about. She pulled her new red sweater over her head and he saw a brief flash of white lace before she struggled into another sweater, this one cream-colored. Then she put her leather jacket on and looked up at him.

"Stop staring! Give me your coat, roll down your shirt sleeves and button the cuffs and your collar. Hurry!" He dropped his jacket and did as she instructed. "Good. Now brush your hair down over your forehead and put on this beret."

He looked at her skeptically. She was on her knees, teasing her hair with a brush, making it stand on end as if she had just stuck her finger in a light socket.

"I don't think—"

"Just do it." Annie applied lipstick, more liberally than was her habit, then checked on Rourke's progress. She frowned. "No, no. Cock the cap to one side of your head."

The little drops of rain had turned into a steady, rather annoying drizzle by the time they were both ready. Annie stuffed everything they weren't using back inside her bag, then stood up and handed it to him.

"You do look like a jerk, Patrick, but this will work. Slip the strap of this across your chest and wrap your arm around me like a lover. We're going to walk to the corner, cross the street and go down two blocks to where we left the other car." She looked at him. "Unless you turned it in yourself to save the pick-up charge?"

"No, it's still—" He blinked. "Stop that! The car is still where we left it and I'll rent another as soon as I can. So there. Now quit fooling around and let's go!"

"Pretty bossy for a pretend husband, aren't you?"

"Come on!" They set off at a casual pace, arms wrapped around each other, acting like lovers huddled together in the cooling rain. "By the way, that purplish lipstick is not your color," Rourke murmured in her ear as they crossed the street.

"A bit garish?"

"Try a lot."

"That's the idea. What's the first thing you see when you look at me?" she asked, her head against his shoulder.

"The lipstick, and you're right, it's what I'd remember most. Clever."

"Want to put some on yourself?"

He squeezed her tightly. "Real cute, Sawyer." Suddenly, Annie slipped out of his grasp and lagged behind. "Now what?"

She was looking at the cluster of curious onlookers milling about in front of the hotel. "Patrick! There's Casey!"

"Where?" Rourke looked in the direction she indicated, scanning the crowd. "I don't see him."

"He was there, I tell you! Using the phone booth."

"Probably trying to call us. If it was him," he said, wrapping his arm around her again. "Walk faster, will you? I want out of this town." They went down another block, then around and back up one to the car. He unlocked it. "Get in."

They zipped through the rain-soaked streets, Rourke at the wheel, navigating with the finesse of a local townsman. He tossed the beret at her as they rounded a curve, his fingers combing his hair back into place.

"Much better," Annie observed. "A beret on you is like purple lipstick on me."

"Both fulfilled their function though." He glanced over at her, smiling. "I must admit, you are resourceful."

"Thanks. Where are we headed?"

"Somewhere safe."

Chapter Thirteen

Casey walked quickly, scanning the street numbers and wondering how much bad luck one poor, tired Irishman could bear. This was the fourth location he had been to looking for Lunn Kendrick. The guy slipped in and out of places like a greased pig. And such places! Roaming the dark alleys of any town at one in the morning wasn't a good idea, but doing so in the rough neighborhoods Kendrick liked to frequent was simply asking for trouble.

At last he found the address he was looking for. Heavy curtains couldn't hide the glow from the lights inside the first-floor apartment. Standing to one side of the door, he knocked. When no one answered, he raised his fist and pounded on the wood, making the rusty hinges rattle.

A very young woman with tousled dark hair opened the door, holding a flowery sheet up to cover her breasts. He could see the empty, rumpled bed behind her.

"Yes?"

"I'm looking for Lunn Kendrick."

"He's not here."

"Is that a fact?" Casey shoved the door open, not hard enough to scare her, but enough to let her know he meant business. She moved aside and he stepped past her into the small room. It was a studio apartment, with doorways on each side of the bed. "Then you won't mind if I look around."

"I'll call the cops," she threatened.

"That's a fine idea," Casey murmured, walking into the tiny kitchenette. A cat couldn't hide in there.

As he turned he realized he'd chosen the wrong place to look first. A man bolted through the doorway on the other side of the bed, heading for the front door.

"Watch out, Lunn!" the girl squealed.

Casey dove headlong over the bed, bouncing off the end of it and tackling the other man before he could reach the door. They rolled across the small open area, bumping into a table. The lamp atop it fell with a crash, spraying shards of pottery and splinters of broken light bulb all over the room.

"Kendrick! All I want is to ask a few questions!"

"Here's your answers!"

Casey gasped as he was hit on the jaw. Another blow landed on his throat. It was obvious Kendrick wasn't going to listen to reason. Scrambling, Casey started getting in a few good blows of his own. At last he managed to roll them both over, this time landing on top. He slugged Kendrick in the jaw and was ready to sock him again when suddenly he couldn't breathe.

Something was wrapped tight around his throat, pulling his head backward and cutting off his air. Casey tried to grab hold of the slippery cloth, struggling to get it away from his throat as he gasped for air.

Kendrick, wiggling out from beneath him, was out the door in seconds. Just as suddenly the cloth around Casey's neck went slack. It slithered across his throat as it was pulled away.

On his knees, Casey breathed in huge gulps of air as he glared at the young girl. In her hands was a colorful scarf, and for some reason she didn't seem to be frightened by him. Evidently she had been through things like this before.

"Do you know where he's gone?"

She shook her head, backing away from him. One more step and she was in the bathroom with the door shut, sliding a dead bolt home. Casey stood there, cursing.

"Saint Patrick's bones!"

Now what? Kendrick really was a greased pig and Casey was no closer to catching him than before. The meeting at the hotel hadn't come off as planned; Casey didn't know how to get in touch with Rourke and he'd also run out of places to look for Kendrick. He was going to have to call Derry.

Casey didn't want to fail him. He owed Derry more than he could ever repay. Not only had the man saved his life, his family had nursed him back to health when he had been left to die after a stupid brawl that got out of hand.

Besides, Casey didn't have the time or temperament for failure. As a free-lancer, he always had many irons in the fire, and his other employers weren't too happy with his latest reports. At the rate he was going, no one would be paying him this month.

Casey slammed the door as he left, not worried about the noise. From what he knew of Lunn Kendrick, the guy wouldn't be lying in wait for him. All he had to worry about was making sure he had really lost the men who had been following him.

ANNIE STRETCHED HER ARMS and legs in the small car. They had been driving for over five hours along narrow, winding country lanes.

"Are you sure we're on the right road?"

"It's not much farther."

It was a coal-black night, the narrow slice of moon overhead giving off little light. She looked at Rourke but was unable to discern his expression in the limited illumination cast by the dashboard lights. "Are you sure this place isn't a figment of your imagination? We're out in the middle of nowhere! I haven't seen so much as a building in quite a while."

"I know where I'm going."

"How?" She sat up straight. "Is this house yours?"

"No. But I'm welcome anytime. So are a few others."

"Then what if it's occupied?"

He shrugged. "We'll have to share."

They were approaching a cluster of hills, their vague outlines etched across the bleak horizon before them like a pen-and-ink drawing.

"There," Rourke said at last. "It's coming right up, straight in front of us."

Annie stared at the hills, looming ever larger by the minute. "I don't see a house, or even any lights! You're having hallucinations."

"You're not supposed to be able to see it. Haven't you heard of bermed dwellings?" He pulled to a stop and cut off the engine. "They're built into hillsides, for privacy and to conserve energy. Come on, the entrance is around this side."

Annie turned on her miniflashlight and walked beside him, around the curve of the hill to a weathered wooden door set in flush with the hillside. "Is it locked?"

"I have a key."

"Then what are we waiting for?"

He glanced at her, his hand on a recessed door pull. "Where are your manners? I rang the bell first to see if anyone was here."

"You call waking someone up good manners?"

"Beats getting shot," he murmured, swinging the door open and preceding her inside. Dim lights directed toward the ceiling cast a soft, hazy glow about the little room.

"This is the mud room," he announced quietly. "We get a lot of rain here." Rourke locked the door and Annie followed him into another, much larger room. In fact it was huge. "Living room. The kitchen is to the left and two bedrooms are down this hallway." He stopped at the second door. "This one is yours."

"Who owns this house?" she asked warily, entering the dark bedroom right on his heels.

"A rich, eccentric Irishman," he replied.

She could hear him moving about the room. "Rich and eccentric, huh? I'll buy that. How do you know him?"

"We did a small favor for him once, Jack, Russ and I."

"How small?"

Rourke turned on a bedside lamp. "That depends on your point of view. We inadvertently saved his son's life."

A double bed covered with a patchwork quilt dominated the room. There weren't any windows, just four white walls. A simple pine dresser, two night stands and a straight-back chair completed the furnishings.

One bed. Would they share it tonight?

"The bathroom's through here," Rourke said, indicating a closed door. "It adjoins the next bedroom. There's food in the kitchen, help yourself to anything you need."

"Where are you going?"

"My room, of course." He closed the door on his way out.

That certainly answered her question. Nothing like being rejected before you've even popped the question. Annie showered and had just climbed into bed when Rourke entered her room without knocking.

In his hand was a glass with an inch or so of amber liquid in it. "Drink?"

Oh, how she wanted one, preferably something strong enough to knock her out and stop her troubled thoughts. With a shrug she reached over and took the proffered glass, draining the contents in one gulp.

It burned all the way down and she sat up, coughing, throat on fire and face flushed, tears welling in her eyes. He took the glass from her before she dropped it on the floor.

"What—what was that?" she finally croaked out, tears streaming down her cheeks. "Battery acid?"

"Home brew."

She took a deep, shuddering breath and flopped back on the bed, one arm covering her eyes. Her voice was raspy, hoarse. "It's worse than the stuff my granny makes!"

"Or better."

Annie raised her arm slightly and peered down her small nose at him. His expression was smug, a smile hovering in his eyes. "You have no taste."

"You're right. I like you, don't I?" With those words he turned out the light and left, shutting the door behind himself.

"Oh, Patrick, you romantic fool," Annie muttered.

Kisses in stairwells, long moonlit rides, strong drink and kind words at bedtime. Even a certain sexy twinkle in his gray eyes. Then he goes off to sleep in another room.

She was fairly certain he wouldn't abandon her again. But he was still running away from her. Whenever she tried to rescue him from his self-imposed prison, he started a game of mental hide-and-seek. Still, she was obviously having an effect on him in other ways. Annie didn't know what game Patrick was playing now, but if he wasn't darn careful he was going to find himself under attack.

"THE POLICE HAVE OUR MAN in custody," Farrell reported, sitting down opposite Brady. "Hagen's grandfather is pressing charges against him for breaking and entering and, given the body count in that barn, they'll probably be trying him for at least one murder, as well."

Brady Adair raised his bushy red eyebrows. "That's what he gets for being the only survivor. With his partner in the morgue, he'll take the fall by himself. Neither of them can be traced back to us, can they?" he asked, already knowing the answer. If he hadn't been sure, he'd be splitting someone's skull open about now.

"No."

"Then forget about them. Anything on the other two?"

"No. Whoever hired them is evidently as careful as we are," Farrell replied. "And they're hardly in any condition to tell us, now are they?"

"That's the thing about dead men," Brady mused. "For one side they're a blessing, for the other a nuisance. At least one of ours came out on top. Anything on Hagen?"

Farrell shook his head. "Not a peep—and I've dug up a lot of our old sources on this one. The reports on his activities over the last few years haven't helped much, but a few things are still being checked out."

"Kid's bound to make a mistake sooner or later," Brady said, puffing on his cigar and blowing foul blue smoke into the air. "What about Rourke and Sawyer? Where are they?"

Farrell leaned back in the leather chair, one ankle resting on top of his other knee. "Haven't a clue. They've managed to elude everyone—the twins, the hotel management, even the police." He coughed. The air was getting a bit thick. "Gone, like I wish your smoke was. And our mysterious informant with the inside source claims the woman hasn't reported in."

"Smart move on her part," Brady noted with grudging respect. "This informant. Do we have an ID yet?"

"No, but I believe we soon will. Whoever it is, their gall is matched only by their greed. So, along with the last payment, I included a phone number and promised extra cash for its use. The number is naturally set up for a trace."

"Excellent. What about Rourke's contact? The one he was supposed to meet at the hotel?"

"A dead end, I'm afraid," Farrell replied. "There was a man seen hanging around prior to the incident and leaving in a hurry afterward. Our man followed, but all he did was go bar hopping. They lost him after the third or fourth pub."

"Damnation!" Brady bellowed, pounding his desk with a big fist. "What do we have left to go on?"

Farrell shrugged. "All of us want Hagen. As he's proving even more elusive than Rourke and the woman, I say we should concentrate our efforts on finding them. If we can keep track of those two, they'll lead us to him."

"We haven't been doing so bloody well on that score, Farrell!" Brady Adair chomped down on his cigar, his ruddy face glowing a bright shade of red. He glared at his partner. "They can't have disappeared completely. Find them, hire more men," Brady ordered. "We don't have time to wait for them to show their faces."

"What do you think I've been doing? Playing pinochle? But if we're too heavy-handed about it, we'll spook Rourke. If he goes underground, we won't be able to find him, and you know it, Brady. You've seen the reports. There are chunks of his life, months at a time, completely unaccounted for."

"Then find Hagen and get rid of *him!*"

"How?" Farrell asked mildly.

"I don't care how, damn your eyes! Just do it! Once he's dead there won't be a clue left to lead anyone to us!"

Farrell intertwined his fingers and rested them on his flat stomach. "Aren't you forgetting someone, Brady?"

"What I'm doing, Farrell, is concentrating on the more immediate threats. Find and kill Orren Hagen. If that means finding Rourke and Sawyer first, do it." Brady was puffing so vigorously on his cigar that he had created a smoke blue haze around his desk that all but obscured him. He looked like a wild-eyed devil pontificating from his smoky pit. "We need to question Rourke, then he can go out with the trash as well. But don't kill the woman unless you have to. I don't want the U.S. government trying to find out why one of their employees disappeared."

"Nor do I. Until we find them, however, the point is moot."

Brady's red eyebrows became one solid line as his eyes narrowed shrewdly. "What about the investigative company we're using?" he asked. "I don't need any of this coming to light right now."

"Solid." Farrell was used to Brady Adair's habit of checking and rechecking every little detail for points of weakness. "They report to me by phone if I call them, and then only if it's needed," he explained. "Otherwise the reports are sent to a post-office box, and the mail is then forwarded to different boxes or faxed to us through a circuitous route."

Brady nodded. They'd used this same routine in the past without any mishaps. And it was still working. "Good. My brother's detectives are snooping everywhere, putting their noses where they don't belong," he reminded Farrell.

"They aren't even close to us."

Brady tapped his cigar on the ashtray. "They'd better not be. This whole situation has become more than a mild annoyance. It's time we put everything on hold."

Farrell calculated the time factor again. "Let's give it another two days. If this isn't settled by then, I'll alert our associates to take cover. But let me remind you, Brady, these people aren't going to react well to delays."

"Hell, I don't like them either." Brady puffed furiously on his cigar. "All right. You have your two days. After that, we'll have to take drastic action and deal with whatever consequences arise."

"Meaning?"

"Meaning that if we don't have Hagen, Rourke and Sawyer by then, we put out the order to kill them on sight."

Chapter Fourteen

Annie leaned back into the cushy sofa, a paperback book beside her bare legs. Her long fuchsia T-shirt was her only garment. She'd taken this opportunity to do some washing and the rest of her clothes were in the dryer.

Though she wasn't too fond of being mostly underground, it was a nice, well-equipped house, pleasantly decorated in a modern style. An oval glass coffee table sat in front of the amply padded sofa, and on the wall facing her were a stereo, a television and a VCR. Matching glass end tables flanked either side of the couch, with a big lamp atop each. On the other side of the coffee table, a pair of comfortable armchairs completed a conversational grouping. Patrick occupied the chair on her right.

It was only midafternoon, but she was already getting restless. Being cooped up together in a house without windows was more than either she or Rourke wanted to deal with. There were skylights overhead, so it wasn't as if the place was gloomy. They simply weren't used to this much inactivity, and not being able to see outside didn't help. Worse, the sexual tension between them was almost tangible, making them both short-tempered.

"How long are we going to stay here?" Annie asked.

Rourke glanced up from his crossword puzzle. "Another day or two."

"I should report in."

"Why?" he asked, raising his eyebrows.

"If I don't they might send out a search party."

"Sure they will."

Annie frowned at his rude tone of voice. What she really wanted to do was call Julie. If Patrick hadn't been in such a snippy mood, she would have told him so. As it was, she just didn't feel like dealing with any accusations he might throw at her.

"You think no one's worried about me?"

"Give her a Kewpie doll for being right," he retorted. "They know you're with me and they're just sitting back in their chairs, fat and sassy, waiting for you to do their dirty work for them."

"It's my job."

Rourke threw the paper down beside his chair. He'd had too much time to think about what had happened—and what might happen. "The hell it is! They're using you. This isn't even close to what you usually do."

"Why, thank you so much! What a vote of confidence!" she exclaimed sarcastically. "Have I let you down yet?"

"You did once before," Rourke reminded her.

Annie jumped to her feet. "That's low, Rourke, even for you. I had a good reason for hesitating then."

"Oh, really?" he inquired, turning away as if he couldn't care less. Actually, he cared a great deal. But he couldn't concentrate properly on her answer while looking at her shapely bare legs. "Do tell."

"All right. I'm tired of you acting so smug about it. It could have happened to anyone. Even you." After all this time, that night still bothered her. She could see the situation clearly, like a movie running in her mind. "I had a choice to make," she told him. "A choice that had nothing to do with experience, that no amount of training could have prepared me for."

"Bull! You froze!"

"Did I?"

"That guy damn near blew my head off!"

"But he didn't," Annie returned quietly. "Maybe a part of my mind took your speed and ability into account. The moment came and went so quickly, I honestly can't say. All I know is that I was faced with a decision and I made it."

Patrick finally looked at her. She was standing there, eyes closed, her fists clenched at her sides, evidently reliving that night long ago. What had she seen that he had missed? "What are you talking about? What decision?"

"It was dark, if you recall," she continued. "And dead still. You were on point and I was covering you, watching your back. A man stepped out of the shadows up ahead, a gun in his hand. I didn't even have time to warn you. If I didn't shoot him, he was going to kill you."

"And you couldn't pull the trigger. You froze."

"Shut up and listen, Rourke!" Annie exclaimed. "I didn't freeze. But I did make a mistake. I had put myself into a position where my field of fire was limited. There was a telephone pole on my left, a Dumpster on my right, with you and the other guy in between. The alley sloped down sharply on the other side of the trash bin, so I could only see his upper body. Still, I had a perfect shot."

Rourke clenched his jaw, remembering that night along with her. "Then why didn't you take it?" he bit out.

"Because, Patrick, as I raised my gun, an instant before I squeezed the trigger, a young boy came out from behind that Dumpster." Annie opened her eyes. "For that one instant he was in my sights, blocking that perfect shot."

Rourke's jaw went slack. "Someone yelled," he murmured. "I remember now. That guy's bullet went right by my ear, so close I could feel the wind of it, but just before that I heard someone cry out."

"That was the boy," Annie confirmed. "He hollered something and took off like a rabbit, but by that time the other guy had fired."

Some long-forgotten pieces fell into place in Rourke's head. The voice, high-pitched, like that of a woman—or a young boy. He'd thought it was Annie, yelling because she couldn't do anything else, couldn't pull the trigger.

He sat there, stunned by this revelation. "Why didn't you tell me this at the time?"

"You've got to be kidding! You came down on me like a ton of bricks," she replied acidly. "Remember?"

"Yes." Patrick sighed, leaning back in his chair. She was right. He wouldn't have listened to anything then, even if Annie had tried to tell him. Then he remembered something else. "I was the one who told you to stay back."

She nodded. "That's right. I should have been in better position, past that Dumpster where there were fewer obstructions. You waved me back. The mistake I made was blind obedience. And it almost cost both of us our lives. The second shot grazed my skull," she reminded him.

"After all this time... You should have told me, Annie," Rourke accused. "You should have forced me to listen."

"My head hurt so much I couldn't think straight and at the time, I didn't care if you knew or not, not even after you were nice to me at the hospital." There had been another pain, too. The look of distrust—even aversion—she remembered seeing in Patrick's eyes. "You couldn't wait to get away from me."

What she said was true; he had been running from her. He realized, perhaps for the first time, that nearly getting killed because of a mistake he had thought she'd made was only part of the reason he'd wanted to get away from her.

Something had been stirring between them even back then. Desire, naturally, but other feelings as well, feelings he hadn't wanted to deal with. Rourke wasn't at all sure he wanted to deal with them now, either.

But he certainly owed her something. "I'm sorry, Annie." That sounded lame, even to him. "I never even gave you the benefit of the doubt. But you really have gotten better."

"Is that the best you can do, Patrick? I've saved your rear end this time out, more than once, and all you can say is 'you've gotten better,' " she said, mimicking him. "I *know* I've gotten better. I also know I have you to thank for the opportunity to learn. The only person who would believe my side of the story about that night is you, because you were there. If you'd told your side then it would probably have ended my career—or sent me back to a desk job. But rather than tell it, you took off and my superiors accepted the more believable story I came up with. That was thanks enough. I don't want your apology."

"Then what is it you want?"

She crossed her arms over her breasts. "You already know what I want."

"I'm glad we're finally working together," Patrick admitted grudgingly. "There. Are you happy now?"

"No! I'm glad we're working together, too, that you finally decided I was capable enough. But I want more, and you know it. I want to be your friend." Actually, deep down, she wanted even more than that, while Patrick was still doing his best to keep her at arm's length. But was that best for either of them? "Why does that frighten you so? Why do *I* frighten you? Do I remind you of your wife?"

He laughed harshly. "Not even close, Sawyer."

His words stung, but she kept her voice soft when she spoke. "Patrick, your wife and child are gone forever. You need to accept that and find peace within yourself. Before you get killed. Think of Bridget—"

Patrick stood up, cutting her off. "Don't push it, Annie. You're good, all right? And you've been a big help. But I don't want or need you interfering in my private life."

She watched his retreating back as he stormed out of the room, fists tightly clenched. A moment later, she heard the front door slam shut.

"Way to go, Sawyer," she muttered, as mad at herself as she was at him. "You handled that with all the finesse and grace of a pregnant elephant."

It was too late to back down now. She was involved, whether she wanted to be or not. She couldn't just walk away. Patrick needed her help if he was going to find Hagen. He also needed someone watching his backside. And for reasons she didn't fully understand, she *needed* to be the one to give him that help.

Annie flopped facedown on the couch, burying her head in the plush cushions. Finally telling him about that night had left her physically and emotionally drained. She decided she might as well give in to it and take a nap. He would probably be gone for hours anyway, walking off his anger.

She was just drifting off to sleep when she heard the front door open. Patrick had calmed down much faster than she had expected.

Half in a doze, her mind wandered down a path it had taken often in the past few days. Even if they couldn't come to terms about her place in his personal life, someday, perhaps soon, she and Patrick would have to confront the desire they felt for each other.

What would it be like? How would it start? Maybe he would approach the couch right now, unable to resist running his hand up the back of her bare thigh. Annie giggled softly, her voice muffled by the cushions. Such pleasant, wishful thoughts were the things dreams were made of and her sleep-clouded mind was filled with just such dreams.

When a hand actually brushed lightly across her thigh, however, her eyes popped open. But she didn't move or moan with pleasure. Patrick's hands, though gentle, were those of a man who spent a lot of time outdoors, strong hands toughened by his active life.

The hand moving up the back of her knee was smooth, uncallused, almost feminine. This was not Patrick.

It continued to slip upward, following the curve of her thigh. She waited for just the right moment. When it came, she flipped over with a quick twist and jabbed the intruder in the abdomen with the heel of her foot. He doubled over with a grunt, gasping for breath. Annie tried to get away, but he fell sideways on top of her and together they rolled off the couch, hitting the coffee table before landing with a thump on the carpeted floor.

She grabbed his dark hair and gave it a vicious yank. Ignoring his yelp of pain, she slammed the palm of her hand sharply into his solar plexus, knocking the wind completely out of him. The stranger lay still.

Breathing heavily, she crawled free and looked around for something to tie him up with. She remembered seeing some thin rope in one of the kitchen drawers and went to get it.

As she finished knotting the rope around his legs, he began to recover his wits and made an attempt to stand up. She pushed him down again. This time he stayed down. All was quiet as she tied his wrists together.

Deciding a blindfold was in order, she went back to the kitchen and got a dish towel. He was still silent when she returned. She looked at his face, noticing that someone else had been pounding on him recently. Both of his eyes were blackened.

"Maybe you should consider karate lessons, sport," she advised. "But I'm glad I didn't see those eyes before I slugged you. You look like a raccoon. And I'm such a sucker for animals."

Sitting back on her heels, she surveyed her handiwork. He wasn't much taller than she, maybe five-six, and he did sort of look like a chubby raccoon. His full cheeks blended into a rounded double chin and pudgy face. She certainly hadn't seen him before; maybe Patrick would know who he was.

Annie smiled, wondering what Patrick's reaction would be when he saw how she'd handled their uninvited guest. In a way, it was too bad this intruder had come along, though. Now they would no longer be alone in the house.

ROURKE WALKED FOR MILES in the misty rain, letting the boiling anger inside him slowly shift back to a light simmer. After the first few miles, he knew in his mind—if not his heart—that Annie only wanted to help him.

But he didn't quite know how to deal with Annie. He was being pulled in two directions, into his past and into the future.

His troubled thoughts disappeared when he rounded the curve of the hill. A quick stab of fear took his breath away. There was another car parked next to his. Who was here? More importantly, was Annie all right?

His sodden pants made his legs feel heavy and awkward as he ran across the side of the hill toward the entrance. The recessed handle slipped from his wet grasp twice before he managed to jerk the door open and run into the living room.

Annie was sitting calmly on the couch, her jean-clad legs curled beside her as she worked on his crossword puzzle. In the middle of the living room floor, next to the coffee table, lay a man trussed up like a turkey.

Chest heaving, Rourke looked from one to the other, his eyes open wide. "You okay?"

"I'm fine," she replied. "But you don't look too good."

Rainwater plastered his black hair to his face and ran down his cheeks in thin rivulets. His shoes and jeans were all spattered with mud, his light blue chambray shirt wet and sticking to his chest. He squished when he walked.

"No worse than he feels, I'll bet. Any problems?"

"Very few. I had to stuff a sock in his mouth about an hour ago." Annie grinned. "His language is atrocious."

Rourke nodded. She hadn't needed him after all. "He can wait. I'm going to take a quick shower."

Patrick stood under a steady stream of hot water, letting the heat permeate his chilled body. Every time he turned around he was underestimating how well Annie could take care of herself. He wasn't used to such self-sufficient women. It was strange, but except for when they were working beside him, he wasn't sure he liked them that way.

Annie set the crossword puzzle aside, quelling the small quivering sensations she felt in her stomach as Patrick came back into the room. He looked good, sexy in black turtleneck and jeans, with his wet hair combed back.

Her earlier fantasies had gotten to her. As crazy as it seemed, all she wanted to do right now was make love with Patrick and to heck with questioning their captive.

Rourke walked over to the man on the floor, pulled the sock out of his mouth and removed the blindfold. "Well, well. Nice shiners around those eyes. What mess have you gone and gotten yourself into this time, Lunn?"

"What's going on here, Rourke? Untie me!" Kendrick hollered. "This is my house!"

"Your father's house," Rourke corrected. "In which I am a welcome guest anytime. Remember, I saved your worthless hide once. By mistake, of course."

"You've been paid back."

Rourke sat down in a chair facing him. "You haven't matured any in the last few years, Kendrick."

"Well? What are you going to do?" Lunn asked. "Leave me tied up on the floor?"

"Maybe. Could be I intend to turn you over to the authorities." Rourke got the reaction he wanted. Lunn's mouth fell open. "Or the other side."

"Not them!" Lunn yelled, pulling on his ropes. But he promptly calmed down. "You wouldn't do that to my old man."

His voice was forceful, but Rourke heard the tremulous uncertainty in his words. "You're right, I wouldn't, but I know someone who would be pleased to do it for me."

Lunn scooted around to glare at the woman sitting on the couch. "Who is she?"

"You should show respect for your captor," Rourke said. Lunn's contempt was obvious. "Her?"

"You're at her mercy."

His eyes returned to Rourke. "What are you playing at?"

"We want a few questions answered. Such as, where is Orren Hagen?" Lunn's head moved back a fraction of an inch in reaction to the question.

"Who?" Lunn seemed puzzled, pursing his full lips. "Never heard of a bloke called Hagen. That's one down. What's the next question?"

Rourke stood up and leaned over Lunn, stuffing the sock back into his mouth. "Take some time and think about that one for a while. I'm too hungry to put up with you right now."

He gestured to Annie and she followed him into the kitchen, where Lunn's muffled protests were barely audible. Still, she kept her voice low. "All right, what's going on?"

"First things first," Patrick said, going to the big white freezer at one end of the room.

To his right there was a microwave oven, then a stove and a sink, with plenty of cupboards above them all. The entire kitchen was done in stark white, except for the kelly-green counters. In the middle of the room were an oblong dining table and four chairs.

Annie leaned against the far counter and crossed her arms. "All right. But it's your turn to burn dinner." One of the first things they had discovered was that neither of them were experienced cooks. "What's made you so chipper?"

Patrick grinned at her over his shoulder. "I was right. Lunn does know Hagen. I'll bet he knows where he is, too, or at least some good places to look." He scanned a list taped to the freezer door before opening it and pulling out a white casserole dish. "Chicken pot pie all right?"

Annie nodded and watched as he set the timer on the microwave to defrost and cook the meal. "As long as it really is chicken pot pie. Are you sure this time?"

"Reasonably sure." He closed the door and hit the start button. "It's sort of yellow and has a crust on top. How else can you tell?"

"You're asking the wrong person. I just know I don't want lentil soup again, like we had for breakfast."

"It was good soup! Besides, I've figured out how to read those charts now. Pot pie, coming right up."

Annie looked at him smugly. "With or without the lovely flavor of molten nonmicrowaveable plastic?"

"Damn." Patrick opened the oven door and removed the rectangular lid. "It's not even to the melting stage this time," he announced, flapping the lid at her as proof before he tossed it into the sink.

"Congratulations. What are we going to do now?"

He opened a cupboard to the right of the sink. "Set the table. Would you get the silverware, please?"

"Patrick!"

"Such a bossy lass. We're going to wait for Casey to show up. He should be here tonight or tomorrow morning."

"How do you know that? We have no means of outside communication here." She watched him take dishes out of the cupboard. "Or have you been holding out on me again?"

"You don't trust me?"

"Not an inch." Trusting him with her life was different from trusting him to part with his precious information. Not that she could blame him. She was playing close with hers, too.

"Smart girl." They began setting the table. "I sent Casey after Kendrick. His showing up here means Casey found him and scared him enough to send him running to the safe haven Daddy built for him."

"That would explain his black eyes, but... Wait a minute!" He *had* been holding out on her. "You mean you planned on coming here all along?"

"Yes."

She was mad. No, she was past that point with him. "This cat-and-mouse game has got to stop or one of us is going to be seriously hurt or killed. Either we're working on this together or we're not, Patrick."

He had come to the same conclusion himself. But it was still hard for him to accept. He rarely worked with a partner. While he appreciated Annie's skills at times he wanted to strangle her out of sheer frustration. And at other times, he wanted to give in to the new-found feelings she aroused in him. There was no doubt she was trying to wear down his defensive wall of anger. In some ways she was beginning to succeed. What bothered him most, he supposed, was that Annie wasn't giving him any choice in the matter.

"Well?" Annie prompted. "Did you mean what you said about being glad we're working together or not?"

He didn't look at her. "Yes."

"Then what's the problem? Is it that difficult for you to accept, Patrick?"

Yes, it was. He wasn't able to separate the woman from the agent. In fact, he knew he'd never been able to, because they were the same person. "It is difficult. But we're in this together as a team," he finally told her.

"Then tell me, who's Lunn Kendrick?"

Patrick sat down at the table and propped his feet up on another chair. "A spoiled rotten rich kid with doting parents." Contempt filled his voice. "The never-ending troubles in Northern Ireland are like a game to him, a lark. It's something he plays at without ever actually getting involved. Most of the people on both sides believe quite passionately in their cause."

"What do you believe?"

He tilted his head back and stared up at the ceiling. "I left it all behind years ago. I have no beliefs anymore." Before she could probe deeper, he stood up and offered her the chair. "Dinner is ready. Have a seat, I'll play waiter tonight, too."

Annie sat down. "Are you a better waiter than a cook?"

"No."

"Then heaven help me. I don't think I'll look very good in chicken pot pie."

Later that night, Annie was huddled under the covers when Patrick entered the room and locked the bedroom door.

"Everything all right?"

"Fine. Lunn's still not talking. He's tied up in the other bedroom. And I set up an alarm on the front door so there'll be no more surprises." Patrick turned out the light, removing his clothes before getting into bed. "No reason we shouldn't all be comfy."

Annie turned toward him, her hand brushing across his chest and down to his stomach. As her hand slipped lower, she heard the sharp intake of his breath.

"Annie, I think I made a mistake. This isn't—"

"Shh, don't think, just feel, let yourself go," she encouraged softly, guiding his hand to her breast.

He needed little encouragement. This was something he had been wanting to do for days.

Their hands and mouths moved, caressing each other, both giving in to their desires. They came together fast, in a wild, frenzied explosion of emotion, swept away without any control. And once was not enough for either of them.

A while later, Annie awoke to find him still beside her but carefully holding himself apart from her. "Patrick?" she whispered into the darkness. "What's wrong?"

"Nothing," he said soothingly. "Go back to sleep."

"Can't you sleep?" She supposed she should be used to it by now. "Silly question. Have you always had insomnia?"

"No," he replied. "Not always. Now get some rest. You're going to need it in the next few days."

"What about you?"

"Don't worry about me."

Annie sat up. "Someone has to worry about you."

"You're not my mother, Annie."

"Hardly," she said in a throaty voice. "Besides, it's not possible. You're older than me."

He sighed loudly. "Go back to sleep."

"Talk to me, Patrick. Aren't we friends?"

"Lovers, certainly," he said.

"That, too. What's wrong with being both?"

"Friends expect more. They want you to talk, bare your soul to them. All that nonsense."

"It's not always nonsense. And friends can also just be there when you need them," Annie told him. "I want to help you, Patrick. You helped me once, remember?"

"Is that what all this is, Annie? You give me your body as a payback for saving your hide?"

"Maybe it started out that way."

Patrick winced. He'd wanted honesty and he'd gotten it, but her words hurt him deeply. "Well then," he said quietly, "I guess we can consider that debt paid."

He was withdrawing from her. She wasn't able to see it, but she felt it and knew she wasn't wrong. If she turned on a light, their conversation would be over, he'd be back hiding from her once again.

"Patrick, I wanted to make love with you. And I want to do it again and again." She resisted the urge to reach out and touch him. "In the beginning, maybe I did think, subconsciously, that I could help you overcome your grief as a way of paying you back for saving my career."

She waited for his reaction but he didn't say anything. "But making love with you was something I did for myself." She paused again, but he still didn't speak. "Patrick, talk to me. I want to help you."

"I know you do. Now go to sleep, Annie."

She chewed on her lower lip, debating whether she had pushed enough for tonight. "Friends?"

"Yes," he said, reaching out, pulling her close into the shelter of his arms. "Friends. We work well together. But please don't destroy that friendship, Annie."

"I just want to help."

There was a hint of a smile in his voice. "I know you care." He continued to stroke her. "Are you comfortable?"

"Mmm, yes."

"Then go to sleep."

He lay awake for a long time, Annie's steady, rhythmic breathing filling his soul as he remembered his wife and son as they had once been. And were no more. Even in her sleep Annie seemed aware of him, her arms tightening around him, comforting him.

But a night of comfort could not make up for all the pain in his heart. He was still awake hours later when a loud buzzer sounded throughout the house. Rourke was up and dressed in an instant, and heading toward the door, gun in hand.

Annie had rolled out of bed, too, and was pulling on her clothes, still struggling to wake up. "What was that?" she asked.

"Someone's here."

Chapter Fifteen

Annie was wide awake and by Patrick's side as they went into the living room. A man was standing in the doorway that led to the mud room, pointing a gun at them. He whistled.

Patrick lowered his own weapon. "Casey. Come on inside." He went to the kitchen and turned on the light, motioning for Casey to sit down at the table. "Hungry?"

"No."

Casey sat at the head of the table, putting his gun down carefully on the spotless surface. He looked exhausted, the jean jacket and dark shirt he wore making the freckles stand out on his pale face.

Annie didn't trust him by a long shot. But, then again, she didn't know him or the truth behind the things she suspected him of doing. For the moment, he was just a tired human being, trusted by Rourke and supposedly on their side. She opened a cupboard and pulled out a bottle of whiskey.

"Then how about a drink?" she asked.

"That I could use." He took the glass Rourke handed him and swallowed the contents, then held out the glass to be refilled.

There was a yellowing bruise on Casey's jaw and a red mark around his throat. "Looks as if you've had a few problems," Rourke said, taking the bottle from Annie and pouring another shot.

"One or two. Nothing I couldn't handle." Casey sipped the whiskey. "I did get lost on the way here, though."

"That's not surprising." Rourke sat down at the opposite end of the table. "Kendrick's here."

"Nice, that. I owe him." With a light touch, Casey traced his bruised jaw. "We had a brief discussion before his girlfriend helped him get away."

"Find out anything?"

"Not from him directly." He shifted in his seat and looked to his left at Annie, who was leaning against the kitchen counter. "But I've got my suspicions."

Rourke followed his gaze. "She's in. Go ahead."

"Kendrick definitely knows Hagen. They've done a bit of business together. And, with a little persuasion," Casey said, popping his knuckles, "he'll tell all. Or else."

Annie arched her eyebrows in surprise. Looks could be so deceiving. Casey hadn't seemed the violent type. "How much 'else' are you planning on using?" she inquired.

Casey grinned. "Don't worry, Annie. Kendrick acts tough, but by all accounts, he's a cream puff. I imagine this will just take some verbal persuasion. You won't be required to bruise your delicate hands."

"You're too late," she informed him. "I already have."

After filling Casey in on Kendrick's capture, Rourke asked him, "Why didn't you meet us in Dublin as arranged?"

"I spotted Annie going into the hotel and waited for you to show up. When you did, I called your room, but the phone was busy, just as it had been for an hour before."

He was looking at Annie again. "Someone had a surprise party waiting for us," she explained. "The phone was off the hook when I got there."

"I see. Well, I knew something didn't feel right," Casey continued. "So I left and went on with my search for Kendrick.'' He shrugged. ''You know the rest. Derry told me about this place and here I am.''

But you didn't take off until after the police had arrived, Annie thought. *What are you hiding?*

''Have you heard anything new on Hagen?'' Rourke asked.

Casey sipped his drink. ''You were right. There are plenty of people looking for him. And at least one group doesn't particularly care what shape Hagen's in when they get him, either. There's a large bounty being offered for his body.''

''And we want to keep him alive,'' Annie murmured.

Casey stared at her. Neither he nor Rourke voiced any agreement with her statement. ''Do you need a few hours sleep before we talk to Kendrick?'' Rourke asked.

''Nah. Let's get this over with.''

After Rourke left the room, an uncomfortable silence descended. Annie still didn't trust Casey, and he clearly didn't seem to trust her, either. That was fine with her. So was the look of respect she'd seen in his eyes when Rourke had told him how she'd subdued Kendrick.

She took a glass from the cupboard, then sat down at the table and poured herself a shot of whiskey, ignoring Casey as carefully as he was ignoring her.

Lunn Kendrick stumbled into the room, cursing. He was dressed in the same rumpled clothes he'd arrived in and looked much the worse for wear. His short, dark hair was all askew, his hands tied in front of him. Rourke was right behind him.

When Kendrick saw Casey sitting at the table, he tried to beat a hasty retreat, but ended up backing right into Rourke, who pushed him into the middle of the room.

Casey chuckled. ''I don't know if I'll have the heart to hit him again. He looks like a raccoon.''

''Doesn't he, though?'' Annie agreed. She realized she was smiling at Casey and quickly reminded herself that it wouldn't be wise to start liking him before she knew she could trust him. "But even a raccoon can be dangerous if it wants to be."

"Come along, Lunn. Have a seat," Casey said, pulling out the chair opposite Annie's. "All's right with the world. We just have a few questions for you."

Kendrick's brown eyes were shifting nervously from one man to the other. "What's he doing here, Rourke?"

"I'm asking the questions." Rourke crossed the room to stand behind Annie's chair. "And you're going to answer them."

"This is a safe house, Rourke!" Kendrick was staring at him with open belligerence. "Just how many other people have you told about this place?"

"The right ones, if you don't cooperate," Casey announced with a nasty smile.

"What's that supposed to mean?"

"Cut the innocent act, Kendrick." Casey paused for a moment, letting him think about it. "You've worked for some very interesting people lately."

"I'm an activist," he said proudly.

"You're a horse's ass! None of the people I'm talking about are involved in the troubles. Dealing in drugs is a dangerous business. If word gets out that you've been talking about it, you're dead."

Kendrick stared at the three people confronting him. Sweat was beginning to bead on his upper lip. "What do you want to know?"

"Where's Hagen?" Rourke asked.

Kendrick's brow wrinkled. "Who?"

"Your father won't be happy if he hears about the drugs."

Kendrick licked his lips nervously but didn't say a word.

"Think about it Kendrick," Rourke told him. "On the run for the rest of your life, cut off from your family and that endless supply of money you don't have to work for."

Rourke knew Kendrick's father quite well. He wouldn't hesitate to throw his oldest son out penniless, disowning him forever, if he learned Lunn was dealing in drugs.

"All right. So I know Hagen. What about it?"

"Where is he?" Casey asked.

Kendrick hooked a leg of the chair with his foot and pulled it further away from the table, then sat down. "I'm not sure. He's been on the run and hiding out for weeks."

"Why?"

Kendrick shrugged. "I don't know."

"But you know where he might be," Rourke said.

"Some possible locations."

"Give them to us."

Still Kendrick hesitated. "Why do you want him?"

"That's none of your business," Casey replied.

Kendrick looked at Rourke. "Are you going to kill him?"

"No. But someone else will if they get the chance," Rourke explained. "We're not the only people after him."

"So I've heard. What's this all about, anyway?"

"That's none of your business," Casey repeated. "Either you give us the locations or I'll help you remember them."

Kendrick lifted his bound hands, running his fingers through his dark hair. "If I tell you this, you have to agree to leave me here where I'll be safe."

"You'll be safe with us," Casey assured him.

"No way," he returned defiantly.

"This isn't multiple choice, Kendrick."

"You leave me here or I'm not telling you anything."

"I wouldn't be so sure about that." Casey popped his knuckles and smiled. "I owe you one, bucko."

Rourke intervened. "You can stay here." He knew Lunn could be stupidly stubborn at times, even when his life was in danger. "If you give us those locations."

"Then you've got a deal."

"Wait a minute." Annie grabbed a pencil and paper out of a kitchen drawer and sat back down. "Okay."

Hesitantly at first, then almost seeming to enjoy the role of informant, Kendrick listed places where Hagen might be hiding. All were in or around Belfast.

"Where's the first place you'd look for him?" Rourke asked, looking at the list Annie had jotted down for them.

He answered promptly. "Second place I mentioned."

"Why?"

Kendrick chewed on his lower lip before answering. "A hunch. There's a hidden room in the house, upstairs."

"Very good, Kendrick. You can go back to the bedroom now. And don't poke your nose out or we'll blow it off."

"Aren't you going to untie me?" he asked, holding out his hands. "This is very uncomfortable."

"Work on it," Casey said. "You'll be free by morning. Now get out of my sight. I want to hear your door shut, too."

Kendrick shuffled out of the room, taking his time.

Rourke leaned over and plucked the glass out of Annie's hand, tossing the whiskey down in one gulp.

"Help yourself," she said dryly.

"I just did." He handed her the empty glass. "Thanks."

Casey looked from one of them to the other. Annie Sawyer wasn't what he'd call a world-class beauty. But, when she wasn't on guard, she radiated friendliness and warmth, a sort of open, innate kindness. Even now there was a twinkling glitter to her hazel eyes. Still, he didn't like her being there.

Derry had assured him of Rourke's professionalism, but Annie Sawyer was an unknown quantity. She wasn't a big woman, but she had to be skilled and fairly strong to have taken Kendrick on her own as she had. Hopefully she wouldn't work out. He had a lot riding on this.

A door banged shut. Casey smiled. "Defiant," he said of Lunn Kendrick, "but obedient. What's our next move?"

Rourke stood up. "First, you get some sleep, Casey. Sorry about making you use the couch, but I prefer Lunn in a place with a door that locks, and nearby so I can hear him."

"That's all right. I can sleep anywhere. I'm dead on my feet." He crossed himself. "So to speak."

"When we're all rested, you'll head for those places Lunn gave us that are on the west side, we'll take the east."

Annie frowned. "But he said—"

Rourke placed his hand on the back of her neck, silencing her. "I've played chess with Kendrick too many times. He's lying about where he'd start looking. It's his nature to lie about everything," he added.

"Then how can you trust him on these locations?"

"I don't," Rourke said. "But I do trust his cowardice, and at the moment we've got the bigger ax. Kendrick won't jeopardize his inheritance or his life."

Casey stood up. "Which room is he in?" he asked. "Just in case he gets frisky and I hear him before you do."

"Down the hall, first door on the right. We're in the second one."

Casey nodded, obviously suppressing a smile. Rourke waited until he'd left the room. "Come on, we haven't had much sleep and tomorrow morning's already here."

"Okay," Annie said, leaning her head back and smiling up at him. "But are you really all that sleepy?"

Chapter Sixteen

The next day Annie and Rourke drove to Belfast, intent on checking out the locations Lunn Kendrick had given them. Their first stop was chosen solely for the sake of convenience. It was a small store and pub on the outskirts of town.

While Patrick was talking to the woman who owned the place, Annie slipped outside to a pay phone. For once the connection was made quickly, but that didn't help; Gerald was in a meeting and couldn't be disturbed. Annie refused to leave a message, telling his secretary she'd check in later.

Then she called Julie, who answered on the first ring.

"Yes?"

"I'm in a hurry, Julie. What have you got for me?"

"Let's start with Casey. He's a freebooter. Among other things, he works as an investigator for whoever will hire him. It took some pretty creative computer work, but I found out he's evidently working for a firm in Ireland right now."

Annie arched her eyebrows. "That's interesting."

"Not half as interesting as what happened when I plugged the name Adair into the equation. It seems the firm Casey's free-lancing for has been hired by one Michael Adair to look into his brother Brady's various business interests in Northern Ireland. And get this," Julie said. "Michael Adair is a heavy-duty political type. He lives in Iowa, has *beaucoup* bucks and a good chance of getting the cabinet appointment he wants—as long as his brother isn't involved in something that could taint the family name. That's why the investigation.''

Annie asked, ''Is the brother clean?''

''Too clean to be believed in my jaded opinion, and that led me to do some more checking,'' he told her. ''Brady Adair's business empire is *quite* profitable.''

There was excitement in his voice. ''What are you saying, Julie?'' she demanded.

''You know that old saw about how money talks? Well, it can also buy a lot of silence. I'm not sure what all this means, but I'm continuing my research.''

Evidently he was rolling around the office, doing it as they spoke. His chair was squeaking so ominously she could hear it over the phone lines. ''Have you found a connection between either of the Adairs and Hagen?''

''No, but something about Brady Adair doesn't sit right with me. All those businesses. I'm in the process of accessing other computers right now, maybe they'll tell me more. If he's left any kind of paper trail, I'll find it.''

Annie didn't doubt it for an instant. Whether it would be useful or not was another matter. ''What about the other names?''

''Nothing specific. Hagen's a crook. Lunn Kendrick's a garden-variety hooligan, though I got a whiff of some possible drug connections. Zip on Flynn, other than what you already know.'' He hesitated. ''I'm, uh, staying on top of that one anyway, so if I can add anything, I'll pass it along.''

''Thanks.'' It worried her that Gerald hadn't taken her call. He'd never done that to her before. ''Julie, do you happen to know if Gerald ever personally worked in Ireland?''

''Sure,'' Julie replied. ''He's worked there at different times over the years. Why?''

"Oh, nothing, I was just curious." More and more she was questioning what Gerald's motivations and involvement were. "Was he working here five years ago?"

"I think so. Let me check." Julie's chair protested loudly as he moved. "Yes, he definitely was."

Annie glanced at her watch. "What about the leak?"

"Same. Nothing's been verified."

"Okay. Thanks Julie, talk to you soon."

Annie left the phone booth and hurried back into the pub, hoping Patrick hadn't missed her. She managed to slip inside with some other people and to circle around to him.

"Hey, handsome. Looking for me?" she asked, tapping him on the shoulder.

He turned and looked at her. "Where have you been?"

"Bathroom."

"Oh. Hagen's not here. Let's go."

After stopping to eat lunch at a lovely little roadside inn, they headed for the next location near the heart of town. Annie was still puzzled by Patrick's logic in this search.

"You're sure this is the one to try next?" she asked.

"No, I'm not sure, but it fits the way Kendrick's mind works when he plays chess. He's a skilled player, but too obvious when he's setting up his moves."

Annie looked at him, her curiosity aroused. "How would you choose if you hadn't played chess with him?"

"I'd guess."

"This could be a setup," she reminded him.

"Life's a gamble."

She couldn't argue that point with him. Annie consulted the street map he'd bought at their first stop. "Take a right at the next light, then go left at the first street we come to."

Patrick followed her directions, slowing down as he passed the address Kendrick had given them. The trim on the brick apartments needed painting. In fact, just about everything was in need of repair. He circled the block, looking the area over, as did Annie.

"There are a lot of people out," Patrick commented. Grass courtyards were set into each section of apartments, and young children were crawling all over, their mothers sitting nearby. "Reminds me of playtime at the park."

"From the looks we're getting, I'd say they all know we're strangers. Let's try the front door," Annie suggested as they parked down the block. "You know, ring the bell, see if anyone's home."

He looked at her skeptically. "You think they're going to let us in to search the place?"

"You never know. Of course, they could shoot us, but I doubt they will with all these people about." Annie raised her eyebrows. "Do you have a better idea to try in the middle of the afternoon?"

"Good point." They got out of the car. "Do you want to do the honors?" Patrick asked. "Or shall I?"

"Follow my lead and keep your mouth shut."

"Cheeky lass."

"We'll discuss my physiology at a later date." Annie smiled as they came upon a group of women, greeting them cordially in passing. She stepped up on the covered concrete porch and rang the bell.

A harried young woman opened the door, a chubby-cheeked boy in her arms and another toddler at her feet. "Yes?"

"Hi!" Annie said with a cheerful smile. "I don't know if we have the right address or not. A friend told us we might find Orren Hagen here."

"Not here." She leaned over and put the squirming child down behind her. When she straightened her hand was on the door, ready to close it. "I mean to say, you have the wrong place."

"Wait, please," Annie said, placing her palm on the door. "We just need to talk to him."

"I—I told you . . ."

The woman was flustered, scared and ready to slam the door in their faces. Annie felt Patrick moving behind her and stepped down hard on the instep of his foot. "We don't want to cause you any problems." A few of the neighbors were watching them with great interest. "Lunn Kendrick gave us your address."

"Maybe you'd better come inside." The woman stepped aside and let them enter. They stopped just inside the door, the two children crawling around them on the floor. "If Lunn sent you, I guess it's okay to talk."

The living room was clean but sparsely furnished with an old sofa, two lamps, one rocking chair and a television. Sunlight poured in through the open curtains at the end of the narrow room. A table and two chairs sat near the window, and an opening to the left of that led to the kitchen. In the middle of the right-hand wall was another open door, leading to a short hallway.

"Is Hagen here?" Annie asked.

"No, he left suddenly last week, in the middle of the night. My husband contacted Lunn right away."

She was extremely nervous, alternately wringing her hands and then wiping them on her faded blue pants. Her bright yellow blouse had food stains on it, matching the ones on the toddlers' white shirts. "Do you know where he is?"

"No. Lunn paid us to hide him here. We needed the money, you see," she explained, using her fingers to comb her short dark hair behind her ears.

Annie watched as she bent down and took a small piece of plastic away from the youngest child. His little face crumpled up into a frown and he was ready to scream when the woman grabbed a yellow stuffed duck off the well-worn carpet and handed it to him.

"Did Hagen leave anything behind?"

She straightened up. "No, he didn't arrive with much, just a few clothes. He stayed in the kids' room. Do you want to see it?"

"Yes, please."

"It's messy," she warned them, opening the first door down the short hallway. "And I haven't gotten the smell of his filthy cigars out of here yet."

Colorful toys littered the threadbare carpet. A crib and single bed took up the rest of the floor space in the small room. Patrick stepped into the maze of toys while Annie stayed outside next to the woman.

"Did anyone else know Hagen was here?" Annie asked, trying to distract the woman's attention from Patrick.

"I don't think so. We didn't tell a soul." She was still keeping a wary eye on Patrick, watching his every move.

Annie tried again. "Has anyone else come here looking for him?"

"No, you're—" One of the children screamed and the woman took off, running to him.

"Find anything?" Annie asked quietly.

Patrick picked his way back out of the room, trying not to break anything on the floor. "No. Let's get out of here."

Annie thanked the woman, who was rocking the crying child in her arms. They let themselves out and returned to the car.

"Using people like that could keep Hagen hidden for a long time," Patrick commented.

"Not when you have a friend like Lunn Kendrick willing to sell you out. Then again, she said he knew Hagen had left."

"He might have thought Hagen would come back. Or he might have lied." Patrick started the car. "Where to next?"

Annie consulted the map and her list. "At the end of this block, take a left and stay on that street awhile. By then I'll have the rest figured out."

Patrick did as she said. In the middle of a block-long row of two-story stucco apartments he slowed down. There were no yards this time, just sidewalks butted up against the buildings, and then the road. Unlike the neighborhood they'd just left, no one here appeared to be home.

"Which one?" he asked.

The doors were painted different colors and set back into the buildings about a foot, distinguishing each entrance. Annie pointed. "The bright blue door."

He drove around the long block and parked behind the place. Reaching under the seat he pulled out a sand-colored chamois sack and removed a gun, then leaned forward, placing it in the waistband of his black jeans up against his spine. His jacket hid the cold, midnight-blue metal from sight.

"If Kendrick was lying to us, this looks to be a good spot for a trap," Annie said. Her fingers were gripping the door handle, ready to move. "How do you want to go in?"

Rourke glanced at his watch, then over at her. "Give me three minutes to get inside. I'll go in the back door, you take the front. Ring the bell."

Three minutes later, Annie stood in front of the blue door, one hand buried in the pocket of her leather jacket, gripping her revolver. By now it felt familiar. She rang the bell a second time but no one answered.

"One more minute and I'm opening this myself," Annie muttered. She tensed up when she heard the dead bolt lock sliding noisily across metal, then the blue door swung open.

"Hurry," Patrick whispered.

One finger was on his lips when she walked past him. She could feel the tension in him, see the readiness in the taut muscles of his hands. He looked up the flight of stairs to his left, then back at her, raising his eyebrows as he motioned for her to check the downstairs.

She did so, finding nothing of interest. The living room was filled with cheap brown furniture, the kitchen and dining area decorated in the same tacky style. All the rooms were empty, including the one downstairs bedroom.

Annie walked quietly up the straight, narrow staircase, listening for sounds. By the time she reached the upstairs landing, she still hadn't figured out where Patrick was. There were four white doors in the dark-paneled hallway and not one of them was open. The first cut-glass doorknob was within her grasp when she heard a door slam shut down below.

Hagen! Adrenaline flowing, she moved quickly, stopping a foot back from the top of the stairs. With her back against the wall she waited to see if he was coming up.

The seconds ticked by. Perhaps a minute later she heard sounds coming from the direction of the kitchen. Annie peeked over the railing, but couldn't see anyone. For a fleeting moment she felt torn. Should she go after Hagen or find Patrick? It only took her a second to decide.

She crept down the staircase and toward the kitchen. A man was at the counter fixing a ham sandwich, his back to her. She waited until he put the sharp knife he was using in the sink and moved away from it.

Then Annie leveled her gun on him. "Liar," she said.

He spun to face her, completely defenseless, with nowhere to go. His raccoon eyes made his expression of disbelief comical.

Annie smiled. "Fancy meeting you here, Kendrick."

He was edging slowly along the counter toward the sink, his hands skimming the surface on either side of this thick waist. "Yeah. Small world, huh?"

"Put your hands high into the air."

He didn't obey, just kept edging toward the knife he'd left in the sink. "You won't shoot me."

"Correction," Annie said with a wicked grin. "I won't kill you. Maybe I'll just take off a couple of chunks."

"I don't believe you." He was still moving steadily toward the sink. "You won't do it."

Annie gripped the gun with both hands. "I will. But sometimes," she said lowering her gun to his waist, "my aim is a bit too low."

"You wouldn't."

"Are you daring me?" She held the gun confidently, her hazel eyes never wavering from his brown ones. "I'm actually an accurate markswoman. Shall I prove it?"

Kendrick was beginning to take her seriously, but there was a gleam in his eyes she didn't trust. If he got the chance, he'd stab her in the back without a second thought.

"You're bluffing."

"Am I? I have nothing to lose, Kendrick." Her grin widened. "And to my way of thinking, you have everything to lose if my aim is accurate or even close to the right neighborhood."

Kendrick raised his hands. "Women! You're all crazy. What do you want from me?"

"At the moment, I want you to have a seat at the table over there. And leave the sandwich behind," she ordered when he reached for the plate.

Empty-handed, he sat down with his back to the rear entrance. "Why? You going to eat it yourself?"

"Shut up and put your hands on the table." Though the sandwich did look tasty, she didn't want it, and she didn't want him throwing it at her as a means of distraction, either.

"Don't you trust me?"

"Why should I? You've shown your true colors. You sold out a person who trusted you to save your own hide," she said. "Or did you? Have you been lying to us? Or did you get disgusted with yourself and come to warn your friend Hagen?"

"What's it to you?" Lunn asked. "I thought you were just along for the ride because you're Rourke's lover?"

Annie ignored his taunt. "I wonder what your parents would think of their oldest son if they knew what a slimy, dirty dealing little weasel you really are?"

His eyes narrowed. "Are you threatening me?"

"Were you insulting me?"

"Isn't that gun getting heavy?"

Annie smiled. "It would indeed be lighter with one fewer bullet."

"Where did you learn to be such a cold-blooded—" He stopped when she aimed the gun at his lap.

"Where did you learn to be such a pile of manure? I don't get it. Your father's rich. He cares enough about you to bail you out of trouble time and again. It seems to me you've been handed the world on a platter and all you've done is make a mess for someone else to clean up."

"She's got your number, Lunn," Patrick said as he came into the room. He'd been standing outside listening to Annie, enjoying the torture she was putting Kendrick through. But there wasn't time for it to continue.

Kendrick jumped up from his chair at the far end of the room. "Where have you been? She was going to make a eunuch out of me!" He glared at her. "Or talk me to death."

"Easy, Kendrick, or I'll tie you up and let her do as she likes," Rourke told him, stopping near the back door. "But, of course, you're unsalvageable."

Kendrick's lips curled into a sneer. "I never knew you had such a cruel streak in you, Rourke."

"There's a lot you don't know about me." Rourke reached into the sink and picked up the knife. "No more games. I want Hagen—or your parents hear everything."

Kendrick sat back down in his chair, lacing his fingers on the table. Rourke always kept his word. "I don't know where he is right now. Honest."

"You don't know the meaning of the—"

"Quiet! Someone's here," Annie interrupted. She moved to the hinged side of the curtained door between her and Patrick.

"Not a word," Rourke warned Kendrick. He crouched beside the kitchen cabinets, right around the corner from the door.

With her back against the wall, Annie watched the door open slowly, the tip of a gun barrel visible at the edge. As the gunman moved forward, she caught a glimpse of his jaw through an opening in the ruffled curtain.

Annie jerked the door open. "Casey! Get in here."

Rourke stood up, studying him. There was a wild look in the man's eyes. His shirt was torn and his short red hair was even more in disarray than usual. He was glaring at Lunn.

"What on earth happened to you?" Rourke asked.

"A trap in a bar on Kendrick's list. Saint Patrick's bones! I really owe him now!"

"What are you doing here?" Annie wanted to know.

He looked at her. "I finished checking out the other addresses without much luck, so I thought I'd try here, the place he suggested looking first. Did you find Hagen?"

Annie pointed at Kendrick. "All we found was this."

"But not Hagen?" Casey didn't hide his disappointment.

Rourke dropped the knife back into the sink. "No, but I did find the secret room upstairs." He glanced at Annie. "It reeked of stale cigar smoke. Hagen was here."

"I've had my fill of this!" Casey roared. "You're going to contact Hagen for us." He advanced on Kendrick. "Now."

"I don't know what you're talking about."

Casey leaned over the table and grabbed Kendrick by the throat. "When was the last time you saw Hagen?"

His face was turning red. "Two weeks ago!"

Annie nudged Patrick and he nodded. Both knew that Hagen supposedly had still been alive a week ago.

"How do you contact him?" Casey demanded.

"I don't know what—"

Casey moved his thumb, applying a different kind of pressure. "Wrong answer. How?"

Kendrick tried to dislodge the hand on his throat, but it didn't budge. "I can't breathe," he gasped out.

"Answer the question."

Other than a flickering of his eyelashes, Kendrick was perfectly immobile now. "How . . . can't . . . if I'm dead."

Casey let go of him, shoving him back into his seat in disgust. Pulling a chair out from the table, he turned it around and sat down, straddling it. "Speak."

"Reason with this ape, Rourke!" Kendrick pleaded, making a show of massaging his throat and taking in huge gulps of air.

Rourke didn't feel very sorry for him at the moment. "I suggest you tell him what he wants to know."

"But I really don't know what he's talking about."

"Yes, you do," Casey said. "When pressure was applied to a chap in that bar you sent me to, he was quite informative. You have a system for contacting people like Hagen and you're going to give it to us."

"But if word gets around about what I've done, they'll kill me!" Lunn protested.

"That's right," Casey told him. "And if you don't tell us, you'll be dead, too. Some choice."

Casey's eyes never left Kendrick. "Rourke, let's drop him down a dry well I know of. If he's lucky, he'll break his neck."

Rourke smiled at the suggestion. "That idea does have a certain appeal. Is it far from here?"

"We can be there in less than an hour."

"Hey! Cut it out, you guys!" Kendrick exclaimed.

Casey shrugged. "Since he doesn't want to cooperate, his usefulness is over. Don't you agree?"

"I do," Rourke said. "He'll just be in our way."

Kendrick jumped up. "Wait a minute! I never said I wouldn't help. What's in it for me?"

"Your life. Start talking," Rourke told him.

"First we make a deal. If I help you find Hagen, you have to get me out of Ireland and into the U.S."

"Why?" Rourke asked him.

Kendrick sat back down. "After this, I won't be able to live here. Over there, maybe I can pass myself off as an Irish folk hero," he said, warming to the subject. "Yeah. Tour the lecture circuit or something."

Rourke considered his options. Right now Kendrick was his only lead to Hagen. He didn't have a choice. "First you make contact with Hagen, then we'll worry about getting you out of the country. And don't double-cross me, Lunn."

"I won't." He was stroking his chin. "Maybe a beard," he muttered to himself. "I'd look real distinguished."

They were ignoring him. Rourke looked at Casey. "Where are you parked?"

"Out front."

"Take Kendrick. I'll pull around and meet you there. We've stayed in one place long enough. Let's go!"

Casey picked up the sandwich. "Mind if I have this? I didn't stop for lunch." Only Kendrick protested as Casey took a huge bite. "Bleah! Too much mustard. Waste of good ham."

Annie and Patrick went out the back door. As Patrick started the car he couldn't resist asking, "Would you really have shot him below the belt?"

"I would have shot him if I had to," she replied. "But probably not there."

"*Probably* not?"

"I might not have had any choice," she protested. "And it's quite effective as a threat. I learned a long time ago that men seem to have this obsession with protecting their male parts."

"I'll say."

Annie reached over and patted him on the cheek. "You have nothing to worry about. I have a fondness for yours." He chuckled and drove around the block.

Casey was waiting for them, with Kendrick in the front seat beside him. "Where are we headed?"

"To a small inn I know of. From there we'll let Kendrick do his tracking. And remember, Lunn," Rourke told him. "The countryside is full of deep, dry wells."

An hour later, Casey and Rourke were standing in the second-story hallway of a quaint bed-and-breakfast inn. They were keeping an eye on Kendrick, who was sitting at a desk at the end of the hall, making phone calls. He'd refused to tell them how to contact Hagen, but he was willing to do it himself.

"Kendrick says Annie threatened to shoot him right in the, uh . . . you know. Would she have?" Casey asked.

Patrick glanced over at Annie, who was sitting in one of the bedrooms reading a thick novel. "I do believe she might have, Casey. But only if she didn't have any other choice."

"When did women become so cold-blooded?"

Rourke revealed a hint of a smile. "I think it started back when Eve offered that apple to Adam." Kendrick finished using the phone and stood up. "Well, Lunn?" Rourke asked him. "What did you find out?"

He walked over to them, a surly expression on his face. "Hagen has friends in London. He's stashed himself away in a place over there."

Annie slipped out of bed and walked past the men to the phone.

"You're not saying that to get out of the country, are you?" Casey asked. "Because if you are, there are plenty of holes to drop you into over there, too."

"He's there, I tell you."

"Where in London?" Rourke asked.

Shaking his head, Kendrick backed away from them. "Oh, no. I'm in it now, and you've got to protect me. Either

I go with you, or you'll never find him. Once word of what I've done gets out, I'm dead.''

"That's the price you pay for squealing," Casey said. "Not that you had any choice." He looked at Rourke. "Well?"

"I don't think we have much choice, either," he replied. "Kendrick goes with us. At least we can keep an eye on him that way."

Annie spoke from behind the three men. "The last flight out tonight leaves in about an hour," she informed them.

"I don't know. Just fly right in? We could have someone arrange an alternative way," Casey suggested.

Patrick was tempted to do so. Derry would never sell him out like Kendrick was selling out Hagen. Unfortunately, there wasn't time. He turned to face Annie and nodded. "We'll fly. Book us all on that flight, Annie."

She grinned. "I already have."

Chapter Seventeen

In a section off the main airport corridor, a sullen Kendrick, sunglasses hiding his black eyes, sat slumped in a seat between Casey and Rourke. Annie was sitting on the other side of Patrick, waiting for their flight to be called.

Casey stood up. "I'm going to make a quick stop before we board. Can't stand airplane rest rooms."

Annie watched him take a left at the end of the short corridor. She touched Patrick's arm to get his attention. "Sounds like a good idea to me. Kendrick is all yours for the moment. Watch my bag."

There weren't many people wandering around, making it harder for Annie to follow Casey down the wide corridor without his noticing her. He walked into the men's rest room and came out less than a minute later, heading right for the phones on the opposite wall.

Annie joined a sudden flood of people whose plane had just landed and moved in closer, looking over his shoulder as he dialed. It was a local call. The phone next to his was being used by a large, overweight man.

Annie slipped in behind the big man and picked up a phone, pretending to use it while attempting to eavesdrop on Casey's conversation. Luckily, he was mad and speaking in a loud voice.

"That's right, London," he said. "Yes, I know Adair is getting impatient. Well, tell him to do it himself if he doesn't like the way I work!" Casey slammed down the receiver and took off.

Annie made her own call, hoping it went through quickly this time. It didn't. With all these extended trips to the bathroom, Patrick was going to think she had bad kidneys.

"What do you have for me, Gerald?"

"Where have you been?"

"Around. I don't have much time. What have you got?"

Gerald became all business, but gave her nothing Julie hadn't already supplied, and noticeably less on Adair. Then he asked, "Where are you?"

"Belfast. Bye."

Annie pressed the lever down, cutting him off, then dialed another number. "Speak to me, Julie."

"I'm not sure what I have, Annie. This Brady Adair guy is good, an expert at hiding things. I've never come across anything quite like it. I'll pick up one paper trail and suddenly it vanishes, like it never existed. The only thing solid I got was a large order of stone billed to that name. No delivery address but, from the price, I'd say it was local."

"Stone?" Annie asked. "You mean building stone?"

"Right. Who knows? Maybe he's refurbishing a castle."

That wasn't very helpful, but it did give them something in common. One of the books she had done with her sister had required a lot of research on castle architecture.

Annie wasn't sure she wanted to have anything in common with Brady Adair. The awe in Julie's voice both surprised and worried her. He wasn't easily impressed and almost never beaten. "Do you have any addresses on him at all?"

"Some shell corporations and a post-office box or two. That's another thing that's got me on the run. I haven't found his personal residence yet."

"Keep trying. I'll check in again. And thanks, Julie."

Annie hurried back down the corridor, more confused than ever. She knew Casey was working for Michael Adair, checking into his brother Brady's past. That was fine, she supposed, except that Brady seemed to be a singularly unusual fellow. Was there a connection between Casey's investigation and the search for Orren Hagen? If so, what was it? When push came to shove, which side would Casey be on? Hagen's, Patrick's or his own? And who was Brady Adair, anyway?

She couldn't chance confronting Casey right now. If he was up to no good, he might panic and they could lose Kendrick in the ensuing ruckus. Besides, Rourke still trusted him.

And, if she went off half-cocked and accused Casey without any proof, Patrick might change his mind about them working together. She'd just continue to keep a close eye on Casey and wait. Over the public address system she heard their flight being called and hurried to join the others at the gate.

"THEY WERE SPOTTED in Belfast," Colin Farrell said, looking at the man sitting behind the large uncluttered desk. "But the tail lost them."

Brady was ready to explode. "What about Hagen?"

"No sign of him."

His balled fist came pounding down on the top of the desk. "Dammit! Who's shielding him?"

"Hard to tell. Some government, perhaps?"

"If that was the case, we'd know about it."

"Maybe not. It could be a ruse," Farrell suggested. "A way to flush us out into the open."

"Then they're sorely underestimating me. We'd never fall for such a simple trap." Brady began pacing restlessly around the room. Suddenly, he stopped and returned to his desk, grabbing a file folder. "What about this friend of

Rourke's?'' he asked thoughtfully. ''Jack Merlin. Isn't he married?''

''To Cassie O'Connor, a very well-known newspaper reporter in Houston.'' Farrell could see the wheels turning in his friend's mind. ''No way, Brady. We're trying to avoid publicity, not create more. It would be like committing suicide. Did you read that file? At the moment Rourke is merely an inconvenience. But if you attack Merlin's wife, the whole band of them will come after us and hound us to the gates of hell.''

Brady dropped the file on his desk. ''It may become our only option. Have someone keep an eye on the O'Connor woman and start setting up the groundwork to have her kidnapped.''

''Brady, think this through,'' Farrell warned.

''I have!'' he yelled, his face turning a deeper shade of crimson. ''It's an option, and if I have to, I'll use it. We need Hagen silenced. If they get him, we'll work a trade.''

In the ensuing quiet the tiny bell ringing on the fax machine sounded like a gong. Farrell crossed the room and picked up the piece of paper that spewed out. He smiled as he read it. ''At last.''

''Good news?'' Brady asked.

''Rourke and Sawyer are on a plane to London. I'll arrange to have them followed. With any luck at all, that pair will find Hagen for us.''

''Quit grinning and get on it!''

DENSE FOG ROLLED IN from the waterfront, blending with the shadows of the huge storage buildings in the industrial area until the horizon became one mass of gray. Casey and Lunn were in the back seat of the car, Patrick at the wheel with Annie beside him. Before coming this way, they had zigzagged all over town to make sure no one was following them. Patrick stopped only once, at the residence of an army officer who owed him a favor, to replace the guns they'd left behind.

"This doesn't appear to be a popular area at night," Annie murmured, surveying the shoddy part of London they were driving through. It was dark, deserted and had the look of decay. "Feels like trouble."

"Hagen chose the location, not me."

"Why couldn't he have chosen some luxurious English estate with modern, working plumbing."

Patrick glanced at her. "Tell me, Annie. When did you develop this obsession with plumbing."

"Growing up in the hills, you learn to appreciate a good bathroom when you find one."

Casey interrupted them from the back seat. "Kendrick says it's the next one on the left up here."

Like everything else, the block-long, three-story building looked abandoned. Many of its small square windows were broken or missing, and no lights were on inside. Patrick circled the block twice before parking at one corner, by a garbage-cluttered curb. They all got out of the car.

Misty fog swirled around them as a sharp breeze blew in from the sea. The cold, damp air cut right through their clothing. The area smelled like rotting fish.

Crossing the street, the group headed for the huge doors in the middle of the building. They were securely locked and the windows had been boarded over.

"Who wants to try?" Rourke asked.

Kendrick pulled his wallet out of his back pocket and withdrew a slender needle of metal. For two minutes he tried to ease the stubborn lock open as the others huddled around him, shoulders hunched against the damp evening air.

"First one I haven't been able to open," he mumbled. "Something isn't right." He looked at Casey. "You try."

Casey stepped forward and twisted the piece of metal experimentally, then he pulled it out and tried to look into the lock. "Seems rusted or clogged with dirt."

"Try this," Annie said, passing a slender black flashlight.

Casey peered into the lock mechanism. "Saint Patrick's bones! It's wired! Get out of here!" he yelled, stumbling over the others in his haste to run for safety.

They scattered in all directions. Annie and Rourke ran across the street and crouched behind the car, waiting for the explosion to come. The seconds ticked by. Nothing.

Patrick whispered in her ear. "Someone is serious about not wanting surprise visitors. What's taking it so long to blow?"

"I don't know. Maybe it didn't trip. But I want to know what's inside that building worth taking such pains to hide." Annie stood up. "Coming?"

They ran back across the street and down a side road, ducking below the level of the warehouse windows just in case. Up ahead they could see the glow of a flashlight, an eerie halo in the fog. The pair sprinted toward it. Near the end of the building they found Casey, his hand firmly gripping Kendrick's arm.

"He tried to run away." Casey let go of him and turned off the light, handing it back to Annie. "What now?"

"We can go in through there." Annie pointed to a section of broken windows in the middle of the building. "If we break the wood out between them, it'll be easy to climb in."

Casey and Patrick nodded at the same time, both moving toward the section she was talking about with Kendrick in tow. Patrick took off his coat and used it to break out the thin wooden slats.

"Kendrick, you'll take the lead," Patrick told him. "We'll follow you in."

"Don't I get a gun?"

"How about a bullet? Just climb in the window, Lunn."

Kendrick grabbed the window ledge where Patrick had draped his leather jacket and pulled himself into the opening. They heard him fall in on the other side, then the echoes of his moaning and groaning.

"Should one of us stay out here?" Annie asked.

Casey pulled himself up into the opening. "Why? This area of town is pretty well abandoned, especially at night."

Annie watched him disappear into the building. Why was Casey so familiar with London and this area? Just how many people was he working for? More to the point, why was he risking his hide to help Patrick find Hagen, and what would he do when they found him?

"Ready?"

"Yes," Annie replied, jerking her mind back to the problem of getting into the warehouse without breaking a leg.

Patrick had his fingers laced together. "I'll boost you up."

Annie placed a foot in the palm of his hands and let him lift her into the opening. It was dark inside, but Casey was standing by to help her over the ledge. If he did have a secret agenda of his own, evidently it coincided with theirs at the moment.

Patrick quickly followed her in, shaking out his coat before he put it on. "Casey, you two take that side, Annie and I will go this way."

Weak, cold light filtered in through the dirty windows, barely enough to see by. The ground floor was dark and completely empty, the few partitioned offices unfurnished. Metal stairs against a far wall led them to a second level, but they found nothing there, either. Together they climbed to the third and final level. Halfway across the room, partitions had been installed, stretching from one end of the building to the other. Cautiously, they moved toward the open door.

Going beyond the partition was like crossing into another building entirely. Inside they found an apartmentlike space, its huge rooms furnished with every amenity, even a kitchen. There was fresh food in the refrigerator. On each side of a cozy living room were large bedrooms.

They went from room to room, checking every dark corner with Annie's flashlight. A distinct smell permeated the place. In the living room by the couch, an ashtray held the still-smoldering stub of a malodorous cigar. Once assured the place was empty and the wiring safe, they turned on the lights.

Kendrick confirmed their guess. "Hagen's brand."

"We must have just missed him," Annie said.

"Just," Rourke agreed irritably. "Convenient, isn't it?"

Annie glanced at Casey, but didn't say anything about the noise he'd made when he'd discovered the lock was wired. Now wasn't the time to press the issue. Besides, she had other things on her mind. "These rooms don't seem as large as they should be," Annie observed. "From the stairs it looked as if half the floor space up here had been partitioned off."

"I thought my eyes were playing tricks on me, but you're right." Patrick looked at Casey. "Did you find a freight elevator in this place?"

"Sure did. It's hidden behind a portable wall near the offices on the first floor," Casey informed him.

Kendrick sat down on the couch. "You three go ahead. I'll wait here and pick up the pieces if it's rigged like the front doors."

Casey grabbed Kendrick's collar and hoisted him to his feet. "How about, we use you as a guinea pig?"

"Hold it. I've got a better idea," Patrick said.

He and Annie crossed the huge room together and stopped in front of the wall at the far end. It appeared seamless beneath the large landscape pictures hanging on its white-painted surface. Annie rapped on it with her knuckles.

"Sounds hollow, all right. We need something to tear a hole in this wall," Patrick said.

Casey snapped his fingers. "I remember seeing an old fire ax down on the first level. I'll be right back."

While they were waiting, Annie removed one of the large paintings from the wall. The other two watched. "What do you think you're doing? Don't just stand there! Help take the rest of them down," she ordered.

They moved to do her bidding. "Anyone ever tell you you're bossy?" Kendrick asked.

"My brothers and sisters did all the time." She took the painting he handed her and stacked it against the other one. "Hurry up, we don't have all night."

There was a neat row of paintings stacked against the wall when Casey returned, carrying a long-handled ax. "You didn't have to do that."

"You weren't here," Kendrick said, glaring at Annie.

"Ahh." Casey stepped up to the wall. "Everybody stand back." He swung the ax, creating a long slit in the pristine white wall. A couple more strokes and he'd made a gaping hole.

Annie took the flashlight out of her pocket and aimed it at the dark hole. The circle of light illuminated row upon row of neatly stacked wooden crates, each stamped with small black letters.

"'Property of the U.S. government,'" Annie read. "I can't make out the smaller print."

Kendrick was breathing down her neck. "It lists the types of guns or ammunition in each box. There's enough in there to start a whole new war."

"Or resupply an existing one," Annie added.

Patrick took the ax from Casey. "Stand back." He waited till everyone moved away. His well aimed strokes sliced through the crumbling white wallboard, sending bits and pieces of chalky gypsum flying everywhere.

When he stopped, there was a doorway cut between the two-by-four wooden wall framing. Patrick stepped through the opening and Annie followed him. A shiver ran down her

spine as she swung her light over the arsenal. It took up all
the missing floor space, lining the area from one side of the
building to the other.

"How did someone get hold of all this?" she wondered.

"That's easy," Casey said. Annie stared at him. "Or so I
hear," he added. "The important question is *why?* Come
on. The elevator should be over this way."

Everyone followed Casey through the dark maze of boxes
to the far wall. Near the corner they found an old-fashioned
service elevator, a small forklift and yet another room, this
the size of a walk-in closet.

Patrick looked at Annie. "Watch Kendrick." He pushed
the door open, then entered. A moment later a light snapped
on in the little enclosure.

Eager to get a look, Annie nudged Kendrick inside. An
elaborate communications setup filled the room to over-
flowing. In front of the impressive radio array were two
coffee mugs and a half-eaten ham, cucumber and tomato
sandwich.

"Someone's been in here recently, too. The coffee in these
mugs is still warm." Annie pressed a finger into what was
left of the sandwich, making a dent in the crustless white
bread. "Fresh."

"It's the preservatives," Kendrick said sagely. "The stuff
is pure poison."

"Shut up, Lunn. Let's get out of here," Patrick said as he
turned the light off. "Whoever this belongs to could show
up at any time." He left the room, then looked back over his
shoulder. "Where did Casey get off to?"

"Over here." He was adding another box to a pile he'd
built next to the elevator. When it was in place, he climbed
up, then pulled himself into the opening he'd exposed on top
of the elevator shaft. A minute later he climbed back down,
dusting off his hands on his dark pants. "It's rigged with
some kind of gas," Casey announced. "I guess they didn't

want to destroy the only means they have of moving this stuff.''

Annie studied his face. "How intuitive you are."

"I'm more than ready to get out of here, if that's what you mean," he said.

"It's not, but I agree."

"So do I," Patrick said, frowning at her. "Let's go."

They wasted no time getting out of the building, using the same broken window they had used before. They were cruising back toward the main part of London before anyone spoke.

"What's next?" Annie asked.

Patrick looked in his rearview mirror at Kendrick, who was fast asleep. "We find a place to stay until sleepyhead comes up with another place to look."

"I know of a small hotel here," Casey told them. "A quiet one. They won't find our happy little group strange."

Following his directions, Patrick drove through the back streets of London that few tourists saw—or would care to see. The hotel was indeed quiet, if a bit seedy, but reasonably clean. The management didn't even ask to see a passport, let alone a marriage license, and there were no questions about who would be sleeping with whom.

Once in their room, Annie turned to face Patrick. "Those weapons have to be confiscated immediately, before anybody has time to move them." The look in her eyes gave him little doubt that she was determined to get her way.

He sighed. "All right. Call your people. Just make sure the conversation is brief. I don't want our present location broadcast to the entire world."

She ignored his taunt. "Thank you."

The phone rang eleven times before a male voice answered. But Annie didn't say a word as she replaced the receiver in its cradle. Patrick looked up.

"What's wrong?" he asked.

"I'm not sure." She picked up the receiver and dialed another number. This time a different male voice answered.

"Yes?"

"Gerald?"

"Annie!" It was rare for her to call him on his home line. "What's wrong?"

"I just called your private office number and someone answered your phone, possibly Bruce."

Gerald muttered an obscenity. "What now? The call should have been switched over to here. Don't worry, I'll take care of it right away."

"Stop telling me not to worry!" Annie exclaimed. Then she took a deep breath and continued in a calmer tone. "Now listen carefully." Quickly and precisely she gave him detailed directions to the warehouse. "And tell whoever you send to be careful, the freight elevator is rigged with poison gas."

"How do you know all this?"

Patrick shoved his watch under her nose. "I'll be in touch," Annie said. Patrick cut the connection for her.

"Why is Bruce still interfering?"

"I don't know." Annie moved away from him and went to sit on one of the beds. "There are some strange things going on in my department," she admitted at last. "Rumor is it's a power struggle, but I'm not so sure. Bruce shouldn't have been in Gerald's office or answering his phone. If it was Bruce at all. I only heard enough to know it wasn't Gerald's voice."

"Tell me something." Patrick sat down in a chair, its loose joints creaking beneath him. "Have you had any personal contact with this Bruce guy? For instance, did you date him?"

His question surprised her, but Patrick's face didn't reveal any emotion. She decided he was looking for a motive on Bruce's part, not just prying into her personal life. It was something Annie had considered as well. "I made the mistake of going out with him once, yes."

"Mistake?"

"Bruce believes he's irresistible to women. He isn't. He also doesn't know how to take no for an answer."

"You rejected him, in other words?"

Annie nodded. "And how."

"Interesting," Patrick murmured. "Is he the type to seek revenge against you for doing that?"

Was Bruce the leak? "Maybe. He's a lot like Kendrick in the spine department, though. I don't think he has the belly for murder. Then again, Bruce is so out of touch, as far as real field work is concerned, that he probably wouldn't even realize his actions could get someone killed."

"This guy is your boss?"

"On occasion," Annie replied.

"You'd better change jobs." She glared at him. Patrick glared right back. "Listen, Annie, we've been pussyfooting long enough. I'm of the opinion someone inside your organization is giving away our position on a regular basis. Think about it. Old man Hagen's place. The hotel. And the minute we have any kind of lead, it seems the world knows about it, too."

Annie flopped back on the bed and stared at the faded wallpaper on the ceiling, her arms tucked under her head. "Like you said, Patrick. Enough pussyfooting." She sighed. "I've been thinking the same thing myself."

"What's your office security like?"

"Excellent. But any security is breachable." Annie leaned on her elbows and looked at Rourke. "Especially if you know where to look for the weak point."

"What's Gerald's weak point?"

"I'm not sure. The fact that someone was able to get into Gerald's office isn't a good sign. But Bruce has no skills as an operative." Annie shook her head. "And I can't believe Gerald is the leak. He desperately wants these men."

"Why does he want them so much?"

Annie sat up. "I've thought about that. Gerald is nearing retirement, and I think these men are the missing pieces of a puzzle he's been working on for years. Without those pieces, the picture is incomplete. That's probably why he took control of this operation. He can't accept incompleteness."

"I don't care if his puzzle is ever completed," Rourke informed her quietly. "Bridget's safety comes first."

"I know that." Annie wasn't going to argue with him, it was a no-win situation. "But as long as we're nominating candidates for fink of the week, what about Casey? He could be the leak, too. He knew where we were going every step of the way." She paused a moment, then added, "Are you aware that he's working on another job while he's helping you?"

Patrick stretched his legs out in front of him. "He hadn't mentioned it, but I don't have a problem with that as long as he's doing what I need him to do. But I'm not stupid, Annie. I'll keep an eye on him."

There was a light knock on the partially open connecting door between their rooms, and the subject of their conversation strolled in. "So far, Lunn's coming up empty-handed," Casey told them. "I get the feeling he's about as welcome around here as a potato blight. Most of those he's called are hanging up on him."

"Little wonder. It is one in the morning, after all." Patrick stood up. "Tell him to pack it in. We'll give it a rest until tomorrow."

Annie got to her feet and picked up her bag. "I don't like this room," she announced brusquely. "I want theirs."

Casey and Patrick looked at her like she was nuts, but by now they knew better than to argue. They made the change and settled down to get some sleep.

FLYNN PARKED HIS CAR at the curb and got out, a mixture of anger and fear building inside of him as he surveyed the scene. White police barricades blocked the entire street ahead of him and beyond those, the flashing red-and-yellow lights of official vehicles illuminated the night sky. People were everywhere, those in uniform and curious onlookers, roaming all over the road and sidewalks. He stepped past one of the barriers and moved toward the action, steering clear of the police.

Joining a crowd of other civilians, Flynn watched from across the street as a large green military truck with a canvas-covered bed rumbled into the warehouse.

A uniformed officer bustled over to the crowd and stopped in front of him. Flynn's stomach churned. But the man addressed the group as a whole.

"You will all have to leave this area," he said, his voice crisp and authoritative. "Only necessary personnel are allowed behind the barriers. Move along."

Flynn turned on his heel and walked back toward his car. The rage building inside of him was beginning to take on a life of its own, speaking to him in a harsh whisper, begging to be fed. It wanted blood. The blood of Patrick Rourke.

To Flynn, Rourke had assumed the shape of an evil wizard, disappearing at will, eluding each carefully planned trap. And now this. The ultimate outrage. Behind him the police were carting away what had been his means of paying back the millions he owed. Another carefully arranged double-cross down the drain. Flynn wanted to go after Rourke personally, carve him into pieces and fling them into the sea.

But he couldn't, and that stoked the fires of his fury even higher. With his debt unpaid, he was well on his way to becoming fish food himself. Now more than ever he would be forced to watch his own back. A black mood descended upon him as he drove away.

And then, suddenly, he began to laugh. He laughed so hard he had to pull over to the side of the road. "Why, thank you, Patrick Rourke!" he said, tears streaming down his cheeks. "How very nice of you to show me the error of my ways!"

Rourke had put him in a desperate situation, and with desperation he'd at last found clarity of thought. He'd been so long at the chess board, immersed in tactics and subterfuge, that he had forgotten the most important part of play. The end game. No more shielding moves and indirect assaults on the pawns. It was time to go for checkmate.

His dream of revenge formed itself in his mind, bonding to the situation like a clear plastic overlay upon which all the correct moves were marked in red. Bloodred. This was the game he'd been born to play—and win. For this he would tap every source he had.

Chapter Eighteen

Three things occurred to Annie as she rolled out of bed and crouched on the floor. First, the hotel Casey had picked for them was no longer quiet. Second, it had evidently been a good idea to switch rooms, because the one next door was the source of commotion. Third, and most important, Rourke was missing. She grabbed the gun she'd hidden under her pillow and peered into the darkness.

"Patrick?"

"Here."

Annie crawled on all fours toward the sound of his voice, finding him crouched in the shadows near the door to the adjoining room. As she reached him, the fight taking place next door reached a new peak. A gunshot rang out, followed almost instantaneously by two more.

"I'll take the connecting door," Patrick said, reaching for the knob. "You take the one in the hall. Be careful."

"No kidding."

She crawled across the carpet to the door and slowly opened it to look outside. The dimly lit hallway was empty. Standing up, she edged her way into the narrow corridor, keeping her back against the wall. A soft glow of light spilled out of the open entrance to the room next door.

Annie crossed to the far side of the hall in order to get a wider angle of fire. With her gun raised before her, she inched closer until she could see into the room. It wasn't a pretty sight.

Two men, dressed in dark clothing and ski masks, were lying on the carpet, their blood pooling around them. The connecting door on her right was open now and Patrick was staring at the same grim scene. Was her face as pale as his? Probably even paler.

Lunn Kendrick was on the nearer of the two double beds, bleeding from a stomach wound onto the off-white sheets. Like Patrick, Casey and herself, he hadn't undressed for bed. But Annie wondered if he had even more reason to expect trouble than the rest of them. She wasn't alone in her suspicion.

Casey was standing over him, the gun in his hand aimed right between Kendrick's pain-filled eyes. "You set us up."

"Doctor," Lunn grunted. He tried to stand, pressing his hands to his stomach. "I need a doctor!"

"You're going to need a priest."

"Casey," Annie said quietly.

He turned his head to look at her. She wasn't aiming at him, but her gun was still raised and pointed in his general direction. His eyes widened. "Hey! They shot him, not me!" Casey looked at Kendrick with disgust. "But I should finish the job and kill him, too. He ratted on us."

"I swear I didn't! Now get me a doctor!" Lunn pleaded.

Patrick entered the room and walked over to the bed, standing opposite Casey. He wadded up a pillowcase and handed it to Kendrick. "Press that against the wound," he told him. "It's the best you're going to get until you talk. Those calls you made. Who did you give our location to?"

"Somebody help me!"

Annie frowned. Had Kendrick set them up? It didn't seem likely, since he was the one lying there with a bullet in him. She couldn't very well pin this one on Casey, either; he'd almost gotten killed himself. Still, Annie didn't lower her weapon until Casey lowered his. Then she came in, closing the door behind her. Ignoring the bodies on the floor, she went back into the other room, picked up the phone and dialed a number.

Kendrick wasn't changing his tune, but he was beginning to get the idea. "You're trying to kill me!" he wailed.

"So were our visitors," Casey told him. "So why all the loyalty? I'm going to let you bleed to death if you don't tell me who you called to set this up."

"Will you take me to a hospital if I tell you?"

"Sure thing, Kendrick old buddy."

"We will, Lunn," Patrick said in a much more reassuring tone than Casey's. "Just tell us what we want to know."

"All right! But I didn't plan this! Honest! Just look at me! All I did was call an old friend of mine. She and Hagen were lovers once and I thought she could help us. I did tell her where we were because she was concerned about me, but Nadia wouldn't have told anyone!"

"Nadia!" Patrick leaned down and grabbed the front of Kendrick's shirt, pulling the man toward him. "Is she married to an earl?"

Annie came back into the room and went immediately to Patrick's side, knocking his hand away from Kendrick's shirt. Kendrick sagged back onto the bed with a groan.

"Leave him alone!" She wadded up another pillowcase and helped Kendrick apply it to his wound. The first one was soaked. Annie looked up at Patrick. "Now go ahead and question him, but you'd better make it quick."

"I intend to. Answer me, Lunn," he ordered. "Is the Nadia you called married to an earl?"

"Yes! How did you know?"

"I'm acquainted with the lady. Believe it, Lunn. She sold you out. You owe that bullet in your gut to her." Kendrick started to object, but Patrick cut him off. "Does she know where Hagen is right now?"

"Yes, but she wouldn't say where," Kendrick gasped out, his voice growing weaker. "Hospital."

"Where is this Nadia?" Casey demanded.

Kendrick coughed. "Her old man's estate."

"Do you know where it is?" Casey asked Patrick.

"No."

"Great," Casey muttered.

"We're wasting time," Annie said. "All I need is her husband's name and a phone. I have my sources."

"One you can use at this hour?" Patrick asked.

"One I can use anytime. But right now, we need to get out of here. Even in a neighborhood like this, people call the cops when they hear gunfire. They'll be swarming all over this place in a few minutes."

Casey nodded and collected his things. Patrick did likewise, returning with Annie's bag slung over his shoulder. She was sitting beside Kendrick, administering some basic first aid. It was the best she could do. In the distance, they could hear the wail of sirens.

"There you go, Lunn," she said. "Just take it easy. I called an ambulance and it should be here soon."

"You're wasting your time," Patrick told her.

"All right, so he's scum. But even scum deserves some compassion. Maybe this will turn his life around."

"Sure," Casey said derisively.

Patrick put his hand on her shoulder. "That's not what I meant, Annie, and you know it."

She knew exactly what he meant, and it didn't make her any happier. Kendrick was seriously wounded, and even a hospital might not be able to save him. By the looks Patrick and Casey were exchanging, Annie could tell they were all thinking the same thing.

It might have been one of them. And it still could be.

"THEY ESCAPED," Farrell announced, hanging up the phone.

"How?"

His partner shrugged. "What would you have me say, Brady? They're good. Very good. Or perhaps we were double-crossed."

Brady focused his attention on the men standing in front of his desk. "What took you two so long to get here?"

"Our flight was delayed, sir."

"Too bad it didn't crash! Report!"

The twins were extremely uncomfortable. They had every reason to be. Their employer was in no mood for excuses. "We're sorry, Mr. Adair," one of them said. "We almost had him. Really. But your standing orders were to set the elevator and vacate the place right away if the door alarm went off, so we did."

Adair was so angry his whole body was shaking. "Let me get this straight," he said, scarcely able to speak. "Hagen and some men attacked the warehouse. Not only did you let him get away, you then abandoned my arsenal to Patrick Rourke. Is that right?"

"No! You had said Hagen was the top priority, so we chased him, figuring the gas would take care of Rourke and the others while we were gone. But Hagen gave us the slip," the other one explained. "By the time we got back to the warehouse, there was no sign of Rourke and the army was swarming all over the place. We barely escaped!"

Brady stood up, a gun in his hand. "Maybe you didn't."

"Brady!" Farrell grabbed his arm, then looked at the twins. "I suggest you make yourselves scarce for a while, gentlemen. For the sake of your health. We'll talk later." The pair beat a hasty retreat. "As stupid as they are, we need them, Brady," he said. "Hagen is still free, as is Rourke, and we have a shortage of reliable help."

"I want blood, Farrell," Brady growled. "And soon."

He put his gun down on the desk and went to pour himself a drink. Farrell took the weapon and put it in his pocket. When his partner was in this mood, it was best to take every precaution.

Brady was beside himself with rage. Even Farrell's rock-steady calm was beginning to show signs of crumbling. He jumped nervously when Brady smashed a crystal tumbler full of Scotch against the stone wall above the fireplace.

"This can't have happened!"

"Well it did!" Farrell snapped. "So just accept it and move on, like you always do."

"No! I want everyone killed! Now!"

"For once, I almost agree with you, Brady." Farrell's eyes gleamed in the firelight. He took a long pull on his own drink, forcing himself to calm down. "But this situation is far too complex for such an easy out."

"Bull!"

"Face the facts, Brady. We haven't been successful in meeting Rourke head-on to date, now have we?"

"And what do you suggest? That we run and hide?"

Farrell took a deep breath and exhaled slowly before answering. "No, Brady. What I suggest is caution. There are too many eager ears listening for word of our every move. Complete, silent success is imperative. Your brother's investigators are still snooping, the U.S. government is still involved, and our own colleagues are watching this situation with great, impatient interest. That arms seizure will make us look very bad if we don't punish those responsible."

Brady sat down behind his desk. "All the more reason to do the job right. And that means doing it ourselves."

"Attractive, but impossible. Remember the last time we did something like that, Brady?" Farrell asked. His partner nodded and turned away, the veins in his neck bulging. "Of course, you do. It was your idea. And it's the reason we're in this mess right now. Don't you agree?"

"Farrell, so help me . . ."

"No offense, my friend. We're in this together as always. I only wanted to remind you that until *all* of the loose ends are tied, leaving our safe haven would be extremely foolish.'' Farrel allowed himself a tiny smile. "Don't worry. I'm already working on a way to make them come to us.''

THE BREEZE WAS DAMP AND COLD, hitting them with a sharp, penetrating sting. Annie pulled on a pair of thin leather gloves, resisting the urge to stamp her feet to keep warm.

Through the tall trees and sculptured hedges surrounding the country estate she could see the hazy orange sun beginning to rise above the distant horizon. Across a wide expanse of dew-covered lawn, the mansion loomed before them. All was quiet. It had only taken an hour to drive there from town. The traffic this early in the morning was almost nonexistent.

Annie glanced at Patrick. "Don't you think it would be just as easy to announce ourselves at the front gate?''

"No. One look at my face, or the mere mention of my name, and Nadia will take flight. And she's good at running and hiding. Nadia trusts no one—with good reason. If the price was right, she'd sell out her own child. Let's go.''

They began crisscrossing the grounds, hiding first behind trees and then low hedges as they got closer to the rear of the Tudor mansion. Though they couldn't see him, they knew Casey was doing the same, coming from another side.

Annie waited until they stopped behind another hedge. "Her own child? You're exaggerating, Patrick.''

"Am I? You don't know her like I do.''

"And just how well is that?''

Patrick glared at her. "She tried, believe me. I turned her down. And the scar on my thigh is her fault.''

Annie's curiosity was definitely aroused. "Is she Irish?''

"Very. Black Irish. Raven hair, violet eyes, a milk-white complexion and a stunning figure. And a lilting voice that can soothe a savage beast—or rip someone to shreds.''

"She sounds like quite a woman.''

"Oh, she is," Patrick agreed, sneering. "And she uses her beauty to get whatever she desires."

"Except you, right?" They were huddled behind another bush. "Admit it. You really like her," Annie teased.

"Sure I do. About as much as I'd like to fall into a pool filled with hungry piranha."

He made Nadia sound like evil personified. Could she really be that bad? Annie knew she would soon find out. The louvered glass doors on the back patio were easy to open.

"Don't underestimate her sweet face, Annie," Patrick whispered. "It could cost you your life."

His grim tone sent shivers down her spine. What Patrick obviously didn't know was that she was prepared to hate any woman responsible for wounding him.

They entered the mansion and moved briskly to a broad staircase leading to the second level. At the top of the stairs, they nodded at each other and took off in opposite directions. Beforehand they had agreed Casey would be in charge of investigating the ground floor.

Annie's wing was empty. It had obviously been closed off, for heat was nonexistent and white sheets covered all the furniture. She was glad to get out of the cold rooms. She paused momentarily on the landing, but Patrick was nowhere to be seen, so she went back down the stairs to give Casey a hand.

Moving through the strange, furniture-filled rooms on the ground floor with only the dawn light to see by wasn't easy, but Annie didn't want to risk attracting attention with her flashlight.

The soft murmur of voices stopped her in her tracks. A woman was doing most of the speaking, but her words weren't clear. Annie rounded the next corner warily, moving in the direction of the voices. At the end of one hallway a set of double doors stood wide open. She crept closer.

"I'm really quite disappointed in you, Rourke," the woman was saying. "You've underestimated me once again."

Annie peered around the door jamb. Rourke and Casey were standing against the far wall while the woman chastised them. The gun in her hand ensured their complete attention. To the right of them was a king-sized bed, the sheets and quilted coverlet in disarray. On their left was a sitting area, with an antique chaise longue and matching chairs arranged in a semicircle.

Nadia did have a lovely, lilting voice and a stunning figure. The rosy light of sunrise streamed through a window, shining right through her white gossamer gown and robe, detailing her every shapely curve.

"But I was surprised by your friend here, Rourke," Nadia said, aiming the gun at Casey. "You've always preferred to work alone, except where Russ and Jack were concerned. Now it's a new partner every week. How are Russ and Jack doing?"

"Nadia, you never cease to amaze me," Patrick said. "They're doing fine, no thanks to you."

"Then why are you here?"

Rourke shrugged. "As you gathered, I'm working with Casey," he replied, indicating the other man with a jerk of his head.

"Casey. What a nice name. What are you working on?"

Annie had taken advantage of the conversation, slipping into the room behind Nadia. "We're working on you, sweetie," she told Nadia, placing the barrel of her gun firmly against the woman's smooth back. "Drop your gun."

Nadia didn't move. "A woman, Rourke? I heard about it, but I didn't believe it. You *have* changed."

"Maybe I should tell you something, dear. Not being a tall, stunningly beautiful woman myself has always made me less than charitable toward those who are."

Annie stepped closer, raising her gun and resting its small, cold point next to Nadia's ear. "I won't kill you, Nadia. I'd much prefer to mar your absolutely stunning beauty beyond all possible cosmetic repair. Now, put the gun down on the carpet, slowly."

Nadia bent down, her finger relaxed as she placed the weapon on the floor. But she didn't let go of it. With the heel of her tennis shoe, Annie stomped down hard on the back of Nadia's hand.

Nadia yelled and straightened up, clutching her hand. "Why you scrawny little wretch!"

Annie pointed her gun at Nadia's nose. "Don't tempt me, darlin'." She kicked the gun toward Casey and Rourke with the side of her foot. "You boys need any more help?"

"Look out!"

Instinctively Annie reached around Nadia's lily white neck and twirled around, using her as a shield. "Which is it to be?" Annie asked. She was completely hidden behind Nadia's tall body and unable to see the person standing in the doorway. She cocked her gun for emphasis. "Nadia or you?"

"Charles, put the gun down," Nadia ordered harshly.

Annie saw Casey move past them, but waited until Patrick said it was safe to release her living shield. The man in the doorway was young, very young, and extremely good-looking.

"You bitch!" Nadia yelled, rubbing the red marks on her neck and examining her injured hand.

"Sticks and stones," Annie returned with a smile.

"For heaven's sake, Nadia," Rourke said. "You always did like robbing the cradle, but this guy isn't even half your age."

"Casey, lock him in the closet."

Charles entered the walk-in closet on his own. Casey shut the door, then tied a long silk scarf to one of the door handles, wrapped it around the other and knotted it tightly.

Rourke had retrieved his own gun from the bed and pointed it at Nadia. "We're short on time and patience, Nadia. No more games. Do you know where Hagen is?"

"Of course, I do. He's in the chauffeur's cottage." She studied her red-painted nails, smiling wistfully. "A woman has to have some male companionship when her husband's out of town, doesn't she?"

"I'll get him," Casey said, brushing past Annie, who was now standing near the open bedroom doors.

"I take it we're going to be here for a while." Nadia sat down on the pink chaise longue and crossed her long legs, showing a lot of creamy thigh. "Don't look so disapproving, Rourke. My charms never did appeal to you, did they?"

The woman was as nervy as ever. "Did you arrange the attack at our London hotel?" he asked.

"No!" She batted her full lashes.

"I told you no games, Nadia," Rourke warned.

"Well, not directly. Maybe I did sell your location to a contact of mine." Pouting, Nadia leaned back on her hands, thrusting her full bosom at Patrick. "How can you be so mean to me?"

"It's easy. And I'm going to get a lot meaner if you don't start talking. What have you been up to, Nadia?"

"Not as much as the old days," she replied with a sigh. "But I still keep my hand in. The intrigue, the excitement." She paused, moistening her lips with the tip of her tongue. "The money. I just love the money. There's a lot of it to be made by a woman in my position. I have so many friends, and I'm a very good listener."

"You're a good talker, too," Patrick said impatiently.

"Especially when someone will pay for what I know," she agreed, not offended in the slightest. "There were all sorts of rumors floating about. People looking for you. People looking for Orren Hagen. And, of course, that *you* were looking for Orren, as well." She smiled. "The possibilities!"

"Which you took advantage of, naturally."

"Naturally! You're not going to believe this Rourke," she continued in a coy tone, "but I found myself in a very strange position."

Annie laughed. "I certainly find it hard to believe." Nadia was incredible. Even with a gun pointed at her, she was flaunting her sexuality in an attempt to get to Patrick. "I bet you're on intimate terms with every position there is."

Nadia shot her a murderous glance, then turned her full attention back to Rourke. "I knew I could sell Hagen out, which was tempting, but he does have such wonderful . . . uses?" She smiled slyly. "Then I discovered that the same people who would pay for information on Hagen were also paying for anything on you, Rourke, as well as anyone connected to you."

"And you couldn't resist," Rourke said. "Just like in the past. It didn't matter who you sold out."

"That surprises you? It isn't as if there was any love lost between us. You and Jack tried to strangle me once. If it hadn't been for Russ, you would have, too."

"You've got that right."

"Who'd you sell the information to?" Annie asked.

Nadia kept her violet eyes on Rourke. "I have no idea. Truly. Until yesterday, it was all done through the mail, post-office boxes and such. Of course, the latest information I passed along via a number they gave me to call. My line here is secure."

Her answer didn't make Rourke comfortable at all. There was no such thing as a completely secure line. "What exactly did you sell?"

"Oh, the location of the hotel where you were to meet Casey." She smiled, showing perfect teeth. "Some details of Annie Sawyer's identity and your progress in the search for Hagen. Things like that. It was a challenge to blur the information around the edges just enough to keep my lucrative game going. But when Hagen called last night and said he needed a place to hide, I decided you were getting too close to him, so I invited dear Orren to my home. Then poor Lunn called and—''

''And you turned around and sold the location you got out of Kendrick, right?'' Annie inserted.

Nadia shrugged. ''But of course! It was worth a great deal, and Kendrick was foolish enough to give it to me.''

Annie was appalled by Nadia's greed and total disregard for human life. She could see why Patrick had wanted to strangle her. ''Who'd you get your other information from and how?''

Nadia grinned at her snidely. ''From your own department.''

The leak! ''Who?'' Annie demanded.

''In the hands of an experienced woman, Gerald's secretary has no willpower.'' Nadia placed a manicured hand on her ample chest. ''Don't look at me! He's much too old. But a dear friend of mine finds him adorable. Together, we actually managed to turn him into a mole of sorts. If I needed to know something my friend would just drop a hint to the poor lovesick fool, who would in turn check the agency's vast network. It was a lovely arrangement.''

''Gerald's secretary?'' Annie couldn't believe it, the man had been with the company forever. Then she realized how naive she was being. ''Of course. With Gerald nearing retirement, his secretary would soon face the task of starting over again with another boss—possibly in a job with a lower security clearance and therefore lower pay. It stinks, but that's the way it works with those who serve under top-level people.''

''And he naturally needed some comforting,'' Nadia said. ''My friend was happy to oblige. When I learned of the liaison, I in turn was happy to pay her for whatever she managed to get out of him between the sheets.'' Nadia preened. ''At times, I had your fellow agents doing my own bidding.''

Her wicked tale explained a lot, but Annie felt a growing uneasiness inside. There were things she hadn't reported to Gerald, things only she, Rourke and Casey had known.

Like the meet at the ruins. Bruce Holloway's agent had supposedly followed Rourke there, but ever since her little chat with the man, she'd had a nagging doubt in his ability to follow anyone anywhere. For a rather poorly informed backup agent, who was only supposed to be keeping an eye on her, he had also seemed overly eager to find out if she knew where Hagen was. And why not? There were people willing to pay handsomely for that information.

Had he known where the meeting was to take place? Was there another information pipeline operating besides Nadia's? If so, who was feeding that pipeline?

Who was the busiest moonlighter of them all?

Casey! Duty to their mutual friend Derry aside, he seemed every bit as eager to find Hagen as Patrick was. What was his real reason for being involved? Then an awful thought suddenly occurred to her. The man was a freelancer who would do almost anything for money. He was also extremely good with a gun.

Had Casey been sent to kidnap or to kill Hagen?

"Watch her, Patrick, I'll be back!"

Annie ran out of the room, down the hallway and out the front door to the side of the house. The gravel path to the chauffeur's cottage was slippery with morning dew. She found the front door open and burst into the cottage, expecting to catch Casey in the midst of eliminating Hagen.

Instead, someone hit her on the back of the skull and Annie saw nothing but the blackness that engulfed her.

Chapter Nineteen

Rourke had his hands full. When Annie bolted from the room, he'd tried to follow, grabbing Nadia by the arm with the idea of dragging her along for the ride. Nadia had other ideas. As he pulled her up from the chaise longue and started toward the door, she stuck her foot out and tripped him. He tumbled to the floor, somersaulting across the thick carpet.

Nadia came after him, a pole lamp in her hands. She swung the base end of it at Rourke, but he rolled out of her reach and the base hit the carpet, slicing a deep gouge.

He got up, his eyes gleaming fiercely. Annie might be in trouble, but he couldn't go after her with Nadia on the loose. Rourke raised his gun. "So help me, Nadia..."

"You wouldn't shoot a lady, Rourke."

"Probably not, Nadia. But you're no lady."

She took another swing at him with the lamp. He ducked and stepped toward her at the same time. Then he clenched his fist and hit her solidly on the jaw, making her perfect teeth click together. She went out like a light, sinking to the carpet in a pool of white gossamer lace.

Rourke sprinted out of the house toward the chauffeur's cottage, slipping on the wet grass as he took a shortcut through an evergreen hedge. The front door of the cottage was open. He stood beside it, checking his weapon before poking his head into the room.

"Annie! Casey?" The cottage was dead still.

He was a few steps into the main room when a man leaned out of the kitchen door. Rourke ducked, trying to dodge the big fist that came his way. It grazed his chin and he staggered backward, just as another man jumped on him from behind, wrapping his hands around Rourke's throat.

Rourke twirled around with the man still hanging on his back and slammed him into the wall behind them. The fingers around Rourke's throat loosened. Taking hold of the other man's coat, he flipped him over his shoulder, smack into a solid iron radiator. The man grunted and fell flat on his face.

Expecting the second man to come from the kitchen, Rourke spun in that direction and saw the man running out the front door with Annie slung over his shoulder, as limp as a rag doll. Rourke only managed one step after them before he realized his mistake. There were three of them.

The third man came charging at Rourke full tilt, plowing into him with such force that they were both propelled back into a small bedroom on the right. They bounced off the metal railing at the end of the bed and fell to the floor.

The man made a desperate grab for Rourke's gun, but Rourke held on to it just as desperately, taking hold of the man's throat with his other hand and forcing the man's head back hard into the metal frame of the bed. The man went limp, but it was a ruse. The moment Rourke eased up, he was hit in the jaw. Reeling from the blow, he lost his grip on the gun and it clattered to the floor. The man grabbed it.

As he was swinging the weapon around to take aim, Rourke pulled another pistol from his jacket pocket and shot him in the arm. The man's hand jerked and he dropped his weapon, grabbing his bleeding arm. Rourke stood up, cocking his pistol again and aiming it at his heavyset opponent.

"Who sent you?" he demanded.

The man grimaced in pain. "Go spit."

Suddenly, Rourke heard the roar of a car outside, its tires squealing on pavement. He collected the other man's gun and hit the man on the back of the head with it, stunning him.

Running out of the cottage, Rourke cut through a tall hedge to get to the circular drive in front of the house. At the end of a long driveway, a man was stuffing Annie into the trunk of a dark green car. Rourke didn't bother taking a shot; they were out of range.

He ran down the long, flat driveway, watching as the man shut the trunk lid and jumped in the car. The driver gunned the engine and took off, through the gates and away down the tree-lined country lane. Once outside the gates himself, Rourke headed for his own car.

All four tires had been slashed.

Nadia's cars! He turned and sprinted back down the drive, cutting through a prickly hedge as he headed for the three-car garage he'd seen set off on the side of the house, near the cottage.

Both the Rolls's and the Bentley's tires were slashed, too. "Damn!"

Murder in his eyes, he went back to the cottage. Both men were still unconscious. Neither was familiar to him. After filling a glass with water, he returned to stand in front of the man lying at the base of the radiator. He threw the contents at the man's face, watching as he shook his head groggily, trying to focus.

Grabbing hold of the man's wet hair, Rourke jerked his neck back and pressed the point of his gun into the man's Adam's apple. "Who do you work for?"

"I don't know," the man gasped out.

"How many are you working with?"

"Three others."

Rourke pushed the gun further into his throat, his rage apparent. "How do you get in touch with your employer?"

"We can't. Everything's always done by phone. We don't even know what he looks like."

"And your orders?"

The man gulped before answering. "To kill everyone here, starting with a guy named Hagen."

"Then why did you kidnap the woman?"

"We couldn't find Hagen. If that happened, we were supposed to grab the woman with the curly hair if she was here and take off. She walked in on us."

"Where did they take her?"

"I don't know. All we have is a number to call."

Rourke pushed the man away. He felt like doing a lot worse. But the man was obviously no threat, at least for now.

Who had Annie? Flynn, possibly, except that he would have told these men his name, as he had the ones in Belfast, so they could let Rourke know who was killing him. He wandered out of the cottage, trying to figure out his next move. In the distance he saw Casey emerging from the woods, with someone in tow. He waited for them to come to him.

Casey had his gun aimed at the man's heart when he stopped in front of Rourke. "Meet the elusive Orren Hagen."

Slender and good-looking, Hagen was dressed in expensive clothes, and had dark brown hair cut short and stylish. His light blue eyes were unmistakable, as was the hard, mean look to his face. Hagen matched the photograph Annie had gotten from his grandfather. Though clearly alarmed by his present situation, he was still defiant, even arrogant.

"Do you have any idea who you're dealing with?"

"A man with a price on his head," Rourke replied. "Face it, Hagen. Right now, you're worth more dead than alive. Who wants you that way and why?"

"I don't know what you're talking about."

All of Rourke's patience had disappeared along with Annie. "Fine, I'll kill you right now and collect the money, then I'll know who it is."

Hagen was one cool customer. He shrugged. "Go ahead, it's your choice," he said, slipping his hands into the pockets of his expensive pants. "But if that's all you wanted, I'd be dead already, right? Maybe we can bargain."

"You want a deal? Here it is. Tell me who put the price on your head and I'll let you live," Rourke countered. "For now." A cold bleakness fell over him. Was he going to lose Annie, too? He put the barrel of his gun against Hagen's temple. "If you think I'm bluffing, just look into my eyes."

"Yeah," Hagen admitted. "You got the look, all right." He shrugged again. "It was Brady Adair and his partner, Colin Farrell. Not that I'm doing you any big favor. If you go after them, I'm talking to a dead man."

Rourke lowered his gun. He'd dealt with enough men of Hagen's ilk to know threats weren't of much use. "So am I if they get their hands on you. Keep talking and maybe we can come to some sort of arrangement."

"Such as?" Hagen asked with studied indifference.

"Protection. There are some other people who would like to get their hands on you. Government people. I take it they want to ask you some questions of their own, and an interrogation is a whole lot better than a funeral."

For the first time, Hagen showed some interest. "All right. You have my attention. What do you want to know?"

"Why do these guys want you dead?"

"I've been asking myself the same question. All I know is something upset them. They've been tying up loose ends in a deadly bout of housekeeping, and I'm on their list,"

Hagen replied. "Right at the top, it seems. It's a good thing I saw them coming."

"The men who attacked the cottage, you mean?"

"Bright boy," Hagen returned sarcastically. "They're men Adair and Farrell have used before. I should know. I did contract work for them, too. So when I saw them creeping through the grounds, I ran into the woods."

Casey had been listening to Hagen with a great deal of interest. Now his eyes went wide. "Rourke, where's Annie?"

"Brady Adair's men have her."

"Oh, Lord," Casey groaned.

He looked ill. Rourke knew just how he felt. "Where have they taken her?" he asked Hagen.

"I have no idea. Could be any one of a thousand places. Our business was done through the mail or by phone. I met them in person only once. I'm a go-between."

"What kind of business?" Casey asked.

Hagen shook his head. "That's the end of the free ride. No more answers until you guarantee my safety. And that means someplace else and anybody but you guys. You go after Brady, you do it without me. He'll come down on you two like a ton of bricks."

"I could still kill you," Rourke informed him.

"Then do it. I don't know where they took your lady friend. And anything else I do know is my ticket out. You said it yourself." Hagen smiled. "I have nothing to lose."

There was no doubt that Hagen meant it. He was the type of man who'd rather die than give something away for free. And none of this was helping Rourke get Annie back.

"Casey, tie up those two I left in the cottage," Rourke said. "I shot one of them, so I guess you'd better bandage him as well. I want him alive for the police later on. When you're done, join me in Nadia's bedroom."

"Will do," Casey said.

Rourke turned to Hagen. "Okay, tough guy. Lead the way to the house."

They found Nadia on the bedroom floor, still unconscious. "Take a seat over there." Rourke pulled the belt from her robe and tossed it to him. "Tie your legs to the chair. And do a good job, Hagen, or I might decide to take a few of my frustrations out on you." He waited until Hagen finished then asked, "What time does the help start arriving?"

"The cook about eight, the others an hour later."

It was seven-fifteen. After filling a glass with ice-cold water, Rourke stood over Nadia and slowly poured it in a steady stream, right into her face. She woke up sputtering and cussing.

"Stay on the floor, Nadia." Rourke sat down on the bed. If looks could kill, he'd be dead. Then again, so would she. "Who's Brady Adair?"

Nadia sat up, gently brushing the water from her face and raven hair. "Who? I don't know any Brady Adair."

"That's hard to believe, since he sent men here to kill you. Ask Hagen."

Nadia turned around and looked at Hagen. "What on earth is he talking about, Orren?"

"Haven't the slightest."

Casey walked into the room. "They're tied up."

"Who?" Nadia demanded. "What's going on?"

"Tie her up in the other chair, then check Hagen's knots," Rourke told him. "If they're loose, break his nose. The same goes for her if she tries to get away."

"My pleasure," Casey said. He meant it, too.

Rourke watched, gun in hand. Nadia compliantly sat down in the chair opposite Hagen. Casey found some cord and bound her hands and feet to the chair. Then he checked Hagen's feet, and tied his hands up as well.

"They're secure," Casey announced. "What now?"

Rourke was glad he'd had a few minutes to think about this. "Brady Adair is the person Hagen's been hiding from, and you, Nadia, were selling information to him."

She gasped. "Oh, no!"

"I see you get my meaning," Rourke said. "Let me make it crystal clear. I'd say it's safe to assume Adair has as many connections as you do, Nadia, probably more. Your secure, unlisted phone line didn't stop us. It wouldn't stop him. He found out who you were and where, then figured you could be the one harboring Hagen, an old flame of yours. When we escaped his men at the hotel, he might even have thought you double-crossed him again and told us about the ambush. Or maybe he thought we'd come looking for you. Whatever, he decided he didn't need you anymore and sent men to kill you, Hagen and us if we happened to be here."

"Let us go, Rourke!" Nadia begged. "We have to hide!"

Rourke ignored her plea. "But they couldn't find Hagen," he continued bitterly. "So they shifted to their backup plan." He walked over to stand in front of her, his gun an inch from her throat. "Their orders were to grab Annie if she was here, and they did. I want to know why they took her."

Nadia's face was ashen and she actually looked worried, an emotion Rourke had never seen her display before. "All right, Rourke. I'll cooperate. If you protect me."

"There's a lot of that going around," he muttered. "We'll get you out of the way, but only because you're too dangerous when you're on the loose. Now talk."

"According to my source at the agency, you and this Annie person have some kind of bond that goes way back. That was part of the information I sold. My contact was immensely pleased with the tidbit, as well as the fact that you and she were after Hagen. They wanted to know why, too, but I couldn't find that part out."

Rourke wanted to strangle her. If he'd done so years ago when she had first sold him out, this wouldn't be happening now. The ringing of the bedside phone was all that stopped him.

He walked over and picked up the receiver, holding it to his ear. There wasn't much doubt about who was on the other end of the line. "Hello, Adair. Or is this Farrell?"

"Correct the first time. Patrick Rourke, I presume?"

"Yes."

"I'm looking forward to meeting you, Rourke. I truly am."

"Hurt the woman and you die, Adair," Rourke said. "It's just that simple. By the way, I have Orren Hagen."

"And I have Annie Sawyer. To get her back, you'll have to personally turn Orren Hagen over to me," Brady Adair informed him. "Or I'll kill her." He laughed. "It's that simple."

Rourke's heart was pounding. "I agree to your terms, as long as you and Colin Farrell personally handle the exchange."

"I wouldn't have it any other way. We'll meet tomorrow, at noon." He gave him the location. "You're acquainted with the territory, I would imagine. It should prove interesting." Brady laughed harshly and then hung up.

"That damn woman is going to get me killed yet!"

Rourke was acquainted with the territory, all right. He also knew there was a remote castle high in those rugged Irish hills. Adair must have bought and refurbished it, for obvious reasons. In days gone by, a handful of men could have fought off a much larger opposing force from just such a stronghold.

Rourke knew the odds were against him this time.

He wasn't fooled, either. There was no doubt in his mind that this was a trap. Adair and Farrell intended to kill everyone. He and Casey would just have to be quicker.

If Casey was willing to help. Rourke looked over at him, his expression grim. "Casey, I know you only signed on to help me find Hagen, but—"

Casey held up a hand, cutting Rourke off. "Say no more. I'm in it all the way. We'll get Annie back, no matter what."

"Thanks."

Rourke was a bit puzzled by Casey's quick answer. This was going to be a dangerous operation. Both of them could end up dead. It was almost as though Casey felt partly responsible, as if he should have been keeping an eye on Annie. Little did he know that she was virtually impossible to restrain. Whatever Casey's reasons, Rourke was glad to have him. His friend, Derry, had chosen well.

"What's next?" Casey asked.

"We need a car to get back to town with Hagen, and we also need someone to watch Adair's men and Nadia. Any ideas?"

Casey pursed his lips. "I know someone who'll baby-sit the lot, for a price."

"Give him a call."

"It's a she," Casey said, smiling at Nadia as he dialed the number. "Sorry, beautiful, but you haven't a chance of wheedling your way past this woman."

Rourke strode across the bedroom. "I'm going to tack a note to the servants' entrance. Nadia's going to give her staff two days off, with pay."

Nadia yelled at his retreating back. "I hate your guts, Patrick Rourke!"

"The feeling's mutual."

Casey made arrangements with his friend, then he dialed another number. He spoke softly, his back to the others in the room. "I have Hagen. Yes, I'll be in touch." As Rourke walked back in, he hung up. "Everything's taken care of," he said. "She'll be here within the hour. We can even use her car. But, of course, that'll cost you extra."

Rourke shrugged. "No problem. While I was looking for some paper to write the note, I found Nadia's wallet."

TWO HOURS LATER, THEY WERE at a small hotel on the outskirts of London. Orren Hagen was in the other room, tied up. He wasn't happy about their plans for him, making as much noise as the gag around his mouth allowed.

Rourke had tried to question him, find out what he knew about the Houlihan murder and why someone was trying to locate Bridget after all this time. But it was soon obvious Hagen wasn't going to talk. At the moment Rourke's main concern was rescuing Annie—and getting a few answers out of her boss.

"Are you sure this is a good idea?" Casey asked. He was leaning against the inner door that connected the two rooms, hands shoved in his pockets.

"No. But there's no other choice," Rourke replied. "We're going to need backup. I have to contact Gerald."

"It's chancy," Casey warned him.

"I know." Rourke sighed and sat down on the bed near the phone. "And I know Hagen said Adair and Farrell have been cleaning house, which might mean they really do intend to handle this personally. But I'm not willing to bet Annie's life that they don't still have access to a few men who'll keep their mouths shut, for a price. In all likelihood, we'll be way outgunned." He picked up the receiver. "Go check on Hagen."

After Casey left Rourke dialed a number and waited for someone to answer. "Yes."

"Julie, I need the number to Gerald's private line."

"Rourke!" Julie exclaimed in a strangled whisper. A chair squeaked noisily in the background and Rourke heard a door slam shut a moment later. "I can't give you that!"

"You have to, Julie. One of his agents was kidnapped."

Julie's chair gave a tremendous squawk. "Oh, no! It's Annie, isn't it! Who's got her?"

"A couple of big-timers named Adair and Farrell."

"I knew it! I just knew Brady Adair was dirty!"

Rourke's eyebrows shot up. "I think you have some explaining to do, Julie."

"Sure. But first things first." He rattled off a sequence of numbers. "Did you get it?"

"Yes, thanks. Now what's going on?"

"Annie's had me checking into the background of Brady Adair, but I still haven't uncovered anything through the computers. I know it's there, I just haven't tapped the right one yet." Julie paused, taking a deep breath before continuing. "She also asked if Gerald was working in Ireland five years ago. I found out he definitely was, in Belfast, but I don't know the significance of it. I've been busy working on the other stuff."

Rourke didn't like the implications of what Julie had just revealed. "That's okay, Julie. I think I know what Annie was trying to figure out." He shook his head in admiration. "Brother. The woman really *is* good, isn't she?"

"She must be. Otherwise I wouldn't be helping her, now would I? Oh. There's something else," Julie said. "Annie suspected a leak in her division. Without her knowledge, Gerald's been using her on this job to flush out that leak."

"Well, he got his wish and it serves him right." Rourke felt he owed Julie for helping him out. And information was Julie's bread and butter. "The leak is Gerald's own secretary."

"Wow!"

"Yeah. Thanks, Julie."

Now more than ever, Rourke hesitated to dial the number Julie had given him. But he didn't have the time to go through anyone else to get what he needed in order to rescue Annie.

Besides, he owed her something else. They were partners now. She was the one who had figured out Gerald's ulterior motives, and Rourke intended to stick the knife in him on her behalf. He gritted his teeth and made the call.

"Yes."

"Gerald?"

"Who is this?"

Good, he already had him worried. "It's Patrick Rourke. You have a loose-lipped secretary, old man, and because of him, Annie's been kidnapped by two men named Brady Adair and Colin Farrell. I think they may be the ones you sent her to find. In my opinion, that puts the blame squarely on your shoulders."

"Oh, no! What about Hagen?"

Rourke stretched out on the bed, easing his sore body into a comfortable position. "I have him."

"I'll make arrangements for you to bring him in."

"Not so fast, Gerald. There's a price tag attached."

"What is it?" Gerald asked cautiously.

"It's twofold. First, I want a few chosen men to help me get Annie back, and since they're going to have to be willing to disobey the orders from you and their superiors, I'm picking them myself."

Gerald's caution grew. "Who do you want?"

"Willie and his men." Willie had been the one to help get Bridget safely out of Houston and away from Flynn the last time he'd tried to get her. They'd worked together before that, too, and understood each other.

"He may not be available," Gerald replied.

Rourke laughed harshly. "Then you'll never see Hagen alive. Am I making myself perfectly clear?"

"Yes." A long silence passed before Gerald asked, "What's the second part?"

"How did you make the connection between my search for Hagen and these men you're after?"

"That's classified information."

"Unclassify it, or you'll never hear what Hagen knows." It was time to use Annie's razor-sharp data. "I know you were in Belfast five years ago, when Bridget's parents were murdered. Why?''

As he waited for a reply, Rourke could hear the furious puffing of a pipe over the phone lines.

"If this ever comes out, I'll deny everything," Gerald began slowly. "None of this is on record, anywhere."

"Just get on with it."

"I convinced the Houlihans to turn on their employers in exchange for getting them off on a gun-running charge."

"And just who were their employers?''

Gerald sighed. "They didn't know, but I suspected they were the criminal masterminds we'd spent years trying to catch. The Houlihans agreed to my terms, and we set up a trap, but they were murdered the night before it was to be triggered."

"Who did you tell about the trap?"

"No one. I was going against orders when I set it up. There was another trap already in the works. Eventually it ended with the death of both agents involved."

That made Gerald responsible for four deaths, maybe more. "That doesn't explain how you knew about my involvement."

"That's why I was in Belfast. I monitored your progress as you searched for the killers and Orren Hagen."

Rourke was furious. "Using me like you used Annie, in other words! Why didn't you mount your own investigation?"

"I couldn't, not without revealing what I'd done, and the penalties would have ruined me. I had no choice but to let it go. But when word came to me that you were once again looking for Hagen, I produced enough information to get the agency involved."

"Thus putting Annie in a deadly situation without all the facts," Rourke bit out. "You *owe* her, old man."

"Has Hagen told you anything about Adair and Farrell?"

"Not a peep, and he's not going to until he's got immunity and protection."

"That can be arranged. I agree with your assessment. Adair and Farrell have to be the men we've been looking for."

"And they've got Annie," Rourke grimly reminded him again. "Right now, except for kidnapping charges, you have no concrete proof of any wrongdoing by the pair. If Hagen doesn't squeal—or live to squeal—you have nothing."

"I understand. I'll find Willie right away," Gerald assured him. "How do I get in touch with you?"

"You don't. I'll call you."

Rourke slammed the phone down, then sat up and called another number. "Jack, turn your recorder on."

"It's on," Jack Merlin replied. "What's wrong?"

"Let me get all this out without questions, then we'll talk." Rourke gave him names, dates and a detailed history of what had happened so far and what would happen next.

"How's Bridget?" he asked when he was finished.

"She's fine," Jack said. "I spoke to her this morning. But Cassie's ticked off at you again."

"Me! How come? I haven't done anything."

"You didn't have tails put on her before you left for Ireland?" Jack asked.

"Well, yes, I did," Rourke admitted, "but it was for her own protection."

"I did the same thing, and it was good we both did. Two days ago, some other goons started following her. They're in police custody, but they're not talking. They say they don't even know who hired them. In the meantime, we're holed up here in the house and you know how much Cassie likes being confined."

So there had been men following Cassie who didn't know who hired them. Rourke was willing to bet he knew who; by now the signature of Adair and Farrell was all too familiar. Their influence really must be vast. Masterminds, indeed.

"Tell her it should all be over by tomorrow. And put that tape in a safe place. You have the necessary information to continue this if something goes wrong."

"Call me when it's over."

Rourke set the phone receiver down and got to his feet, unable to sit still. Adair and Farrell wanted Hagen because of what he knew about their empire. When they failed to grab him, they'd taken Annie to force a trade. Presumably, they had put those men on Cassie O'Connor with the same idea in mind, a sort of backup hostage in case they needed one, knowing Rourke was on the trail of Hagen and might get to him first. And he had. No doubt about it, the pair were as sharp and careful as they come.

They seemed to know so much. It was possible they could shed some light on the murder of Bridget's parents. Rourke intended to question them—if they lived through the battle that would undoubtedly take place tomorrow.

If he lived through it himself.

Patrick forced himself to sit down and rest, refusing to think about that or what might be happening to Annie. He had to believe she was all right. Right now, it was all that kept him going.

Chapter Twenty

Annie slowly opened her eyes. For a moment everything was blurry and unfocused, including her thoughts. Then, as her vision cleared, so did her mind, and she gingerly touched the back of her head, wincing in pain.

Somebody had clouted her a good one. Casey? Hagen? Another of Flynn's men or maybe the people Nadia had been selling information to? There were too many choices.

She looked around, finding herself on a plush sofa in the middle of a cavernous room with stone walls. There was a fire in the huge fireplace directly across from her. And there were two men looking at her, one with bland disinterest, the other with a severe intensity. The second man's face was florid, his eyes full of a barely contained rage.

Annie didn't know either of the men. They were new players in the game and, somehow, she didn't think they were on her side. Her training had taught her very specific ways of dealing with situations like this. The first rule was to keep your mouth shut for as long as possible. Unfortunately, they already knew she was awake.

"Our little bargaining chip has come around."

"About time," red face said irritably.

The other man left his position near the roaring fire and approached her. "We have a few questions we'd like you to answer, Ms. Sawyer."

Answers. That was a good one. All Annie had at the moment was questions. It didn't seem like a very smart idea to let them know that, however. Her life might depend on how much she knew, how much they thought she knew, and how long she could keep them thinking she was valuable.

"You already know my name," Annie said. Talking made her head hurt. She tried not to let it show. "I don't have a rank or serial number. What else is there to tell?"

The one with the red face strode across the room toward her, his fist raised. The calmer one stopped him. "Wait! We can't question her if she's unconscious." He looked at Annie. His eyes were hard and cold. "Don't play games with us, Sawyer. U.S. agent or not, you're balanced on a very fine thread at the moment, between being useful and simply a nuisance we'd as soon be rid of. Tell us why you and Rourke were after Orren Hagen."

"Why don't you ask Rourke yourself?"

"We intend to. He'll be joining us shortly, to bring us Hagen in exchange for you. If you want to live that long, I suggest you stop being flippant and cooperate."

Some answers at last. These were the other people who wanted Hagen. Or one pair of them, at any rate; Hagen was a popular guy. It was nice to know Patrick was coming after her, too, but Annie was hardly elated by the circumstances. The two men glaring at her were not the type to let her or anybody else inimical to them get away from them alive.

But she could do something useful in the meantime. They seemed extremely well-informed. If she could keep them talking, they might let something slip that could help her figure a way out of this mess. That didn't mean she had to cooperate, though.

"I'm just a humble government servant who was sent to help Rourke track Hagen down," Annie replied at last. "Nobody tells me anything, including Rourke."

"That's bull!" red face bellowed.

"My partner doesn't believe you, Ms. Sawyer," the other one said in a tone that made her skin crawl. "Neither do I. As much as we'd enjoy beating the answer out of you, we're pressed for time. There is another, more important piece of information we need. And you *will* give it to us."

"What's that?" Annie asked.

"The whereabouts of Bridget Houlihan."

Annie's head throbbed viciously. That certainly answered another of her questions. Unfortunately, it also made her realize just how desperate her situation might be.

The walls around her were stone, this room enormous. Like a castle. Her surroundings were baroque but elegant, rife with very expensive furnishings and art objects. These men were well-dressed, virtually oozing the aura of wealth. And yet they had hard eyes, the sort Annie had seen before during this operation. These, however, were not common criminals, but the men who hired them. Heavyweights. Masterminds.

They'd kidnapped her to get answers and to use her as a bargaining chip. They wanted Hagen. And they wanted to know where Bridget Houlihan was. That was a difficult name to come by. The implications were clear—and frightening. Her quarry and Rourke's were one in the same. She was being held hostage by the heads of a vast criminal network and by the murderers of Bridget's parents as well.

She struggled to regain her composure. Her life depended on it. "I haven't the slightest idea where Bridget is," Annie replied. "Sorry to disappoint you—"

Red face came forward again, fists clenched at his sides. "You're the one who's going to be sorry, you—"

"Wrong answer, Ms. Sawyer," the other man interjected smoothly. "This is your last warning. Be assured we can and will make you tell us what we want to know. You'll talk and talk and then beg for death."

Annie didn't doubt it for a moment. That, too, was in their eyes. Not just ruthless. Cruel. "I'm telling the truth. I don't know where Bridget is, nor does Rourke. We set it up that way from the beginning, so it couldn't be tortured out of us."

"Damn! This is totally useless!" the volatile one exclaimed. "Let's get the twins in here. They'll make her sing a different tune!"

The other shrugged. "I'm sure of that. But different doesn't mean better. I think she's telling the truth."

"You must be joking!"

"With what we know of Patrick Rourke, that's precisely what he would do. A very large nuisance, that man. I'm going to enjoy taking care of him personally."

Annie managed a curt laugh. "Fat chance."

He dismissed her remark with a wave of his hand, as if shooing away an annoying fly. "I'm not concerned with your opinions, Ms. Sawyer. What does concern me is what you know about us. If, indeed, you know anything at all."

His smug tone made her mad. But she was well aware he was baiting her, trying to trick her into telling them everything. The trouble was, they were right. She didn't have much to tell.

It was time to go on the offensive. She could play the baiting game, too. "I know you're vicious killers," she said.

"Us?" he asked mildly. "We're simple businessmen."

"Right. In the business of death. You're wanted by my government, undoubtedly by many others as well. I also know why you want Bridget Houlihan. You'd like to silence her, just like you silenced her parents."

Eyebrows arched high, the man with the florid face shot a glance at his companion. "She knows, Farrell. I told you this was coming apart at the seams."

"Calm down." Farrell stepped closer to Annie. Somehow, his quiet, suave manner was even more frightening than the other's more overt anger. "Go on, Ms. Sawyer."

It wasn't a request. Annie was on treacherous ground now. One misstep and they would realize that she was running mainly on supposition. That realization could very well end her usefulness and her life, as well. But she was certain she was right, and the pieces of the puzzle these men could inadvertently put together for her were worth the risk.

The only thing she really had was a name. She would have to use it, play her trump card and hope for the best. "What more is there to say? Regardless of what happens to me, you'll pay for your crimes, Farrell," Annie told him with blithe assurance. Then she looked at the other man. "As will you, Mr. Adair."

It worked. Adair's eyes went wide and that florid complexion of his drained to ashen gray. He opened his mouth to speak, strangling on the words. "Kill her!"

Farrell bent down and grabbed her by the shoulders. For a horrible moment, Annie thought he was going to carry out Adair's demand. She braced herself against the back of the sofa, ready to try to defend herself.

"How did you come by those names?" Farrell demanded.

Now what? She didn't have time to think up a good lie, and a bad one might trip her up. "I overheard a man I was tailing use it during a phone conversation."

"What man?"

Another step closer to the abyss. But her confidence was building by the moment. She had one more name, that of a man who had so subtly played both ends against the middle.

"One of your partners in crime," Annie said. "Casey."

"Casey?" Farrell let go of her shoulders and stood there looking at her. "Is that his first or last name?"

"Who the hell is Casey?" Brady Adair demanded.

Annie clenched her fists. She'd made a mistake! All she could do now was blunder onward, hoping for a chance to regain the upper hand. But how?

They had been expecting her to name one of their hirelings. Casey obviously wasn't one of them, but she couldn't change her tune now or they'd know she'd been bluffing. Patrick had inadvertently told her there were four men responsible for the Houlihan murder. She would have to be creative.

"How would I know if Casey is his first or last name?" she returned sarcastically. "It's the only one I know him by. He's your accomplice, not mine. I would think the four of you would at least keep track of each other's aliases."

"Four? Four what?" Farrell asked.

"Murderers. All of you had a hand in killing Bridget's parents. And you'll all pay for it. Rourke will see to that."

That was it, the end of the line. All she could do now was sit back and wait to see what happened. Annie did just that, trying to look as comfortable as she could, considering the lump on her head and the company she was in.

Farrell simply looked thoughtful.

Brady Adair, on the other hand, seemed ready to burst a blood vessel. "That's why Rourke was after Hagen!" he yelled. "He found out Hagen was in on that deal. By now he probably knows everything!"

"Calm down, Brady," Farrell demanded. "Hagen won't talk until he's under protection, and Rourke can't turn him over because we've forced this trade. Besides, it doesn't matter what they know. By this time tomorrow, they'll all be buried in an unmarked grave."

That thought did seem to placate Brady. "Yes," he said, almost smiling. "They will, won't they?"

"You're a very smart woman, Ms. Sawyer," Farrell said. "Too smart for your own good, I'm afraid. By now you either know or have surmised how we came by much of our information. The leak in your department. We are therefore aware that you haven't reported any of this to your superiors."

"And if you had, it wouldn't matter, either," Brady added. He was much calmer now that he had poured and drained half of a large tumbler of Scotch. "Without proof, they can't touch us."

Suddenly, Annie didn't feel quite so smug. Except for the identity of the fourth man, she had it all now. But it wasn't going to be any use to her dead. Escape was essential. She wracked her brain, trying to remember her architectural studies. Just how did one escape from a fortress?

Farrell spoke again, breaking her concentration. "You really are a remarkable woman," he said. "It's a shame both you and all your hard work will go to waste."

"You'll never get away with any of this."

"Oh, but we will, Ms. Sawyer. Hagen will soon be in our grasp. We'll find the Houlihan girl eventually. And this Casey, as you call him, is already in our bad graces. No alias or masterful disguise will save him this time. He, too, will soon die," Farrell assured her. "Of course, you won't be around to see any of this because we're going to take care of you, Rourke and whoever comes with him, first. Afterward, we'll simply go underground. With our money and connections, we can go very deep indeed."

"I'll call the twins in now," Brady said.

To the left of the large stone fireplace was a set of double doors, at least eight feet high and made of heavy wood, with large wrought iron pulls. Brady opened one of them and spoke quietly to someone in the corridor.

Annie tensed, looking for a way to escape.

Farrell chuckled. "Don't worry, Ms. Sawyer. We'll let you live for a while longer, in case we need you to lure Rourke and company into the castle tomorrow."

He turned away and went to pour himself a drink. Brady joined him. Obviously, she was being dismissed.

The two big men who entered the room were the same twins who had been after her and Patrick at the Dublin hotel. They were still dressing alike, and by the way they both leered at her, they were still as nasty as ever. Annie cringed when one of them reached out and grabbed her arm, hauling her off the couch. The other laughed and poked a gun in her ribs.

"Nice to see you again, missy," he said in that deep, gravelly voice she remembered only too well.

His brother grinned. "You were right. She does have a nice set of—"

"That's enough!" Farrell bellowed. "I want your minds on business and nothing else. Just take her and lock her up, then come back here. We have plans to make."

The pair didn't bother concealing their disappointment, but they obeyed instantly. They each put a beefy hand on her shoulder and escorted her out of the room, with Annie wedged between them like the filling of a sandwich.

In sharp contrast to the room she had just left, the maze of corridors down which they led her was cold, damp and dimly lighted. She had half expected to see flaming torches on the walls, and indeed there were sconces of that design, but the lighting was electric. Still, it was a gloomy walk, bringing memories of old horror movies to Annie's mind.

That impression increased when they took her down a flight of broad stone steps, deeper into the bowels of the castle. But, of course. Every good castle had a dungeon.

Annie managed to fight off the feeling of dread the place gave her by concentrating on the layout, taking note of the distance covered and the changes of direction, making a mental map of what she could see. At last, the twins stopped in front of a door and opened it.

Although the hinges squeaked ominously, the little room they pushed her into was an anticlimax compared to the image she had formed in her mind. It was Spartan, with only a cot, crude toilet and a single light bulb dangling from the ceiling, but it was not a torture chamber. The twins slammed the heavy wooden door and locked her in.

She smiled. The lock was modern. They would have been wiser to keep the old iron crossbar the room had probably been fitted with originally. A lot of her castle research was coming back to her, and more would surface as soon as she could prowl around a bit.

Escape was way down on her list of priorities now. Adair and Farrell had to be stopped. Withdrawing a thin wire lock pick hidden in the waistband of her jeans, Annie got busy on the door. There was much to learn before tomorrow.

Chapter Twenty-one

There would be only one rule in this encounter: Adair wasn't going to play fair. Rourke didn't intend to, either. He couldn't afford to give his opponents any added advantage. At dawn he was already in place with his handpicked cadre of men, waiting and watching. As if foreshadowing events to come, the day arrived dressed in gray, accompanied by a slow procession of dark, somber clouds. They hung overhead, pressing in on him like a smothering blanket as he lay stretched out on top of a hill, peering through binoculars at the scene below.

The castle, built of blond stone, was roughly square and three stories high, with a single round turret jutting up into the sky. At first glance the turret appeared windowless, but after adjusting his binoculars, Rourke noticed small squares of stones missing on each level, all the way up to the top of the five-story cylindrical structure. He had the uneasy feeling someone was watching him from inside that lookout tower. But Willie and his men were down at the base of the hill, out of sight, and the tall grass surrounding Rourke gave plenty of cover.

The castle appeared deserted, but Rourke knew otherwise. Inside, Brady Adair and Colin Farrell were expecting him, and they had Annie. Somehow he had to get in there without anyone knowing he had arrived.

The first obstacle was the ten-foot-high wall, also of blond-colored stone, that completely surrounded the castle. In some spots it had been erected directly against the hillside upon which the castle sat, like a foundation wall, while the rest stood alone, with a broad swatch of open territory between it and the fortress wall proper.

Studying the barricade more closely, Rourke noticed that along the top, indentions had been carved out every few feet. For hundreds of years the previous owners of this castle had probably defended themselves against invasions from those battlements. At the moment, however, they weren't manned and, unlike their ancestors, Rourke and his men had the modern equipment necessary to scale that wall. But he doubted they could do so undetected.

So far the only other entrance he'd found was where a dirt road led up to a huge set of wooden gates, built right into the outer stone wall. Would they be reduced to storming those gates like conquerors of old?

Casey crawled up beside him. "Find a way in?"

"Not yet. I'm going to check it out, up close."

"I'm right behind you."

They kept low, using the field around them for cover. The verdant landscape was wet and slippery beneath their feet as they headed for the nearest section of wall. At the base, out of sight of the castle, they split up and slowly moved around the curving sides for a hundred feet or so in each direction, searching for any hidden entrances or weakness in the stone structure. In a few minutes, they returned to where they had started and hunkered down in the tall grass.

"Useless," Rourke said.

"I agree. Some of this has been repaired recently and the top couple of feet is all new. I don't think there's a way in, except over the top." Casey sighed. "From the looks of things, what we need is a miracle."

"Then we'll find one," Rourke told him. Something grazed the back of his head and he brushed at it irritably. "With all the hardware we brought, there must be a way."

"It's your call. Do we go over or not?"

"It looks like that's our only choice, but getting in that way undetected is—" Rourke stopped midsentence and slapped at his neck. "Darn it! That's all we need."

Casey was looking at him strangely. "What?"

"Bugs. Pesky critters!"

Suddenly they heard a low chuckle and both turned toward the sound. On the downslope of land directly beside them sat Annie, hidden in the weeds and looking totally at ease in her jeans and cream sweater. "Lovely morning, don't you think?" she asked softly. She climbed up the slope and crouched down in front of Rourke, enjoying his stunned expression immensely as she tickled him with the fuzzy end of the weed she held in her hand. "Buzzzz! Better watch out! I bite!"

"I should have known." He touched her face, running a finger across the curve of her cheek, caressing the soft skin. "You okay?"

"I'd kill for a cup of coffee, but otherwise I'm fine." She reached up and traced a scratch that ran down his face and into his black turtleneck. "You didn't get into a fight with Nadia, did you? I'm sure *she* hasn't had her shots."

Rourke chuckled. "No, I got these from a prickly hedge while chasing after the guys who took you. How—"

"Later." She wrapped her fingers around his and held them to her breasts for a moment before letting go. "It's good to see you. Now give me a gun."

Still not believing his eyes, Rourke handed her his. Annie promptly turned it on Casey. "Don't even twitch, darlin'. Just drop the armament."

Casey held his hands up. "What are you doing?"

"I already know how good a shot you are. If you don't want to find out how good I am, drop the guns." Casey carefully dropped his weapons at his feet. "Now back up."

He backed up to the wall. Annie followed, as did Rourke, out of sight of the fortress beyond. She kept her gun trained on Casey.

"What's going on, Annie?" Rourke demanded.

"We had an interesting chat, Adair, Farrell and I. I found out they're the masterminds Gerald is after. They are also two of the murderers you've been searching for. Hagen is the third."

"And you think Casey is the fourth? That's crazy!"

Casey's eyes went wide. "It sure is! I don't even know what you're talking about! What four murderers?"

"Keep your voice down, Casey," Annie ordered. "They're busy cooking up an ambush in there and I don't think they've had time to notice I'm gone yet, but there's no sense calling attention to ourselves." She glanced at Rourke. "I know he's not the fourth man. But he has been reporting to someone. I want to know who."

Casey was not at all happy with the way Annie had taken aim. "All right! Just watch where you point that thing!"

"Your answers will determine that. Who are you working for? Nadia? Hagen? Brady Adair as well as his brother, Michael? Or are you working for all of them and selling each one out in turn?" Annie asked.

Casey looked at Rourke, then back at Annie, a sorrowful expression on his face. "I'm sorry. I should have told you sooner but... Sometimes I'm too tricky for my own good! I'm not working for any of them. Well, maybe Michael Adair in a way. Mainly I've been working for myself."

"Explain."

Casey rushed to do so. "When Derry asked me to help Rourke find Hagen, I thought it was an easy way to pay back a favor to a friend who saved my life, as well as get a bit of extra cash on the side. You see, I was already looking for Hagen. He was supposed to have the goods on Brady Adair, and Adair's brother, Michael, was paying for that kind of information. I didn't see anything wrong in earning two fees at the same time."

"Who have you been reporting to?" Annie asked.

"An investigative firm here in Ireland. They wanted daily reports to turn over to Michael Adair, a political hopeful in the States."

Rourke frowned. "Why didn't you tell me about Brady? Surely you realized he was up to no good, if only because of the people we kept running into in our search for Hagen."

"Sure, I figured he was bad. But I didn't know how bad," Casey replied. "And how was I supposed to know that Brady Adair was one of these murderers you were looking for? The only guy you ever talked about was Hagen!"

"I didn't even know it until just now," Rourke said, looking appreciatively at Annie. "You have been busy. Any more surprises?"

Annie grinned. "A few."

"Do you have any solid proof of wrongdoing on Brady's part?" Casey asked eagerly.

Annie stepped closer, still not convinced of his innocence. "I have proof of yours."

"Wait a minute, I'm too young to die, I'm getting married next month! And besides," Casey protested, trying to crawl up the wall behind him backward, to get away from her. "I really haven't done anything wrong!"

Another unsolved glitch occurred to her. "Did you tell your firm about the meet at the ruins?"

"Yes."

"This is starting to make more sense," Annie said, stepping back from him. "Bruce's agent must have gotten the location of the meet from the company you were working for. Between Gerald's secretary and the firm you talked to daily, people were always able to find out what we were going to do next, except when we told no one of our plans. I'll bet your investigative firm sold all your information to anyone with the money to pay for it."

"But that's not my fault!" Casey exclaimed.

No, it wasn't. Annie lowered her gun, deep in thought. Casey sagged against the wall with a sigh of relief.

"So who *is* the fourth man?" Annie wondered aloud.

"I'm very impressed with all you've found out, Annie, but, meanwhile, we still have a job to do," Rourke reminded her, taking his gun back. "The answers we're both looking for await us inside the castle, in the form of Farrell and Adair." He frowned. "Providing we can get in, that is."

Annie knew it was pointless to ask him not to go in there. Bridget would never be safe until all four of the men who'd killed her parents had been dealt with, in one way or another. But Annie wasn't going to let him do this alone.

She looked at Rourke. "I can show you a way in, but Adair has a small army in there. They began arriving last night. Everyone forgot I was there, which left me free to roam the castle—after I picked the lock on my cell door. We'll need help to take on so many."

"You aren't the only one who's been busy. Follow me." Rourke led the way over a hill to a small valley. "How does this look?"

There were over twenty men present, dressed in black, their faces smeared with camouflage makeup. Two other men were dressed otherwise, and one of them shocked her. He wore his usual wool tweeds. And he looked very relieved to see her.

"Gerald! What are you doing here?"

"It's a long story, dear." He took her hand and patted it, as if trying to reassure himself that she was really there. "I'll explain after this is all over."

"You're coming inside?"

"No." Gerald glanced at the handcuffed man at his side. "I'll stay out here and baby-sit Hagen. We brought him along just in case. Thank heaven you're safe!"

She tapped Rourke on the arm. "I want to talk to you privately." They moved away from the group. "I'm not convinced Gerald is completely trustworthy." Her mind was spinning with possibilities. "We still don't know who the fourth man is."

"I agree with you, and I'm not leaving him here alone with Hagen." Her suspicions of Gerald mirrored his own.

After all, Gerald *had* been in Belfast on that night five years ago. "These men have orders to disobey all of his commands, and they'll do so without a second thought." Rourke turned as one of the men approached them. "Willie, you know what I want done."

"Gottcha boss, loud and clear. We ready to move out?"

"Yes, Annie Sawyer will lead us in. But first, she needs a gun."

Annie checked the gun Willie handed her and tucked it into the waistband of her jeans. Then she walked over to the assembled group. They were heavily armed and had the hard look of men who only needed to be told their objective to know what had to be done.

"We'll stay in the shallow ravine all the way to the base of the surrounding wall," she told them, indicating the direction. "Right there, where the wall meets that hill, there's a hidden entrance and a tunnel into the castle."

She gave them a brief layout of the place, then they took off, Annie keeping them below a ridge that hid them from the lookout she knew was stationed inside the castle turret. As they got closer to the hill, she led them into a concealed entrance that looked like a small dead-end cave.

Gradually, however, the cave acquired stone walls, then a floor that was slimy with moisture that had leached from the ground. At last the passageway ended and they edged past a crumbling opening in the castle foundation, to emerge behind a large oak barrel. The small wine cellar was dark and cold, its sparse furnishing dusty with age and disuse.

From there they moved through a maze of damp, dimly lit corridors, up into the castle proper, the men going off in pairs at the various intersections Annie pointed out.

"We're almost to the central rooms," she whispered.

Rourke stopped, his hand on her arm. "Will you wait here?" She shook her head. "I didn't think so. At least stay behind me. Maybe they don't know you're gone and we can surprise them." He turned to Willie and the few men still with him. "Hang back and wait for my signal."

At the end of the narrow corridor, a set of large wooden doors stood open, almost inviting them into the room beyond. There was a roaring fire burning in the massive stone fireplace. A plush sofa and matching chairs faced the blaze, and there were expensive art objects scattered about. To one side of the fireplace was another set of doors, also open.

And on the balcony above the huge chamber stood a group of armed, efficient-looking killers.

"Come in," a deeply brogued voice invited. Brady Adair rose from one of the chairs in front of the fire and turned toward them. "I've been expecting you, Patrick Rourke."

Rourke stayed in the shadowy corridor just outside the entry. "Where's Annie?"

"Where's Hagen?"

"Produce the woman first."

Brady chuckled. "That's difficult for me to do when she's already with you. It would seem you hold all the cards, except that I have all these men." He gestured to the balcony. "With their weapons aimed at you. One wrong move and you're dead."

Suddenly, a man stepped into the open doorway beside the fireplace. He had a pistol in each hand and a broad grin on his face. "I can't possibly let you deprive me of that particular pleasure, Brady."

Brady spun on his heel. He gaped at the man, his face turning crimson. "I don't believe it!"

Farrell jumped up out of his chair. "Flynn!"

"Only you would have the gall to show your face here, considering the money you owe us." Brady glowered at him. "It will be a pleasure to hand you your head, Flynn. After I find out what you're up to."

Annie peered over Rourke's shoulder. As she watched, the twins joined Flynn in the doorway. Last night they had been following Adair's orders; now it seemed they were taking orders from Flynn. That would explain how he'd gotten into the castle. From the looks on their identical faces, she figured they had more in mind than a simple double-cross. If the heavy automatic weapons slung over their shoulders were any indication, they were ready to kill.

But who would be their first target?

"I've come to make amends," Flynn announced in a jovial voice. "To make up for all the trouble I've caused you."

As he spoke, Flynn positioned himself for an easy escape. This was the opportunity of a lifetime for him. In one fell swoop he could wipe out a huge debt, get rid of Rourke at last, and place himself in control of Brady and Colin's empire. All it would take was one vicious killing spree that he and his henchmen would enjoy thoroughly.

But the timing had to be perfect.

"And just how do you propose to do that?" Brady asked.

Two more armed men appeared in the doorway behind Flynn. "I know how and where to get hold of that shipment of arms you lost the other morning," Flynn replied.

"You think that's worth the millions you owe us?"

Flynn smiled. "I know it is. You see, I had every intention of stealing it and then paying you back with the proceeds."

"You what!" Farrell cried.

"Hagen told me about them when he sought refuge at my house. He and the twins were helping me." Flynn jerked his head, indicating Rourke in the opposite doorway. "Then these meddlers came along and scared them off. Too bad. But I still know how to get the weapons." He cocked his pistols. "This time, though, I think I'll keep the money for myself."

"Traitors! Kill him!" Brady yelled with outrage as he ducked behind a chair. "Open fire! Kill them all!"

Shots rang out from every direction, the staccato crack of pistols joining the chatter of automatic weapons. Total chaos reigned, with chips of stone and flying glass spraying everywhere. A man cried out and fell from the balcony, while those in the doorway sprinted into the room, diving for cover.

Rourke pushed Annie back into the narrow corridor out of harm's way as he gave the signal for Willie and his men to come forward. They advanced into the room with methodical precision and joined the melee.

Staying within the safe confines of the corridor, Rourke kept his eyes on Flynn. He was watching the fight from behind the twins, safely outside the doorway. They were all firing wildly into the room, not bothering to aim. Flynn was laughing.

Under cover of his own gunfire, Brady ran toward the doorway where Flynn stood. But Flynn must have seen him coming because he took off, the twins disappearing with him. Brady followed, hot on his heels.

Rourke moved closer to the entrance, looking for a chance to go after them. Suddenly, Annie shoved him aside as she shot at a man on the balcony. "Back this way," she yelled.

He ran after her, following her through corridors until they ended up in a main outer room. "Wait here," he said.

She ignored him and took off. "They had to go this way. These stairs are the only way out."

They ran up the stone steps, coming to a screeching halt before the second-level landing. Brady Adair lay in their path, shot in the chest. Annie squatted down and felt for a pulse.

"He's dead."

The sound of gunfire in the upper levels had Rourke running up the next flight of stairs. He was one step behind Flynn, as he'd been so often in the past. Occasionally he caught a glimpse of Flynn running through the empty stone corridors of the third level, but he couldn't get a clean shot at him.

Annie was close by his elbow. "We've got him now," she said, huffing and puffing a bit. "The twins cut him off for some reason. There's no way out of this section, except past us."

They were in the round turret that towered above the castle, running up the spiral staircase. On each level, stones in the wall were missing here and there, enabling one to see a great distance across the countryside. But their enemy was up ahead, inside, with no way out.

At the very top, Flynn turned on them and fired one wild shot down the stairs, then his pistol clicked, empty. Frantically, he looked for a way out, backing up against the curving stones, arms stretched out to either side.

Rourke approached the landing cautiously, his emotions tearing him in two. The man before him was responsible for the death of his family. No one would ever know of all the untold evil Flynn had caused, the many lives he had taken and would gleefully take again.

Such a man deserved death. Rourke raised his revolver, finger on the trigger. Still, something deep inside of him made him hesitate. The killing had to stop somewhere.

Life must go on. He knew that now, because Annie Sawyer, who was standing right beside him, had helped him to see it. Flynn's death wouldn't bring him release from his own torment. That he had to find within himself.

Flynn was enjoying the moral dilemma he could clearly read on Rourke's face. "What a fool you are, Patrick Rourke!"

He tossed his empty pistol at Rourke, who ducked, giving Flynn the tiny bit of distraction he needed to pull his knife from the sheath strapped to his back. A second later he was lunging for the woman beside Rourke, jerking her arm hard, causing her gun to clatter to the ground as he forced her in front of him, the sharp blade against her slender throat.

"At long last, Rourke," Flynn said. "We meet face-to-face, without a single disguise between us. No more false names, no more hiding. And how appropriate that a woman is the cause of your downfall."

Annie gasped. Aliases. Disguises. Colin Farrell had mentioned both, saying they wouldn't stop them from finding and killing their partner in crime. She knew from Flynn's file that he was adept at hiding his identity, considered a master of misdirection. He and Hagen had been in cahoots, working against Farrell and Adair, men who wanted them both dead for what they knew.

The last piece of the puzzle fell into place in her mind. It all fit. Flynn was the fourth man!

"Shoot him, Patrick! You have to! He helped kill Bridget's parents and I'll never forgive you if you make me the one responsible for letting him get away!"

His face pale, Rourke took aim.

Suddenly, Flynn shoved Annie into Rourke. Patrick fell backward, his gun hand striking the wall with such force that his fingers went numb. The weapon slipped from his grasp. Annie tumbled to the floor. Flynn took advantage of the new opportunity, charging at Rourke with his knife raised.

Annie dove for her own gun where it had fallen on the top step. She picked it up and twisted around, laying back across Rourke's feet and firing without hesitation, shooting Flynn right in the chest.

Eyes wide open, Flynn staggered one step closer to Rourke. "Houlihan," he gasped. "That little girl...Bridget *Houlihan!*" Then he crumpled to the floor and was still.

Annie stood and approached him carefully, kicking the knife aside, still not believing he was dead. She knelt beside him and felt for a pulse.

Annie looked up. "It's over."

"Over," Rourke repeated. The word sounded strange to him. He didn't know how to thank her. Annie had saved his life more than once since they'd joined forces, but more importantly, she had saved him from carrying this one more death on his conscience.

A noise startled them both and they whipped around, Annie still on her knees, weapon raised. The twins stood a few steps below them, unarmed.

"Why did you help us?" Annie asked curiously. "I saw one of you blocking Flynn's only escape route, forcing him into the tower."

"We want the body."

Annie stood her ground, her gun pointed at them. "You can have it, after you tell me why you helped us."

"A Middle Eastern country is offering a reward for Lian Francis Dougall. We're going to collect it."

"Well, why didn't you just kill him before now and be done with it?" Annie asked, incensed.

The twin holding his injured arm answered her. "We had to wait and see. Flynn might have been able to pull this coup off. If he had, we'd have been in an even better position than we could be with the money for killing him. But we'll take what we can get."

She moved aside. Rourke didn't object as one of them picked up the body, slung it over his shoulder and went back down the stairs. He was too glad that he and Annie had survived to care about the twins, Flynn's corpse or anything else.

Anything except the woman standing beside him. Rourke touched her on the shoulder. "Are you okay, Annie?"

"I will be." She looked at him, as white as a ghost. "I've never killed anyone before," she said. "I've never needed to. All the target practice in the world doesn't prepare you for how that feels."

Patrick wrapped his arm around her shoulders, offering her comfort as they descended the stairs, knowing there was nothing more he could do for her right now. He knew the feeling well. Hopefully, he would never have to feel it again.

"Does this mean Bridget is safe now?" Annie asked.

"Yes, yes it does, thanks to you," Patrick told her. "Now Bridget will be free to do anything she wants with her life." He felt like the weight of the world had been lifted off of his shoulders. "Finally."

At the base of the stairs, on the ground floor, Willie was waiting for them. "Did you tell those twins they could leave with Flynn's body?'' Rourke nodded. "Fine with me then, it's Gerald's problem anyway. Farrell is dead, too. He was shot by one of the men on the balcony.''

"I thought those were his men. Were they being paid by Flynn?'' Annie asked.

"No, it seems someone else was offering a bonus for bodies,'' Willie explained. "But these men don't know who's paying them.''

Annie looked around. "Where's Casey?''

"On the phone,'' Willie told her.

"What!'' Annie shrugged off Rourke's arm and ran into the huge room with the fire. At one end Casey was sitting on the edge of a desk, talking on the phone. "What are you doing?''

Casey turned away, spoke for another minute, then hung up. He faced her. "Turning in a report. Why?''

"For what?'' Annie demanded. "Haven't you and your zest for free enterprise caused enough trouble?''

Casey jumped up. "For crying out loud, are you still suspicious of me?''

"Yes,'' Annie said glaring at him, her arms crossed.

"I'm just trying to make a living! It's for a bonus,'' Casey explained. "I need the money. I'm getting out of this business when I get married. We're buying a bed-and-breakfast place.'' He glared at her. "Is that okay with you?''

Annie thought about it for a minute. "What are they paying a bonus for?''

"For information on any wrongdoing by Brady Adair.''

She looked over at Patrick, who had quietly come into the room. "Brady's politically minded brother is going to try and cover everything up. I wonder if he paid those men to kill his brother and his brother's partner?''

"If he's anything like his brother, you'll never be able to prove it,'' Patrick told her. "Besides, that's Gerald's problem, not ours.''

"What's my problem?'' Gerald asked, entering the room.

"I'll tell you later," Annie said. "Right now I want to know if you ever found out why Bruce was constantly interfering in this operation."

Gerald lit his pipe. "Bruce suspected a leak within our department and was sure we were going to try to pin the problem on him. After his recent actions, if I could find a way to do it, I would." He puffed on his pipe. "And I want to talk to you, Annie, about using Julie without authorization."

"I don't think that's necessary," Rourke said. He was looking at Gerald with his eyebrows raised, passing along a silent communication. "Is it, old man?"

Annie looked from one man to the other. The tension was so thick between them you could cut it with a knife. "What's going on?"

"I'll give you the details later," Rourke assured her. "I don't think we have a problem, Gerald, unless you'd like me to create a few for you?"

Gerald cleared him throat. "No, there's no problem. Why don't you two run along? I'll mop up here," he said. "Oh, by the way, someone claiming to be a friend of yours contacted my office. He said he's ready for you to take him to America as soon as his stomach wound heals. Something about a promise you made. Does that make any sense?"

Rourke laughed. "Perfect sense."

"Well what do you know?" Annie said. "I guess raccoons have nine lives just like cats."

ANNIE WALKED BESIDE PATRICK across the rugged Irish countryside. It had turned into a beautiful day and the sun was shining brightly. The silence was deep and satisfying.

But finally she felt compelled to speak. "Would you like to come home with me for a visit?"

Patrick smiled. "And meet your booze-making Granny? Does she carry a shotgun?" he asked.

Annie looked up at Patrick, not wanting things to end between them, indeed, having no intention of ever letting him get away from her again. "You'll have to meet her to find out. Her home brew alone is worth the trip."

Rourke paused for a moment, then continued walking down the hill, Annie one step ahead of him. Progress had been made in coming to terms with Ireland and what it had done to him. It looked as if he would have to come to terms with the woman who had helped him make that progress, as well.

If he did go home with her, meet her family, it would be the start of something very special between them. They were already friends and lovers. That was a pretty big commitment for him. And a step in the right direction.

"You do know my weak spots, Annie," Patrick admitted. "All right, I'll come, but only if you stay beside me, not one step ahead."

Annie stopped and held her hand out to him. Patrick slipped his fingers between hers, holding on tightly as they continued across the rolling hills.

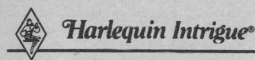

Harlequin Intrigue®

A SPAULDING & DARIEN MYSTERY
by Robin Francis

An engaging pair of amateur sleuths—Jenny Spaulding and Peter Darien—were introduced to Harlequin Intrigue readers in #147, BUTTON, BUTTON (Oct. 1990). Jenny and Peter will return for further spine-chilling romantic adventures in April 1991 in #159, DOUBLE DARE in which they solve their next puzzling mystery. Two other books featuring Jenny and Peter will follow in the A SPAULDING AND DARIEN MYSTERY series.

If you missed the debut of this exciting pair of sleuths and would like to order #147 BUTTON, BUTTON, send your name, address, zip or postal code along with a check or money order for $2.50 plus 75¢ postage and handling ($1.00 in Canada) for each book order, payable to Harlequin Reader Service, to:

In the U.S.
3010 Walden Ave.
P.O. Box 1325
Buffalo, NY 14269-1326

In Canada
P.O. Box 609
Fort Erie, Ontario
L2A 5X3

Canadian residents add applicable federal and provincial taxes.

Everyone loves a spring wedding, and this April, Harlequin cordially invites you to read the most romantic wedding book of the year

ONE WEDDING—FOUR LOVE STORIES FROM YOUR FAVORITE HARLEQUIN AUTHORS!

The church is booked, the reception arranged and the invitations mailed. All Diane Bauer and Nick Granatelli have to do is walk down the aisle. Little do they realize that the most cherished day of their lives will spark so many romantic notions....

Available wherever Harlequin books are sold.

You'll flip . . . your pages won't!
Read paperbacks *hands-free* with

Book Mate • I

The perfect "mate" for all your romance paperbacks

Traveling • Vacationing • At Work • In Bed • Studying • Cooking • Eating

Perfect size for all standard paperbacks, this wonderful invention makes reading a pure pleasure! Ingenious design holds paperback books OPEN and FLAT so even wind can't ruffle pages – leaves your hands free to do other things. Reinforced, wipe-clean vinyl-covered holder flexes to let you turn pages without undoing the strap . . . supports paperbacks so well, they have the strength of hardcovers!

Pages turn WITHOUT opening the strap

SEE-THROUGH STRAP

Reinforced back stays flat

Built in bookmark

BOOK MARK

BACK COVER HOLDING STRIP

10" x 7¼ , opened.
Snaps closed for easy carrying, too

H A R L E Q U I N
American Romance®

RELIVE THE MEMORIES . . .

From New York's immigrant experience to the Great Quake of 1906. From the Western Front of World War I to the Roaring Twenties. From the indomitable spirit of the thirties to the home front of the Fabulous Forties. From the baby boom fifties to the Woodstock Nation sixties . . . **A CENTURY OF AMERICAN ROMANCE** takes you on a nostalgic journey through the twentieth century.

Revel in the romance of a time gone by . . . and sneak a peek at romance in a exciting future.

Watch for all the **A CENTURY OF AMERICAN ROMANCE** titles coming to you one per month over the next three months in Harlequin American Romance.

Don't miss February's **A CENTURY OF AMERICAN ROMANCE** title, #377—TILL THE END OF TIME by Elise Title.

A CENTURY OF
AMERICAN ROMANCE
1970s

The women . . . the men . . . the passions . . . the memories . . .